Pra
Carlton

CW00740716

"Easily the craziest, weirdest, writer in America."
—*GOTHIC MAGAZINE*

"Carlton Mellick III has the craziest book titles... and the kinkiest fans!"
—CHRISTOPHER MOORE, author of *The Stupidest Angel*

"If you haven't read Mellick you're not nearly perverse enough for the twenty first century."
—JACK KETCHUM, author of *The Girl Next Door*

"Carlton Mellick III is one of bizarro fiction's most talented practitioners, a virtuoso of the surreal, science fictional tale."
—CORY DOCTOROW, author of *Little Brother*

"Bizarre, twisted, and emotionally raw—Carlton Mellick's fiction is the literary equivalent of putting your brain in a blender."
—BRIAN KEENE, author of *The Rising*

"Carlton Mellick III exemplifies the intelligence and wit that lurks between its lurid covers. In a genre where crude titles are an art in themselves, Mellick is a true artist."
—*THE GUARDIAN*

"Just as Pop had Andy Warhol and Dada Tristan Tzara, the bizarro movement has its very own P. T. Barnum-type practitioner. He's the mutton-chopped author of such books as *Electric Jesus Corpse* and *The Menstruating Mall*, the illustrator, editor, and instructor of all things bizarro, and his name is Carlton Mellick III."
—*DETAILS MAGAZINE*

Also by **Carlton Mellick III**

Satan Burger
Electric Jesus Corpse
Sunset With a Beard (stories)
Razor Wire Pubic Hair
Teeth and Tongue Landscape
The Steel Breakfast Era
The Baby Jesus Butt Plug
Fishy-fleshed
The Menstruating Mall
Ocean of Lard (with Kevin L. Donihe)
Punk Land
Sex and Death in Television Town
Sea of the Patchwork Cats
The Haunted Vagina
Cancer-cute (Avant Punk Army Exclusive)
War Slut
Sausagey Santa
Ugly Heaven
Adolf in Wonderland
Ultra Fuckers
Cybernetrix
The Egg Man
Apeshit
The Faggiest Vampire
The Cannibals of Candyland
Warrior Wolf Women of the Wasteland
The Kobold Wizard's Dildo of Enlightenment +2
Zombies and Shit
Crab Town
The Morbidly Obese Ninja
Barbarian Beast Bitches of the Badlands
Fantastic Orgy (stories)
I Knocked Up Satan's Daughter
Armadillo Fists
The Handsome Squirm
Tumor Fruit
Kill Ball
Cuddly Holocaust
Hammer Wives (stories)
Village of the Mermaids
Quicksand House

CLUSTERFUCK

CARLTON MELLICK III

ERASERHEAD PRESS
PORTLAND, OREGON

ERASERHEAD PRESS
205 NE BRYANT
PORTLAND, OR 97211

WWW.ERASERHEADPRESS.COM

ISBN: 978-1-62105-117-6

AUTHOR'S NOTE

I'm on an airplane returning home from a convention in Las Vegas that I attend every year called KillerCon. It's a fun little event of about 150 people at the Stratosphere Hotel that tends to attract the more extreme writers of horror like Edward Lee, Jack Ketchum, and Wrath James White (who also runs the event). Being the top extreme horror publisher, Deadite Press is always in attendance and I always go along for the ride. I don't consider myself a writer of extreme horror, but I have written a few books for that audience—Apeshit, Zombies and Shit, and the book you now hold in your hands.

There was a panel at KillerCon this year featuring some originators of the splatterpunk genre such as John Skipp, David J. Schow, and John Shirley, as well as some of the modern champions of extreme horror Wrath James White, Monica O'Rourke, and Ryan Harding. All amazing writers. One recurring theme on the panel was how they appreciate when writers of splatterpunk attempt to elevate the genre, turn it into something smarter, deeper, and relevant. Now, on my flight back home, I'm wondering if Clusterfuck might fit into this style of elevated splatterpunk. Is it smart? Is it deep? After a split second of thought, I decided that no, Clusterfuck is definitely not any of these things. Clusterfuck is just pure stupid. It's a B movie in book form. There's nothing deep about it. Like Apeshit, it's a celebration of trash horror. And I like it exactly as it is.

As I said in the first book, I love B horror movies. Crappy, terrible, hilarious B horror movies. I also love movies that are intentionally bad for comical purposes. If you can't make a good movie then at least make it funny. I always appreciate when filmmakers (or other creative types) don't take themselves too seriously. Apeshit was my version of a B movie in book form. Clusterfuck is the sequel to that book (although you don't need to have read Apeshit first to enjoy this one).

There are a few big differences between Apeshit and Clusterfuck. For starters, Apeshit is a parody of cabin in the woods stories. Clusterfuck is a parody of spelunking horror. *The Descent* and *The Cave* are the two most obvious spelunking horror films, though I'm pretty sure spelunking horror has been done a million times before either of those films were made. Another difference is that Clusterfuck's more comical than Apeshit—it's definitely more comedy-driven than gore-driven, but only slightly. The last difference is that instead of high school jocks and cheerleaders, this book stars college girls and frat boys.

Frat boys are both the worst human beings on the face of the planet and the funniest human beings on the face of the planet, at the same time for the same reasons. In order to capture the frat boy mentality, I read every blog written by every frat boy I could find. This took quite a lot of endurance. I don't recommend anyone ever attempt this, but the experience was horrible, funny, sad, terrifying, annoying, and strangely enlightening. And I hate to admit it, but I have since grown to empathize with the average American frat boy despite all his faults. He's not just the douchebag hooting in the back of the keg party, thinking he's the toughest/hottest dude in the room. He's also a human being with hopes and dreams and rich parents who sometimes don't buy him every single thing he wants. And when nobody else is looking, he sometimes cries when he thinks of his chocolate lab, Stinko, who had to be put to sleep while he was away at college. He had Stinko ever since he was a puppy. He didn't even get to say goodbye… It's not fair, bro. It's just not fair…

My plane is about to land so I need to turn off this electronic typing device. I hope you enjoy Clusterfuck as much as you did Apeshit. It's 50% longer and at least 50% more *extreme*.

—Carlton Mellick III 9/23/2013 6:14 pm

CHAPTER ONE
EXTREME DEAN

THE BRO CODE #125
A bro is always psyched. ALWAYS.

Dean Brockman had no idea he was a douchebag.

You'd think it would've been obvious to him. He was a frat boy. Just that should have been enough to tip him off right there. But even among other frat boys he was considered a douchebag. Perhaps it was because he constantly quoted Jay-Z lyrics at irrelevant times, called all women *flaps*—presumably as a reference to the outer labia of their genitalia—and was utterly obsessed with all things *extreme*, as if he grew up idolizing those extreme sports douchebags from Mountain Dew commercials of the 90s.

At any given moment, you could find him pacing through the frat house yelling at the top of his lungs, "This weekend is going to be *extreme*, bro! FUCKING EXTREME!"

His frat brothers at Sigma Alpha Epsilon would just shake their heads and say, "We know, we know. Chill, bro."

"FUCKING EXTREME!" And then he'd smash an empty can of Natty Ice on his forehead.

Just the sight of him screamed douchebag. He wore socks with his Brooks Brothers flip flops, a pair of croakies rested on the brim of his backwards preworn hat, and there were always at least three popped collars on his multi-layered Abercrombie & Fitch polo shirts. He also had spiked hair with frosted tips, which was perhaps the douchiest hairstyle in the history of the entire world.

He earned the nickname *Extreme Dean*, but it wasn't meant to be a compliment. His frat brothers called him that because the idiot would never shut up about doing *extreme* things all the time. Dean, however, thought he received the nickname because he was just that fucking awesome. He was under the delusion that everyone saw him as the toughest, smartest, funniest, most extreme bro in the frat house. That couldn't have been further from the truth.

"You wanna go *extreme* kayaking?" Dean asked his two best bros, Trent and Gravy.

They were in their room, hitting a bong. Hard.

"Nah, bro, no time," Trent said, blowing smoke at the television.

"Extreme skydiving then? Or how about extreme wakeboarding? I'm in the mood for doing something EXTREME!"

Of all the guys in the frat house, Trent and Gravy were the only two who could tolerate Dean for more than two minutes at a time. Trent could tolerate him because the dude was the fucking Alpha Bro. Nothing bothered that guy. Ever. And Gravy tolerated him because the goofy fat-faced bastard loved everyone when he was stoned out of his mind, which was always.

"Save your energy for the weekend, bro," Gravy said.

"Then how about a game of extreme beer pong?" Dean asked.

Extreme beer pong was just normal beer pong.

"Nah." Trent was only half-listening, looking up Facebook photos of girls he'd banged on his iPhone.

"Extreme hacky sack? Extreme tetherball?"

Gravy pulled his face out of the Italian sandwich he was munching on between bong hits. "What the fuck is extreme tetherball?"

Dean shifted his weight from side to side. "You know, it's like regular tetherball only fierce and intense."

"Where would we even play it?" Gravy hadn't even thought about tetherball in at least twelve years. "We don't have a tetherball pole."

"You want a tetherball pole?" Dean said, getting all intense and serious. "I'll MAKE a fucking tetherball pole. Give me a ball and some rope. I'll put that shit together RIGHT NOW."

Dean was that particularly annoying kind of person who always claimed he could accomplish anything within seconds, even when he lacked the proper knowledge or experience required to complete such tasks. Many guys in the frat were like this, but Dean was the worst of the bunch by far. Need your car fixed? He'd say no problem he'll take care of it for you. Need a sushi chef for a private party to impress some girl? He'd say he was trained by a sushi master when he visited Japan last summer, just leave it to him. Need to get more alcohol after the liquor stores close? He'd claim to know a secret technique for whipping up instant moonshine in a bathtub, just give him an hour or so. If he actually ever went through with trying to accomplish one of these tasks it would always be a total disaster. Then he'd blame something or someone else for his failure.

"Forget the tetherball pole, bro," Trent said. "We're going to REI to get the gear today."

"What gear?"

"The caving gear, shithead. For this weekend."

Dean's eyes lit up. "You mean we're doing it? We're really going *extreme* caving?"

"Of course, bro. First thing in the morning. I set it all up."

"EXTREME!" Dean cried, about to have a brogasm. "Fuck the morning, let's do this shit right fucking now. Let's drive up there RIGHT NOW." He pumped his fist as hard as he could. "I'm going to spelunk the fuck out of that cave."

Dean was getting intense again.

"Bro, chill," Trent said. "It's a six-hour drive. We'll wait until morning."

Dean tried to relax, taking deep breaths, "Who's all going?"

"The three of us and three slam pieces," Trent says.

"Girls?" Dean groaned. "This trip is supposed to be about extreme *man* shit. We can't take flap into the bro zone."

"What are you gay or something?" Trent said. "I'm not going into a cave with just a bunch of dudes."

"I like flap as much as the next bro, but I don't want to deal with them getting all scared and wanting to go home to change their tampons right when we get into the *really* extreme caving shit."

"Don't worry, bro. It'll be fine."

Dean shook his head. He did *not* think it was going to be fine.

"Let's at least bring Lance with us," Dean said. "That way the flap-to-bro ratio will be more in our favor."

"Whatever, bro," Trent said. "But you two are going to have to share the same slam piece."

This was enough to satisfy the extreme one. Without saying another word to his bros, Dean pumped his fist and danced out of the room. Then he yelled into the empty halls, "Who wants to go to Taco Bell for some Extreme Fiesta Nachos?"

None of his bros responded.

Extreme Dean didn't bother to tell Lance that he was coming with them on their caving expedition until the next morning when they were packing up the SUV and getting ready to go.

"Come on, bro, we're leaving in five minutes," Dean told Lance.

Lance looked up from his economics textbook.

"Huh?" Lance said. He had no idea what Dean was talking about.

"In the car, five minutes." Then Dean punched the wall, knocking pictures of Lance's parents onto the floor, as he said, "This is going to be THE MOST EXTREME FUCKING WEEKEND EVER!"

Lance was the frat's Token Black Bro. He was only a first year nib, but he was already treated like frat royalty on the account of his much cooler ethnicity. Dean, more than anyone, absolutely loved the guy, even though he knew next to nothing about him. *Most* guys in the frat knew next to nothing about him. He was black, and that's all that mattered to them. They thought he gave them street cred.

But what the other frat guys didn't know was that Lance, for all intents and purposes, was actually the whitest bro in the frat house. His name was *Lance* for fuck's sake. You can't get any whiter than that. He also came from a wealthier family, attended better private schools, and was raised in a much nicer neighborhood than any bro on campus. By the time he was sixteen, he owned his own yacht and a private island in the Bahamas. Not that he was actually allowed to do anything with them yet, but a fucking island and a yacht? His parents were beyond loaded.

"So… what's up?" Lance asked as he walked off the fratio toward Trent's SUV.

Trent and Gravy were packing the car with supplies for the trip.

"Going caving, bro," Gravy said. "You ready?"

"Caving?" Lance said. Even the way he talked made him sound like a rich white guy. "You mean like *spelunking*?"

"That's right," Trent said. "You ever been before?"

Lance shook his head. "No, never. Is it hard?"

"*Pshh*," Trent said, rolling his eyes. "Not for me. I've been doing it since I was like nine years old."

"I've been doing it since I was five," Gravy said.

"Bullshit, you haven't been caving longer than me," Trent said.

"I've been caving longer and my dick is longer, too, wook," Gravy said.

Without dropping the equipment in his hands, Trent kicked Gravy in his pudgy ass.

"Did you just call me a *wook?*"

If anyone else had said that, Trent would have knocked his teeth out, but Gravy was his bro. And if he hoped to smoke any weed at all during the trip, he knew not to piss Gravy off.

"I don't think I could ever go caving," Lance said. "That shit's not my thing."

"What are you talking about?" Trent said. "You're coming with, aren't you?"

Before Lance could answer, Extreme Dean came up behind him carrying six 18 packs of Natty Ice and said, "Hells yeah he's coming with. L-Dawg wouldn't miss this shit for anything."

"I don't know…" Lance said.

"What don't you know?" Trent said.

"I've got an exam Monday and…"

"We'll be back tomorrow morning," Trent said.

"Yeah, bro," Dean said. "You can just cram for that shit tomorrow night. Easy-peasy."

Lance inched back and forth, trying not to look weak in front of his senior frat brothers.

"But it's not…" Lance just went out and said it. "I'm not cool with confined spaces. I'm claustrophobic."

His three frat brothers stopped and stared at him. Lance just made a huge mistake admitting such a weakness. There was no way they would let him get out of going after saying something like that.

"Then I guess it's about time we broke you of that phobia," Trent said.

"Yeah, bro," Dean said, putting his arm around Lance's shoulder. "It's no big deal. I've been caving since I was two years old. I'll show you the ropes."

Lance wanted nothing to do with caving, but as a nib he had a hard time arguing with his seniors. The Old Balls weren't going to budge. He just surrendered to their wishes and allowed them to shove him into the back of Trent's SUV.

"Let's go, bros!" Dean yelled, sitting in the seat next to Lance, pounding his fist out the window.

As they pulled out of the frat house parking lot, Lance drooped his head against the window and let out a long sigh. He wished he would have stood up to them and stayed back at the house. He didn't really even like Trent, Dean, or Gravy. He didn't really like *any* of his frat brothers for that matter.

He was just too big of a pushover. If the frat recruiters weren't so forceful when they offered him a bid, he never would have joined Sig Alp in the first place. He went to school for the education, not the party.

"This is going to be extreme, bro!" Dean screamed directly into Lance's face. "FUCKING *EXTREEEEEMMME!*"

Dean's lips stayed in a wrinkled up O-shape, like he was giving an angry blowjob to an invisible man as he dragged out the enunciation of the word *extreme.*

"I can't believe I let you talk me into this," Selena said to Lauren, as the two girls waited outside of their dorm for the guys to pick them up, a pile of backpacks on the sidewalk at their feet.

"Relax, it'll be fun," Lauren said in her excited Chihuahua-like voice. "You'll thank me later. I promise."

"But spending the night in a cave in the middle of nowhere with Sig Alp guys?" Selena said. "Yeah, that sounds *real* safe."

"Come on, caving isn't that dangerous," Lauren said. "Plus, these guys have been doing this for a long time. They're like experts."

"It's not the cave that I'm worried about," Selena says. Then she nodded toward the SUV as it barreled down the road toward them, Extreme Dean hanging out the window hooting at the top of his lungs. "It's *them.*"

As the vehicle screeched to a stop in front of the curb, Lauren whispered into Selena's ear, "Just put up with them for one night. I *really* like this Trent guy."

The tinted driver's side window rolled down to reveal Trent behind the wheel. He had one eyebrow raised and a half-smile parting his cheek—the kind of look that bros only use when in the company of members of the opposite sex.

"Ladies," he said. It was all he needed to say.

Lauren ran to the car with her bags, a giddy smile on her face. Then she shoved her tongue down Trent's throat. The frat boy didn't object. But as he sucked on Lauren's tongue, his eyes were locked on Selena. Trent undressed her with his eyes, imagining what it would be like to tear off her jeans and tight red t-shirt, rub his hands all over her warm Latina skin, suck on her glossy lips and squeeze her big doughy breasts. These thoughts always went through Trent's mind whenever he saw any hot girl on campus.

But she just rolled her eyes at him.

Selena wasn't the average sorositute these frat boys were used to dealing with. She was in a league even higher than the porn models they usually fap to. Selena was a Brazilian goddess, far too good for any one of the frat boys in that vehicle, and she knew it. The bros, on the other hand, thought they had just hit the jackpot.

"Oh, *damn!*" Extreme Dean said to her, hanging halfway out the window. "*That's* what *I'm* talking about!" He bobbed his head back and forth as he chugged a can of Natty Ice.

Selena glared over at Lauren as if to tell her with her eyes *You owe me big time for this.* At the same time, Trent looked back at his bros as if telling them with his eyes *The hot bitch is mine,* even though he already had Lauren all over his nuts.

"This is Selena," Lauren said to the frat guys, once she noticed all of them had their eyes locked on her.

Then Trent introduced his bros to the ladies.

"I thought you said there'd be three of them, bro," Dean said. "Where's the other flap?"

Selena got into the backseat next to Lance. He politely moved into the middle, so that she wouldn't have to sit next to Extreme Dean. She *really* didn't want to sit next to Extreme Dean. Lance gave her a timid smile as she buckled her seatbelt, but she wasn't really paying attention to him.

"My sister, Marta, is at another dorm," Selena said. "We have to swing by and pick her up."

"Is she as hot as you?" Dean asked, cracking open another Natty Ice.

Selena did not warrant that question with an answer.

Dean leaned forward and whispered toward his bros in the front seat, "I call the hot chick's sister." But everyone in the car heard him say it.

Selena always hated frat guys, but at that moment she also hated Lauren for telling her *but these guys aren't like other frat boys, they're actually really cool* and she hated herself for not giving in to the instinctual urge to hop out of the vehicle and run for her life.

Trent's SUV pulled up to Marta's dorm, but the bros didn't see anyone out front who could've possibly been Selena's sister. The only person out there was some behemoth 350-pound chick with a mustache.

"Where is she?" Trent asked. "I thought you said she'd be waiting out front for us."

"She *is*," Selena said, pointing at the large woman on the curb. "She's right there."

The bros dropped their mouths as Selena waved the big girl over.

"Holy *shit*..." all the bros said in unison.

Then they recognized who she was. They'd seen the fatty around campus many times. They even had a nickname for her.

"Oh, my God..." Dean yelled. "It's *Giant Gonzales!*"

The large woman opened the door and dropped her backpack inside. Then Selena introduced her to everyone. The girl quietly said *hi* but did not make eye contact. She sat in the middle row next to Lauren, her abundant weight leaning the SUV to one side.

Nobody knew what to say for the next few minutes. Dean stared into his can of beer. Gravy held his hand to his face, hardly able to hold back the laughter. Then Trent broke the silence.

"You called her, bro!" Trent yelled at Dean, laughing his ass off.

"She's all yours!"

Gravy exploded into laughter and gave Trent a high-five.

"Fuck you, bro," Dean cried. "There's not enough Natty Ice in the world for that!"

The bros didn't even care the other girls could hear them.

"Wooly mammoths need love too, bro!" Gravy said.

"More cushion for the pushin', bro!" Trent said.

"Fuck off!"

Marta was getting annoyed, but didn't say a word. She knew these frat boys well and hated them more than anyone else on campus. They always taunted her and yelled insults at her whenever she walked past the Sig Alpha house on her way to class. Seeing that *they* were the cute frat boys Lauren had been talking about all week made her want to cry.

"How the hell are *you* related to Giant Gonzales?" Trent asked Selena. Gravy giggled in the front seat next to him.

"Who's Giant Gonzales?" Lauren asked.

Extreme Dean freaked out when he heard that Lauren didn't get the Giant Gonzales reference.

"You don't remember Giant Gonzales?" he asked, speaking far louder than he needed to. "The professional wrestler from the early 90s? He was this massive, furry Hispanic dude who used to fight the Undertaker. He was fucking awesome!"

Pro wrestling was kind of Dean's thing.

"But…" Lauren was still confused. "But why are you saying that Selena is related to him?" She turned to Selena. "Are you related to a professional wrestler?"

Lauren was clueless. Almost all the time.

"Forget about it," Selena said. "They're just being assholes."

"No, I'm serious," Trent said, trying to get back Selena's attention. "Look at the two of you. You're like a *Porsche* and she's like a *monster truck*. Does. Not. Compute."

Selena didn't let the assholes bother her.

"And you're like a Dodge Viper," she told him. "Just drive, jackass."

Trent said nothing more. He didn't like being compared to a Dodge Viper, which was a really lame douche-mobile that tried to pass itself off as a sports car. He adjusted his rearview mirror, shifted into gear and drove forward, taking them off campus toward the highway.

Selena's attitude toward him didn't sit well with Trent. He was used to girls being all over his dick all the time. A girl who thought he was a worthless idiot instead of the hottest, smartest, funniest dude on campus? The Alpha Bro did not think such a thing was possible…

A few hours outside of town, the frat boys blasted Jay-Z on the stereo and Dean freaked out with excitement. He bounced in the backseat, throwing his arms around, rapping along with the lyrics right in Lance's face as if trying to get him to join in. Trent should have known playing Jay-Z when Dean was around was the worst thing he possibly could have done to everyone else in the car.

"Now double your money and make a stack!" Dean yelled, spilling Natty Ice all over Lance and the girls.

Once Lauren screamed at the shock of cold beer splashing the back of her neck and drizzling down the back of her pink and white collared shirt, Trent turned the music down.

"How much longer do we have?" Selena asked.

"We're halfway there," Trent said.

Dean pounded the back of Lauren's seat. "I'm so fucking pumped. This is going to be the most extreme shit ever."

His face was getting bright orange. Dean's face always got bright orange whenever he had more than two beers.

"Where are we going, anyway?" Lauren asked. "I thought it wasn't that far away."

"It's a place my dad used to take me caving as a kid," Trent said. "I haven't been there in ages."

"What's it called?"

"You wouldn't have heard of it," Trent said. "It's a small area in the middle of nowhere called Turtle Mountain."

Lauren's mouth dropped open. "You're messing with me, right?"

Selena put her face in her palm. "Just great…"

Trent didn't know what the problem was.

"Why didn't you tell me we're going to Turtle Mountain," Lauren said. "Are you crazy?"

"You've heard of it?" Trent asked.

"Of course I've heard of it," Lauren said. "Who hasn't? I never would have come with you if I knew we were going *there*."

"What are you talking about?" Trent said.

"You don't understand," Lauren said. "Six of our friends were murdered near Turtle Mountain."

"We don't know if they were murdered," Selena said. "They disappeared."

Lauren looked back at her friend, "They were *murdered*."

They had the frat boys' attention, but the bros weren't actually taking them seriously. The frat boys rarely took flap seriously.

"So what happened?" Trent asked with a smile on his face.

"It was back when we were in high school," Lauren said. "Crystal and Des were on the cheerleading squad with me. They went with their boyfriends to a cabin up near Turtle Mountain. I was one of the last people to see them alive."

Selena continued the story. "Their vehicle was found smashed up at the bottom of a cliff. The cabin was covered in blood. Nobody knows what happened to them. Their bodies were never found."

"But it's not just them," Lauren said. "Since then, other people went camping up in that area and never returned."

"Those were just rumors," Selena said. "I don't think anyone else ever went missing up there."

"They say anyone who goes there will get killed or *worse*," Lauren said.

"What's worse than getting killed?" Trent asked.

"I don't know, but it's bad," Lauren said. "The area is cursed. Anyone who goes up there is going to die."

"It's all bullshit," Selena said. "The kids at our school made up dozens of stories to explain what happened to Jason, Crystal and the others. There was even a story involving an unkillable deformed maniac named *Buddy the Lobster Boy*. Nobody seriously believes any of it."

But Lauren was just shaking her head at everything Selena was saying.

"We can't go there," Lauren said. "We have to head back."

"Are you kidding me?" Trent asked. "We're not going back just because some of your friends disappeared."

"But it's dangerous," Lauren said.

"So where on Turtle Mountain did they disappear?" Trent asked.

"It wasn't exactly Turtle Mountain. It was nearby, though. Maybe a couple miles away."

"Then what's there to worry about?" Trent said. "It didn't even happen in the same area."

"I was devastated after what happened to them," Lauren said. "That's the last place I'd ever want to go to." She turned to Selena. "Tell them."

Selena shook her head. "Don't worry, Lauren. Whatever happened to Crystal and her friends isn't going to happen to us."

"But don't you think it's dangerous?" Lauren asked.

"Going to Turtle Mountain?" Selena asked. "No, I don't think that it's dangerous. Now, going caving with these jokers is a different story. I don't think I've done anything more dangerous in my life."

Trent snickered from the front seat.

"Don't worry, babes," Trent said. "You're safe with us. We're pros."

"Yeah, they should make a fucking documentary about us," Gravy said. "We're *that* good."

"How often do you go?" Selena asked.

"All the fucking time," Trent said.

Selena looked at the equipment in the back. It was all brand new. Most of it hadn't even been taken out of the boxes yet.

"Are you sure?" Selena asked. "All your equipment looks like you just bought it yesterday."

"Well, I haven't gone for a while," Trent said. "All my equipment is at my dad's. But I used to go every weekend. I've even *discovered* new cave systems singlehandedly."

"Oh yeah?" Selena laughs. "Singlehandedly?"

"Hell, yeah," Trent said. "They've fucking *named* cave systems after me."

"They've named cave systems after *my dick*," Gravy said.

Then the bros all gave Gravy mad props, as if it were actually possible for somebody to get a cave system named after their dick.

"It's true," Gravy said. "There's an area of a cave in Montana called *Gravy's Dick*. It's a long vertical tube. And when I say long, I mean *long*."

All of the bros gave him high-fives.

Ten miles away from Turtle Mountain, Trent pulled over at a small gas station/food mart/boat rental/fishing supply shop. The whole building seemed like it was slapped together with driftwood.

"All we need to do is pick up the boats and we'll be set," Trent said.

"Why do we need boats?" Lauren asked.

"The cave is on a lake," Trent said. "The only way to get to it is by boat."

"What?" Lauren cried.

Extreme Dean hopped out of the SUV and hooted at the top of his lungs; empty beer cans tumbled from his lap onto the gravel drive.

"Let's get this party started, bros!" Dean yelled. "This shit is going to be extreme!"

"Dude, pick that shit up," Trent said as he stepped out of

the driver's seat, pointing to all the cans on the ground.

Dean was too busy chugging another beer to hear what he was saying.

Trent went inside and got the boats he reserved. Lance and Gravy helped him attach the canoe trailer to the back of his SUV.

"Will two canoes be enough?" Gravy asked.

"They're supposed to be enough to accommodate 3-4 people each," Trent said. "But with Giant Gonzales on board, I don't know."

"She's like 3-4 people by herself," Gravy said.

"If it looks like she's going to sink the canoe the bitch is going to have to swim," Trent said.

When the two of them realized Selena and Marta could hear every word they were saying from inside the vehicle, Trent just smiled and waved at them. He was glad she could hear them. It meant he didn't have to explain it to her later.

Once the girls turned back around, Gravy said, "How the fuck is that fat bitch going to even get inside the cave? If she gets stuck and confines me in a tight spot I'm going to be pissed."

"No way, bro," Trent said. "It's *good* to bring fat people with you caving."

"Why's that?"

"They make good guinea pigs," Trent said. "See, we'll have Giant Gonzales lead the way through the cave. If she can fit through a tight squeeze then the rest of us will have no problem getting through whatsoever."

Gravy bobbed his head in agreement. "I see what you're getting at, bro. Smart thinking."

While the frat boys hung out in the parking lot, acting as if they owned the place as they always did wherever they went, they didn't notice all the locals staring at them. The place was in the middle of hillbilly country and city folk didn't visit all that often. They'd probably never seen a frat boy in their lives.

All of the people inside the shop stared at them with funny faces, wondering what these college douchebags were doing in their little town. Dean, however, had no clue they were irritated by his presence. Like everyone else he'd ever met, he assumed they all thought he was the most awesome human being they'd ever laid eyes on.

"Hey bros, where's all the flap in this bitch?" Dean said to two locals who were leaning against a pickup truck.

These two were hunters. Redneck hunters. Pissed off, trigger-happy, racist-as-all-hell redneck hunters. The last kind of people Dean wanted to be fucking with in the country, especially since they already looked like they were ready to put a tire iron in the back of his skull before he even came over to them.

"We're about to go caving, bros," Dean said, waving his hands in their faces as he spoke. "You ever go caving? It's going to be extreme, bros. Fucking *extreme*."

A dead deer lay buzzing with flies in the back of the rednecks' truck. It didn't look as if it were a fresh kill. The thing was rotten, like they found the body on the side of the road and were on their way to dispose of it. Dean, however, thought the hunters had just shot the rotten animal and were on their way to get it butchered. Dean was impressed. He offered them a high-five. They didn't even look at his hand.

"You guys killed that shit?" Dean said, still holding up his hand for a high five. "You deserve mad props, yo."

The rednecks stared him in the eyes. One of them chewed a scab off of his lip.

"I'm kind of an expert hunter myself, you know. Been killing deer twice that size since I was old enough to hold a gun. I prefer hunting bear myself, though. Grizzly bears. Ever kill a grizzly bear?"

The rednecks looked like they were two minutes away from cutting his nuts off.

"I got a sweet gun I keep under my bed in the frat house," Dean said. "Ain't nobody fucks with me on campus. I can hunt grizzly, moose, I could even kill a fucking dinosaur with that shit if they still existed."

One of the hunters finally spoke. He spit tobacco at the frat boy's feet and then asked. "And what kind of gun is that?"

Dean shrugged. The only thing he knew about guns was what he learned from playing *Call of Duty: Black Ops*.

"Sniper rifle," Dean said. "Military issue. No big deal. I can take out a squirrel from a mile away, right between his eyes and shit. *Booya!*"

He meant to say *Oorah*.

After that, Dean didn't know what else to say. The rednecks just stared him down. He turned away from them and bobbed his head as if rapping Jay-Z lyrics to himself.

Then Dean yelled, "FUCKING EXTREME" and chugged the last of his can of Natty Ice.

The other frat bros watched him from across the parking lot, wondering what the fuck he was doing.

"Bro," Gravy yelled over to him. "Stop fucking with the locals. Come on."

When Dean looked back at the others he realized the boats were already hooked up and everyone else was waiting for him.

"We ready?" Dean said.

"Yeah, let's go," Trent said.

Dean turned back to the rednecks. "Later, bros!" Then he jogged over to his friends, but instead of getting in the SUV he turned left toward the gas station.

"Just a minute," Dean said. "I've got to go to the bathroom."

Everyone in the SUV groaned.

While waiting for Dean to go to the bathroom, which must have been one of his epic leaks because the bastard took forever, a cop pulled up next to the SUV. It was an off-roading police vehicle.

A Law Enforcement Ranger, with the most pissed off, grumpy expression any of them had ever seen, stepped out onto the gravel drive and glanced over at the fratmobile. The man walked as if he had a ten-day-old tampon stuffed up his ass that was starting to give him toxic shock syndrome. He had his hands on his hips, cop-shades covering his eyes. It didn't take him long to notice the empty beer cans on the ground next to Trent's SUV.

"Are those yours?" the officer asked Trent, pointing at the cans.

The frat boy was leaning against his SUV, trying to act completely sober and relaxed. Trent looked down at the beer cans.

"No, sorry, bro," Trent said. "They were there when we got here."

The cop scratched one of his earlobes.

"Hmmm..." he said. Then he stepped forward, investigating Trent's vehicle.

Trent just watched the Law Enforcement Ranger as he circled the vehicle. It was obvious the SUV was full of the same kind of beer that littered the driveway, but the cop didn't seem to care about that.

"Where you boys headed?" the cop asked.

"Just up the road," Trent said. "Turtle Mountain."

The cop pointed into the back of the truck.

"You've got a lot of gear here," he said. "What's that for? Mountain climbing?"

"No, no," Trent said. He looked closer at the ranger's badge. The name on the badge was Roy. "We're not mountain climbing, Officer Roy. We're going caving."

The cop looked away from the frat boy, as if taking in the beauty of the mountains in the distance.

"You wouldn't be planning on caving in my jurisdiction, now would you?" the cop said. "There aren't any caves open to the public around here."

"What?" Selena said from the backseat.

"The caves around here are dangerous," Roy said. "Nobody's allowed in them. Nobody. Especially not a bunch of college brats like you. It's a $5,000 fine if I catch you trying to go into any of them."

Trent didn't break a sweat. He just smiled at the officer and patted him on the shoulder. Roy gave him a *get your damned hand off me before I put a bullet in your chest* face.

"It's all good, bro," Trent said. "We're just going to go boating in this area for a couple hours or so. But we're not going caving until we get up to Bear Point."

Officer Roy just stared Trent in the eyes, searching for a lie. Roy was a cop, so he was good at spotting lies in people. But Trent was a frat boy. He was a master at making his lies convincing. Otherwise, he'd never get laid.

"There are better lakes up near Bear Point," Roy said. "I suggest you wait until you get up there before you go boating."

Trent tried to hold back a giggle. "Sure, bro. I mean *officer*. Whatever you say."

As the cop turned around, heading away from the frat boy's vehicle toward the store, Dean charged out of the doors and yelled, "Dudes, I've got the most extreme boner for that cave right now. Let's go spelunk the fuck out of it."

The cop looked at Dean and then turned back to Trent. The frat boys in the SUV just gave him a salute and held back their laughter. Officer Roy shook his head. Then he pushed past the frat boy in his way.

Dean was too busy pumping his fist and banging his head to notice the cop was even there. He shoved a pickled sausage in his mouth and hopped into the backseat next to Lance, spilling more empty beer cans onto the gravel drive.

"What the hell was that shit?" Selena yelled at Trent once they were back on the road.

"What?" Trent said.

"That cop," Selena said. "What was that about all the caves in this area being off-limits?"

"Fuck that cop," Trent said. "He didn't know what he was talking about."

"He said they were too dangerous."

"He's full of shit," Trent said. "He's just saying that because he doesn't want us going on private land."

"It's still a $5,000 fine," Selena said. "I don't have that kind of money. Are you going to pay it?"

"Relax. We're not going to get caught. We'll hide the truck and set up the camp in the cave. There's no way anybody's going to find us."

Selena wanted to strangle the idiot.

"Trust me. I know what I'm doing. I do this shit all the time and I've *never* gotten caught. Nobody will ever know we were even there."

Trent turned off the highway and took a dirt road deep into the mountains. The path to the lake he wanted to get to was blocked by a barbed wire fence. He had to send Gravy out with a pair of wire cutters so that they could travel on. Gravy not only cut the wires but also reattached them as soon as Trent drove through, and then he wiped away the SUV's tracks in the dirt so it wouldn't look as if they came that way.

"My family used to go to this lake all the time," Trent said. "They liked it because it was private. Nobody ever comes here."

"Why was it fenced off?" Lauren asked.

"It's private property," Trent said.

"Somebody lives out here?" Lauren looked through the trees around them as they drove, but there were no signs of any homes in sight.

"Nobody lives out here," Trent said. "It's privately-owned land. The owner probably hasn't been out here for decades."

The path opened up to a large lake against the side of a cliff face. Waterfalls poured down the rocks into the water below. Tightly grown trees surrounded the lake like a green cage.

"It's beautiful," Lauren said.

The grass near the water was speckled with dandelions and small white flowers. Cattails grew from the water near the bank. It looked like something out of a fairy tale picture book.

They pulled over and stepped outside. The air was cool and fresh. It was totally quiet except for the sound of the wind in the trees, the bugs chirping in the grass. The whole area seemed like it hadn't been disturbed by human beings in at least ten years.

"This is tight, bro," Gravy said, giving Trent props. "Where's the cave?"

Trent pointed to the end of the lake where it met the side of the mountain. "It's over there, bro. We take the boats right into the cave there."

The girls squinted in the direction Trent was pointing.

"I don't see any cave," Lauren said.

"Trust me," Trent said. "It's there."

They unpacked the SUV and launched the boats into the water. Gravy passed out the gear to everyone. They strapped on their knees pads, elbow pads, sturdy climbing boots. When Lauren looked at her harness, she didn't know what to do with it.

"What's this?" she asked, holding it up.

"It's for climbing and rapelling," Trent said. "I'll show you how it works once we're in the cave. You connect ropes to it and shit."

"You mean, it'll be like mountain climbing underground?" Lauren asked. "I can't do that. I'm afraid of heights."

"Don't worry," Trent said. "We might not have to."

Lauren also saw the scuba gear Gravy was loading into the canoes.

"And what about that stuff?"

"It's for cave diving," Trent said. "Just in case some parts of the cave are only accessible underwater."

"What?" Lauren cried.

Extreme Dean pushed his way between them hooting at the top of his lungs, carrying all the 18 packs of Natty Ice.

"Hell yeah," Dean screamed. "This is going to be so fucking extreme. I'm so fucking PUMPED."

He put the beer in the boat, then turned to the others.

"Are you ready, bros?" Dean yelled. "Are you ready for the MOST FUCKING EXTREME ADVENTURE OF YOUR LIVES?"

Then Dean ripped off his shirt and flexed his steroid-ridden muscles. As he pumped both fists, his large jiggly breasts bounced in the air.

Trent and Gravy diverted their eyes and blocked their view of his breasts with their hands. The others just stared at him in shock.

"Aww, man, put your shirt back on, bro," Trent cried. "We don't want to see that shit."

Dean put his hands on his hips and said, "What?"

He had no idea what they were talking about.

"Just put your shirt back on and cover that shit up," Trent said.

A few months back, Extreme Dean had been the butt of a rather cruel practical joke. One of his less tolerant frat brothers convinced him to use a special new muscle-building formula that would help give him large bodybuilder pecs. Little did Dean know that what he'd really been taking for the semester was a female hormone supplement that caused him to grow bitch tits.

Most of his frat brothers had thought the joke had gone way too far. They tried to discretely convince him to stop taking the hormone supplement. It was incredibly embarrassing for Trent knowing that one of his bros had the breasts of a woman, but Dean never noticed what was wrong with him. He thought his breasts were actually muscular Conan-esque pecs. He couldn't have been more proud of them.

"Yeah, bro, that's indecent and shit," Gravy said.

"Why?" Dean said. His breasts juggled as he spoke. "My muscles need to breathe, bro. They need to BREATHE."

Then Dean began squeezing and massaging his breast muscles. He had no idea how weird that looked to the rest of them.

"Why does he have boobs?" Selena whispered into Lance's ear.

Lance didn't answer. He just slowly shook his head. He was one of the few people in the frat who didn't know about the hormone prank against Dean.

"His nipples are bigger than mine," Selena said. "He could milk baby cows with those things."

Dean didn't hear her making those comments to Lance. He was too busy flexing his muscles and allowing the wind to tickle the sweat glistening in the cleavage of his breasts.

The bros changed into waterproof clothing, but there wasn't anything for the girls to wear outside of their cotton clothes. Gravy wondered why the girls didn't have the right attire for caving.

"I did that on purpose, bro," Trent whispered to Gravy, while the others were packing the boats.

"But you can't go caving in cotton clothing, you know that," Gravy said. "We talked about this."

"I know," Trent said. "What happens when you go caving in cotton clothes? You get all wet and your clothes get all torn up." He pointed at Selena. "Can you imagine what she's going to look like with her clothes torn off her?"

Gravy looked at Selena as she bent over toward the canoe. He could imagine what she'd look like. He could definitely imagine it. *God, yes.*

But then he thought about the women's wellbeing. "But it

gets really cold down there, bro. They could get hypothermia."

Trent punched Gravy's shoulder. "That's the best part, bro. If they start getting hypothermia, they'll be forced to take their clothes off and get naked with one of us inside of a thermal bag." He looks at Selena. "Once I save her life by warming her up with my body heat, she won't have any choice but to do me right there on the spot."

Gravy lit a bowl and took a hit.

"Dude, you're so fucking smart. That's totally what's going to happen."

"I know! It's going to be awesome. Caving with these slam pieces was the best idea we've ever had."

The two frat boys high-fived each other.

"Guide me into the bushes over there," Trent said, pointing to a thicket of trees. Then he hopped into his SUV, backing it up into an overgrown area of the woods where the Law Enforcement Ranger would never find it.

As Trent locked the SUV and went toward the boats, he felt raindrops hitting him on the neck and forehead. He held out his hand and felt the water sprinkling on his palm.

"It's raining," Gravy said.

Trent nodded.

He said, "Let's get inside the cave as quickly as we can. We'll be safe from the rain in there."

Gravy wholeheartedly agreed. He hated smoking bowls in the rain.

"Check it out," Dean yelled from the canoe. "The boat's staying afloat! Giant Gonzales isn't sinking it!"

Dean, Lance, and Marta occupied one boat. Trent, Gravy, Lauren and Selena shared the other. They paddled their way through the cool, crystal lake, staring down beneath the surface at what seemed to be hundreds of fish swimming below. The whole area was a hidden paradise. Every single one of them understood why Trent's family treasured the place so highly.

Marta looked over at Selena in the boat ahead with a miserable expression on her face. She hated frat boys even more than her big sister—especially Extreme Dean, who was doing fat person impressions in front of her while paddling the boat. She was seconds away from tossing him in the water. For having to endure these douchebags, Marta was going to have to kill Lauren the second they got home. No mercy.

"Where's the entrance?" Gravy said, scanning the edge of the mountain.

They were getting close to the end of the lake where the water met the rocky cliff. Selena looked up. The sheer rock face towered above them, leading to the tip of Turtle Mountain. The top was green with vegetation. Vines and rose bushes grew down the side of the cliff, like red speckled hair flowing down the back of a snarling backwoods princess.

"It's straight ahead, bro," Trent said, pointing at a region of the mountain in their path.

All they could see were rose bushes growing out of the rocks and dangling into the water.

"Rose bushes?" Lauren asked. "I've never seen wild rose bushes before."

"Oh yeah, they grow like weeds here," Trent said. "My mother loved coming here for the wild roses."

When they got to the bushes, Trent grabbed one of the long stems to steady the boat. Even with the gloves on his hands, he felt the thorns pierce his palm.

"Where's the opening?" Selena asked.

"Through here," Trent said, pointing at the bushes.

They heard the sound of rushing water beyond the bushes, but did not see a cave entrance. Trent pulled out a machete attached to his thigh and hacked at the bushes dangling in the water. With just one whack, the others could see a small passage beneath the rocks.

"My dad discovered this place when we came here one summer," Trent said. "I don't think anybody's ever been here besides me and him."

Trent hacked at the bushes until a path was cleared. The roof of the cave was only three feet off the surface of the water. There was hardly enough room for their boats to fit through, let alone the people inside the boats.

"We have to go in *there?*" Lauren asked.

"Yeah, this is the way," Trent said.

"That's not a cave, that's a *crack*," Selena said.

"How are we going to fit?" she asked. "It's too small for these boats."

"The water level was much lower when I came here as a kid," Trent said. "But I think if we just duck down enough we'll be able to get through."

"How are even going to be able to paddle in there?" Selena asked.

"Don't worry," Trent said. "It'll get easier to paddle after the first fifty feet or so."

"What?" Selena yelled. If it were five feet of a tight squeeze she might have done it, but fifty feet? "Fuck no."

But it was too late. Trent ducked down and paddled the boat into the crack in the rocks. Selena had no choice but to lean down and bear the pain of rose bush thorns cutting into her flesh as she was dragged into the darkness.

The three in the other boat watched with amazement as the first canoe squeezed into the tight passage. They heard the two girls screaming as they were cut apart by thorns and sharp low hanging rocks.

Dean yelled back to Marta, "Giant Gonzales, squeeze down as far as you can. I don't want you getting us stuck in there."

"Fuck off," Marta said, but it was too quiet for Dean to hear.

When Lance saw how tight the opening was, he contemplated jumping out of the boat and swimming for shore. He did not sign up for this kind of shit.

"No way in hell am I going in there, bro," Lance said.

"Fuck yeah you are," Dean said. "This is going to be EXTREME."

Dean paddled the canoe inside, unbothered by the rose thorns clawing at his face and shoulders. Marta squeezed down without problems. Because she was so large the rose thorns attacked her body more than anyone else's, but the denim jacket she wore provided enough protection that she couldn't really feel them.

Lance, on the other hand, was having a panic attack. His fear of confined spaces was making him dizzy and tense. He didn't duck down when Marta did. Instead, he held out his hands and grabbed the rocks. He pushed against the opening of the cave, resisting Dean as he tried to paddle.

"I think we're stuck on something," Dean yelled, not yet realizing it was Lance who was keeping them from going deeper inside.

"I'm not going in there," Lance said. "Fuck this shit. No way am I going in there."

"What's wrong, bro?" Dean said, turning back. He couldn't really see Lance past Marta and the vegetation dangling over the opening.

"Nobody told me it was going to be like this," Lance said.

"Come on," Dean said. "This shit is *extreme*. Just duck down into the boat. It's not really that bad once you're in here."

Lance glared at the opening. It was three feet wide but the more he looked at it the smaller it appeared. In his reality, the space was only a foot wide or less.

"No way, bro," Lance said.

Dean kept paddling forward, trying to force Lance inside.

"Come on," Dean said. "We have to catch up to the others. It's no big deal."

Lance couldn't hold on anymore. The canoe lurched

forward, further into the passage. Lance lost his grip and was thrown backwards, hanging off the back of the canoe as he was pulled into the cave.

"Stop," Lance yelled. "Go back."

His face scraped against the rocky ceiling, scratching up his nose and forehead. But the worst part was all the roots growing down through the rocks. They filled his face like a wig of human hair, brushing against his nose and mouth, making it difficult for him to breathe.

"Go back," he yelled again. But Dean wasn't listening to his pleas.

There was only darkness in front of them. Lance was sure the tunnel would eventually end, trapping them inside. He closed his eyes, trying to imagine he was somewhere else, even as his face was attacked by roots and mud. The fact that he was leaning backward over the edge of the boat, rather than tucked forward safely like Marta and Dean, made the experience several times more devastating. He turned his head to the side and took deep breaths, praying that he would die quickly so that it would all be over with.

The passage went on for quite a ways, much longer than fifty feet. And it got smaller before it got bigger. It also got a lot darker. Trent turned on the light on his helmet. It didn't really do much good, though. With his head leaned down he couldn't really see where he was going.

Trent could hear all the people he was leading. All the girls were crying and whining as cold mud brushed against their backs, Lance was somewhere way in the back crying and pleading to go back, and Dean's voice echoed through the cave as he yelled, "This is so fucking extreme, bros! I'm having a brogasm in my pants right now!"

When the cavern opened up, it didn't open up to much.

It was a small area the size of a men's bathroom. The ceiling was high, though. A small waterfall came down from the rocks above and emptied into the stream leading out to the lake.

"The water in the lake all comes from here," Trent said, pointing up at the waterfall.

The girls turned on the lights on their helmets so they could see better. Normally they might have thought the waterfall was pretty, but instead it made them nervous. They were in a rather small chamber. The waterfall came down with such force that it made them feel as if the room was going to flood within minutes.

When Dean's canoe reached this chamber, Lance gasped for breath so loudly that it seemed as if he'd been underwater the whole time. Based on how rapidly he was breathing, it wouldn't have been too far off. His anxiety had seized up his lungs through the entire passage.

They pulled their canoes onto the rocky shore of the cavern, which was really only the size of a hotel balcony. With the boats pulled up onto the rocks, there was hardly enough space for all of them to stand up.

"My father discovered this place," Trent told them. He had to speak loudly so they could hear him over the sound of running water. "Because he discovered it, he was able to name it."

Then Trent raised his voice so that it would echo through the chamber.

"Welcome to the Devil's Kidneys," Trent said, his voice reverberating against the walls.

"Why is it called the Devil's Kidneys?" Lauren asked.

"Because it's kidney-shaped," Trent said. "It's also wicked as fuck."

"Sweet, bro," Gravy said. "But this is it? We came all the way out here just for this?"

Trent shook his head.

"No, no," Trent said. "This is just the entry room of a grand palace, bro. The way inside is up there." He pointed up to the top of the waterfall.

Selena looked up. "You've got to be fucking kidding me…"

"It's completely unexplored," Trent said. "When I was a kid, my dad checked it out once. He used to be a fucking master at caving back in the day. But when we used to come here when I was a kid, he only went in there once, for only about ten minutes. He said there was a vast cave system inside of there just waiting to be discovered. Ever since then, I've always wanted to go inside and discover firsthand what was in there. It's got to be something amazing. I just know it."

"So are we gonna check it out or what?" Gravy asked.

"Hells yeah," Trent said. "Let's make this cave *ours*."

CHAPTER TWO
LANCE

THE BRO CODE #68
A bro will always verify another bro's story
when he is trying to score.

Lauren noticed that Lance was having a panic attack. Nobody else seemed to realize what he was going though, but Lauren could tell. Everyone was huddled together so they could all fit on the small area of dry rock, but Lance was off to the side, standing in a shallow section of water so that he wouldn't be so crowded. He didn't have his helmet light turned on, as if he hadn't even thought of needing to see. His eyes were locked on the exit and the small amount of light coming from the water in that direction. Going deeper into the cave was unthinkable for him.

"Don't worry," Lauren said to Lance, stepping into the water and putting her hand on his shoulder.

Although Lauren wasn't very bright intellectually, she was a genius at reading body language. It was easy for her to pick up on what was going on inside of people's heads. A lot of her friends thought she was psychic whenever they interacted with her, but it was just that she was good at reading people based on their body posture and expressions.

"It doesn't matter about what happened to you before," Lauren said. "You didn't have control then. You have control now."

Lance looked at her with a confused face. "What?"

"It's okay," she said, rubbing his back. "You just have to relax. Take deep breaths. Loosen up. Nothing bad is going to happen to you."

Lance had no idea how she was able to know what was going

through his head. He'd never told anybody about what his brothers made him do when he was young.

"Here," she said. "I'll help you relax."

Lauren massaged a small section in the center of his back. Almost instantly, his muscles loosened up. It was a tense spot he never even knew he had.

"Eat some of this," Lauren said, pulling an oatmeal cookie out of her pack. "Food calms the nerves."

Lance took it and held it up to his face. He didn't realize he was squeezing it so tightly his fingers were breaking through the middle.

"I made it myself," she said.

Lauren watched carefully as Lance ate the cookie. Her eyes widened and her breath quickened. She made sure he ate every single bite.

Trent climbed first. He only had to go fourteen feet up, but even that high was difficult for him. The rocks were wet and muddy. His gloves felt unnatural on his hands, making it difficult for him to get a good grip. He slipped down three times.

"What's your problem, bro?" Gravy asked. "Forgot how to climb?"

"It's just slippery," Trent yelled.

"I could climb that with just my index fingers, bro," Gravy said.

"I could climb that with just my dick," Dean said.

Trent was pissed off. He was making a fool of himself, which was completely unacceptable for the Alpha Bro. His job was to be the embodiment of pure awesome at all times, which meant he had to be flawless even when doing something he'd never done before.

"Shine your lights at my hands," he said in a pissed off tone. "I can't see shit."

The others did as he asked. Then Trent got all serious, bro-down serious, and forced himself up the rock wall. When his fingers began to slip, he gripped the rocks so tightly that he felt his fingernails crack inside his glove. His groans echoed through the cavern, but he did not fall.

The others watched from below, shining their lights at the rocks above to help him see. Only Lance did not shine his light. Just looking at the small opening Trent was climbing toward made him uncomfortable.

"I have this nightmare," Lance said to Lauren. "It's pretty much the worst thing that could ever happen to me."

As Lance continued, he didn't realize that everyone else could hear him speak. Even with such a quiet tone of voice, it echoed in the cave. He said, "I dream that I've fallen into a well. It's not one of those wide open water wells. It's more like an oil well, something that was drilled by machine."

When Lance realized everyone was listening to him, he paused for a moment. But then he decided to continue, perhaps so that everyone would understand where he was coming from and empathize with his phobia.

"The opening is not even as wide as the opening of a child's sleeping bag," Lance said. "But I still fall in. I go headfirst. The hole gets even smaller the deeper it gets. I fall thirty or forty feet and then get stuck halfway down. Then things get really bad."

Some of the people listening began to wonder if this had actually happened to him before. They heard about children falling into wells or getting trapped in confining spaces. They wondered if Lance was one of those boys they heard about on the news.

Lance continued, "Even though my body is too large for the hole, I am still pushed down deeper. The walls of the hole are wet and muddy and act like a lubricant. My weight forces me deeper and the passage keeps getting smaller. The walls constrict around me. It's like I'm in the belly of a snake. The air is crushed out of my lungs. I can't even breathe or scream anymore. The hole keeps getting smaller and smaller."

Trent made it up to the top of the waterfall and looked back to see everyone had stopped paying attention to him and were more focused on Lance. He had no idea what was going on, nor did he care. He sat at the top of the waterfall, almost a foot of water pouring over his lap, and pulled the rope from his backpack.

"Then somebody else falls into the well," Lance said. "He slides all the way down until his upper body becomes entangled in my legs, overlapping me. I don't know who he is or how he got there. He also cannot scream because the air is crushed out of his lungs. The man struggles, but his movements only cause us to sink deeper and become more constricted."

Trent lowered the rope down and Selena took it. She was athletic and regularly went to the rock climbing gym by the campus. It didn't take her much effort to climb the wall.

"Another person falls into the well," Lance said. "And then another. One by one, people drop down on top of me, all of them struggling and pushing. Their weight forces me even deeper into the shrinking passage."

Once Selena dropped the rope for her sister to climb, Trent went on ahead by himself, climbing up the passage where the water was issuing.

"The hole becomes the width of a drain pipe, not even large enough to fit my head, but I am still forced downward. My body is squeezed and crushed into an unnatural shape. I have no idea why, but I'm still alive."

Selena helped Marta climb to the top. It was slow going, but Marta was more physically capable than the frat boys would have thought. She wasn't agile but she was very muscular. She could probably bench-press more weight than Trent or Gravy.

"By the end, there are at least a dozen people on top of me," Lance said. "That's when someone starts filling in the hole. I have no idea who, but there are people outside the well who know we're all down here. They might have even been the ones to put us all down there in the first place. They shovel dirt into the hole and bury us alive. They pack the dirt all the way to the surface and lay down concrete, so that nobody will ever know we were there."

After Marta was halfway up, Extreme Dean took his turn. He laughed and pointed at the girl's massive ass as he climbed up beneath her. Nobody else was paying attention.

"The worst part of it isn't just that I'm buried alive," Lance said. "It's that it doesn't kill me. I pray for death but I do not die, nor do any of the other people buried with me. It is the worst hell I could possibly imagine."

When he was done with his story, Lauren hugged him and told him that nothing like that was ever going to happen to him. But Gravy did the complete opposite of comfort the guy. Consoling a friend after a story like that was definitely not bro code. It was Gravy's obligation to give him shit for being such a scared little vagina.

"What the hell is that pussy shit?" Gravy yelled. "What's so scary about that?"

Lauren said, "So you're saying it wouldn't bother you if you were trapped in a hole like that?"

"Fuck no," Gravy said. "I'm not scared of shit. If I fell in a hole I'd just climb up backwards."

"And what if people fell on top of you?" Lance asked.

"I'd just kick their ass until they got out of my way," Gravy said. Then Gravy took the rope.

"You're next, bro," Gravy said.

Lance looked at the rope and shook his head.

"We're not leaving you here," Gravy said. "You're coming with."

"Yeah, but I'm not ready," Lance said. "You go next. I'll go after you."

"Bullshit," Gravy said. "I'm going last to make sure nobody stays behind. No pussying out."

He handed Lance the rope. Lance took it, held it in his

hands, and looked up. He wasn't worried about the climb. It was the hole in the wall he was supposed to go through that panicked him. The others were already up there, crawling deeper into the mountain. He didn't want to join them.

"This is it," Lauren said. "You can do it. Deep down, you know you can."

But Lance's body language responded to her, *There's no fucking way. No fucking way in hell.*

Then Lauren turned on his helmet light for him.

At least five minutes passed before Lance could build up enough courage to climb the rope. But eventually, with enough support from Lauren and bullying from Gravy, he was able to climb up into the fissure.

It was even tighter than he expected, but Lance was able to go through the opening without having a panic attack. He looked above, in the direction the others had gone. The water cut through the rock like a tube of wax, creating a smooth sloping passage. It was wider than it was high. He'd have to climb up on his hands and knees.

He turned around expecting to see Lauren behind him, but she hadn't climbed up yet.

"You guys coming?" Lance asked.

Neither Lauren nor Gravy said anything to him. He peered down, but he didn't see anyone. The only light down there was coming from the water.

"Hello?" His voice echoed through the chamber.

No response. It was as if they'd disappeared.

Lance waited for a few minutes, but they did not come. He decided to go on without them. He didn't know what else to do. He had to catch up to the others.

It was like entering the mouth of a dinosaur as he crawled upward. Sharp rocks dangled from the ceiling like toothy jaws, the rock floor was smooth and wet like a tongue, and the water running through his fingers and legs was a cold stream of saliva.

He moved slowly, one foot at a time. Because he was so focused on balancing himself on the slippery rocks, he didn't have time to be afraid of the constricting walls. He quickly learned that the tightness of the passage was not nearly as hard to endure as he imagined. He couldn't stand up, but he didn't feel as if he were trapped. He felt like he could go back at any time if he wanted.

There were much worse things he had to endure than the confined spaces. For instance, the water he climbed through was freezing. The cold temperature was not something he was expecting. The icy droplets splashing him in the face felt like needles. And although his clothes were waterproof, he could still feel the freezing temperature through the fabric.

There was also the darkness. All he could see was what was immediately in front of him, just barely made visible by the beam of light on his head. It was the darkness that was the most terrifying to him. It was crushing. The walls were not nearly as constricting as the darkness. But Lance just took it one foot at a time, focusing only on what he was doing and not what was waiting for him in the darkness.

"Where'd you guys go?" Lance asked.

He didn't see anyone up ahead. There were lights flickering up there a while ago, but not anymore. He wondered if the flickering light was ever there to begin with. The slope was getting much steeper, the rocks much more slippery.

"Lauren?" he yelled, looking back the way he came. "Gravy?"

The other two had never come. He wondered what happened to them.

"What's taking you so long?" Lance asked, not that anyone was listening. He turned to the path ahead. "Dean? Trent?"

Even if they were up there, he couldn't hear them. The noise of rushing water was so loud it drowned out every sound.

At first, Lance wanted to panic. He was in the middle of the cave all by himself. He wondered if his friends had all ditched him on purpose, just to fuck with him. But then he closed his eyes. He took deep breaths. Then all his worries were gone.

Caving was not nearly as bad as he thought. It was calm, peaceful. The sound of the running water was soothing. Even though the air was thick with the smell of soil, it was still cool and refreshing in his lungs.

He thought back to what had made him claustrophobic in the first place. When he was a child, his big brothers forced him to play a game called *Time Machine*. He was the youngest of four boys. All of them were much larger than him. There was no way he could ever get out of doing whatever they wanted him to do.

Time Machine was a game they'd play where all four boys would enter a sleeping bag at the same time headfirst. They would pile in there with their heads at the end, then zip up the bag the rest of the way so there was no way out. All four boys could hardly fit inside the bag, but they forced themselves into it like tamales in a can. Lance could hardly breathe. The only air inside came from the sweaty warmth issuing from his brothers' shirtless bodies.

Then the four boys would pretend to travel back in time. They did this by rolling around on the floor. It was bad enough with how crowded it was inside of the bag, but when they rolled around, tumbling on top of each other, their limbs tangling together, it would send Lance into a panic attack. He was so small that he was compressed by the massive weight of his older brothers. They practically drowned him in their sweat. Then, when it was over, just before they left the Time Machine to enter a new make-believe world, his older brothers would spray each other with what they called *time juice*. They opened plastic bottles of warm milk and squirted it at each other within the sleeping bag.

Every time they played Time Machine, Lance would always have a panic attack. When they finally unzipped the bag, he would be screaming and crying uncontrollably. And since the game bothered him so much it only made them want to do it even more. Lance had no choice but to suffer through it.

But in this cavern, Lance didn't have the same problems he had with his big brothers. He was all by himself. Nobody was crowding him. Then he realized that it wasn't the confined spaces that he was afraid of. He was afraid of being trapped in a confined space with other people.

Lance smiled and continued climbing upward. His spirit felt lighter, his mind at ease. He was lost in the middle of a cave, in a tight squeeze he couldn't even stand up in, and he was not afraid.

When Lance got to the top of the sloping passage, he realized he couldn't go up any further. The water he was following disappeared into cracks in the rocks. He'd come to a dead end.

"Hello?" Lance asked, looking around him.

His friends were not up there. He thought he was following them, but they were nowhere in sight.

"Where are you guys?"

He went into his pack and pulled out his extra light source, wondering if there was another passage he wasn't seeing. Flipping on the flashlight, he scanned the shadowy corners.

"Where'd you go?"

There was only one way they possibly could have gone. It was a deep hole in the rock, just enough for a human to fit through. He shined his light inside.

"Are you in there?" he asked, yelling as loud as he could.

The running water was still too noisy for him to hear anything. He leaned into the hole headfirst, putting his ear as far inside as he could.

"Hello?" he yelled again.

Then he leaned in further, listening carefully. He thought he might have heard voices down there, but he wasn't sure if they were actually real. It was very possible he could have been imagining the sound of voices within the white noise of the running water.

"I'm coming down," Lance said.

He looked back. Still no sign of Lauren or Gravy.

"You guys better be down here or I'm going to kill each and every one of you," Lance said.

He crawled in headfirst. It was the only way he'd be able to see where he was going. The hole went straight down five feet, then made a hard left into the rock. To get inside, Lance had to guide his way down with his hands, then twist his body to get through the hole. He took it slowly, taking deep breaths, trying to keep calm. Pushing himself like this was giving him a rush of confidence. He'd never done anything so brave in his life.

"You guys down here?" Lance yelled.

The passage dropped again, going down another seven feet, and then turned right. Lance continued to push himself. He wanted to get over his fear and crawling through this thin snake-like passage was exactly what he needed to go through in order to kill his phobia.

"Why can't you just go straight?" Lance said to the passage as he came to another downward curve.

It was like a spiral staircase descending into the earth; only this spiral staircase was barely big enough for a man to crawl through lying prone on his belly.

While inching his way forward, Lance felt as if somebody else was in his body taking over the controls. He just watched from the outside, wondering what the hell this person was thinking as he went through such a tight winding hole.

Then Lance stopped and realized what he was doing. He was all by himself, with absolutely no caving experience, going deeper and deeper into the ground.

"What the fuck was I thinking..." he said. "This isn't a passage, this is a goddamned worm hole."

There was no sign that anyone had ever gone this way. He couldn't imagine Dean or Trent fitting through here, let alone Giant Gonzales. He was all alone in there. He must have gone the wrong way. He had to go back.

"But how do I…"

He had no idea how to go through the passage backwards. Part of the way was possible, but not the steep sections. Is it even possible to climb a vertical drop in reverse? He might as well have tried to climb a mountain while upside-down.

He didn't know which he should do, push forward or attempt to go back. Part of him wanted to push forward and just believe the others had come that way. But the further in he went the harder it would be for him to get out and the harder it would be for the others to find him. So he just lay there, breathing heavily, wondering what to do next.

"Hello?" he yelled. "Can anyone hear me?"

He listened. If only somebody would respond. If only he knew he was going in the right direction.

"Is anybody there?" he said, staring into the black void beyond his headlight.

Then he heard something. It was a low rustling noise, like somebody moving through the dirt toward him. He stood motionless, straining to make sense of the sounds. As he listened more closely, the noises started to sound like voices.

"Trent? Dean?" Lance yelled. "Is that you?"

He continued forward, crawling toward the sounds of the voices. But the further in he went, the further away the voices sounded. He kept going. He prayed he wasn't just imagining things.

The walls became tighter, but he pushed himself through. Lance wondered if the passage was going to just get tighter and tighter until it hit a dead end. Then there'd be no way out for him. He'd have to just wait there until somebody eventually found him.

But then an even worse scenario entered his head… What if the others did come this way and were stuck up ahead somewhere? What if the others realized, just like Lance, that they could only go forward and not backward, and kept pushing forward until they hit a dead end? What if Gravy and Lauren were going to come up from behind Lance and also get stuck? He'd be trapped in there, surrounded by other trapped people, unable to leave, and nobody would know they were down there. It was Lance's worst nightmare come to life.

Although he was calm before, the idea of being stuck down there with other people sent him into a panic attack.

"Hello?" Lance yelled. "Where are you guys?"

He crawled forward toward the sound of the voices, moving faster, frantically pushing his way through the tight space.

"Answer me," he screamed.

The passage continued spiraling into the earth and Lance continued to force his way through. But as he shoved his way forward, he stopped paying attention to how narrow the passage was becoming. He jammed himself right into a tight squeeze without thinking. He could go no further. No matter how hard he pushed in either direction, he couldn't move.

He was stuck.

The first thing Lance did was struggle. He pushed back and then forward, whipping his arms around, breathing rapidly.

"Help," he called out to the darkness in front of him. "I'm stuck."

He stared at his beam of light. The cave seemed to get even tighter up ahead.

"Trent? Can you guys hear me up there?"

He listened for a response. The voices were still ahead, but they did not respond to his call.

"I need help."

Lance screamed until his throat hurt but nobody heard him. He dropped his head into the mud and closed his eyes. If the others were up there they had to have gotten through this tight area somehow. Lance was smaller than the other guys. It should've been easier for him to get through.

Then Lance heard the voices. They sounded closer, clearer. "Hello?"

They weren't loud voices. They were soft, more like whispers.

"Who's up there?" Lance asked.

As the whispers grew louder, he realized they didn't sound anything like his friends. They were the whispers of children.

"Hello?"

He continued to listen. The children whispered to each other. He couldn't make out what they were saying.

"Hel—" Lance cut his words short after a thought entered his head.

Something else was in the passage with him. It couldn't have been the voices of his friends. It couldn't have been the voices of children. Why would children be down in a cave like this, hiding deep underground in the dark? It had to be something else.

The walls closed tighter around him, holding him in place. As the whispers grew louder, Lance shut his eyes and looked away. Something was crawling out of the darkness toward him.

It came closer. A cloud of dust swallowed Lance's face. He kept his eyes closed but he could feel it against his skin, the flavor of rust filled his mouth and lungs.

He heard somebody else breathing. The whispers were so close they were practically inside his ear. He still couldn't understand what they were saying.

"What the heck are you doing down here, bro?" a voice said from behind.

Lance opened his eyes and saw a light shining on him.

"Dean?" Lance asked.

"Yeah, bro," Dean said, pushing his way through the cavern toward him.

Lance looked ahead. There was nothing there. He wondered if the whispers were just the sound Dean was making as he crawled through the passage. From a distance, their waterproof suits brushing against the muddy rocks could have sounded like anything.

"This is some *extreme* caving shit right here, bro," Dean said, excited by the tight passageway. "I can't believe you beat me to it. I wanted to be the first person to discover this place."

"Where are the others?" Lance said. "I thought you guys went this way."

"I *wish* we went this way," Dean said. "This is way more extreme than the way we went."

"Where'd you go?" Lance asked. "I couldn't find any other passage once I got to the top of the waterfall."

"We didn't go up the waterfall," Dean said. "We took a passage close to the bottom. It was way easier, just a small dead-end tunnel you can get through standing up. Totally lame."

Lance dropped his head into the mud. He couldn't believe he went through all of that for nothing.

"I left their pussy group and went exploring on my own," Dean said. "I wanted to do some extreme crawl space shit like this."

The sound of a can of Natty Ice being cracked open echoed through the cave.

"You mean you're not here to get me out?" Lance asked. "Didn't you guys realize I was gone?"

Lance had to wait for Dean to chug half his beer before he got a response.

"No, we thought you were with us the whole time. You hardly ever talk. It's easy to forget you're even there sometimes."

"They know *you're* down here though, right?"

Dean shrugged. "I don't know. Maybe." He drank some more beer. "Probably not."

"Great…"

Dean chugged his beer, crushed the can, and tossed it aside.

"Let's keep going."

"What?" Lance cried as he heard the guy crawling up behind him, squeezing up against his legs.

"Let's do this, bro," Dean yelled. *"LET'S DO THIS!"*

The large frat boy lay on top of Lance's legs as if trying to get alongside him.

"No, *get back*," Lance screamed back at him. "I'm stuck. Don't come any closer."

"Don't sweat it bro. Just force yourself through. Here, I'll help you."

Dean shoved Lance's butt, pushing him deeper into the tight space, getting him even more stuck.

"STOP," Lance cried. *"Don't fucking push me!"*

Then Dean pushed his arms under Lance's armpit.

"Then let me squeeze through," Dean said. "I'll go first."

"No fucking way, bro," Lance cried. "You'll get us both stuck."

"Ain't nothing going to get me stuck," Dean said.

As Dean tried to force his way alongside, Lance freaked. The idea of being stuck in that tight space next to Dean was too much for him. He kicked his legs and pushed at Dean, but the large frat guy didn't seem to notice him struggling.

Dean continued, "If a space is too tight for me I'll just break the walls until it's big enough. Ain't no cave too tough for *Extreme* Dean."

The panic took over Lance. He kicked off of Dean and pushed himself forward, forcing his way through the tight space. The rock walls crushed his shoulders together, ripped his flesh, and bruised his ribs, but he didn't care. He would not let himself get stuck in that passage with Dean.

"There you go, bro!" Dean yelled. "Force your way through that bitch."

Lance continued forward until he realized he was no longer stuck. He was able to crawl freely again. He shined his light ahead. The passageway was widening. Although he had no idea where he was going or just how deep this passage went into the cave, a wave of relief rushed over him.

"We should call this area of the cave *the snake*," Dean said, as he crawled through the tunnel behind Lance. "Cause it's totally like a snake coiling into the ground."

"I guess," Lance said.

"No, wait…" Dean said. "It should be called *Jake the Snake*, as in Jake "the Snake" Roberts, the pro-wrestler. That guy was *awesome*."

"Yeah…" Lance said, not paying attention to him.

Lance heard something up ahead. The whispers he'd heard earlier… They were back.

"He used to take these giant fucking boa constrictors into the ring and wrap them around his opponents," Dean said, getting really excited about it. "And they'd like totally freak out about it."

This time, Lance could tell they were definitely whispers. The noise was distinctly different from the sound of their clothes brushing through the mud.

"And while they were all freaked out about it," Dean continued, "Jake the Snake would kick their asses and give them like twelve suplexes."

Then there was a giggle. A child's giggle.

Dean was too busy talking about wrestling to notice. "And then in the 90s he became an alcoholic and would come to the ring all drunk, dropping his snake all over the place. He was the shit."

Lance stopped in his tracks and listened.

"What's up?" Dean asked.

Lance hushed him.

"Do you hear that?" Lance asked.

Dean listened.

"Hear what?" Dean asked.

There was whispering again and more laughter.

"*That*," Lance said. "Did you hear that?"

Dean didn't hear anything. "What the fuck are you talking about?"

Lance listened longer. They sounded like they were just ahead of them.

"It sounds like children," Lance said.

"Children?"

"I know it sounds crazy, but I swear I hear children laughing up ahead."

Dean cracked up. "Dude, you're just hearing things. That's what happens in caves. You hear shit and see shit that isn't there all the time. Just ignore it."

Lance nodded and continued forward. He knew Dean was right and just needed somebody else to tell him it was all in his head. If the voices were real, there would be no way that Dean wouldn't have heard them.

The passage widened. They were able to get to their feet and walk in a crouched position. Then the cave opened into an area about the size of a child's bedroom. Although the floor was rocky and hard to balance on, Lance was no longer restricted. He stretched his limbs and cracked his back. His muscles ached from being on his hands and knees for so long.

"Finally…" he said.

But Dean seemed to be disappointed.

"A dead end?" Dean asked, searching the walls of the room. "We went through all of that just for this?"

"At least we'll be able to turn around," Lance said. "We'd never have made it out of there if we had to crawl backwards."

"Shine your light into the corners," Dean said. "There's got to be another tunnel somewhere."

They scanned the area.

"There." Lance pointed at a pile of rocks against the wall. "Is that a way?"

At first, Dean didn't know what he was talking about, but then he saw it. Beyond the rocks, there was a massive opening. Dean shined his light through.

"Help me move these rocks," Dean said.

Lance helped him clear the passage. They could tell there was a wider area beyond the rocks, but they had no idea just how wide until they climbed through.

"Holy shit..." Lance said.

The cavern was enormous. It was so large the beams of light from their helmets didn't even reach the other side. Their lights could hardly even reach the ceiling. Like a queen's ballroom, the cave was expansive and majestic. Rock formations twisted like surreal sculptures throughout the room. Giant stalactites, maybe thousands of years old, hung from the ceiling, pointing down at them like mammoth tusks. A forest of stalagmites grew up from the cavern floor, creating a maze of shadows.

Neither of them could speak as they stared up at the glorious scene, overwhelmed by its natural beauty.

Then Dean looked at Lance and said, "Bro..."

Lance nodded back.

"We *found* this, bro," Dean said. "We fucking *discovered* this shit."

Lance couldn't believe his eyes. "I bet we're the first people to ever lay eyes on this place."

"Boom!" Dean said, then high-fived Lance as hard as he could. "Now that's what I'm talking about, bro. This is what I call *extreme* caving."

"I can't believe it," Lance said, shaking his head. "We actually found this."

Dean ran down the sloping floor toward a rock formation, pumping his fists in the air. "This is so fucking EXTREME." He pulled a warm beer from his backpack and cracked it open, then raised it over his head. "We're extreme explorers, bro.

We're like Marco Polo and shit."

As Dean chugged his beer, Lance went down to the forest of stalagmites, to get a closer look. They were so smooth, almost waxy. It looked almost like they were made of ivory.

After he was finished with his beer, Dean tossed it over his shoulder. It clanged against a stalagmite before falling to the ground.

"Wait here, bro," Dean said, running back the way they came.

"What do you mean? Where are you going?"

"I need to go get the others," Dean said. "They *have* to see this."

"What am *I* supposed to do?"

"You can come with if you want," Dean said.

Lance shook his head. It was going to be a while before he could build up the nerve to go back into that tight space again.

"No thanks," Lance said. "The next time I go through that will be the last."

"Suit yourself," Dean said.

He left his backpack behind so it would be easier to get through the narrow passage. Then he took off, leaving Lance alone in the massive cavern.

As he waited for the others, Lance explored the area, taking it one step at a time. The rock formations created an army of dramatic shadows across the floor. Any one of them could have been hiding a bottomless pit.

Although he knew he was all alone in there, he felt as though somebody was staring at him. From a distance, the forest of stalagmites looked like an army of disfigured stone people wearing pointed hats—all of them standing at attention, watching his every step.

"Ten-hut!" Lance said to the rock formations, as if a superior officer talking to his troops.

He paced in front of the stalagmites, his hands folded behind his back. "You call yourselves marines? I've never seen a sorrier group of soldiers in all my life."

He steps up to one of the tall rocks. "Private Benson, why are you slouching? Are you a soldier or are you a lazy pot-smoking wook?"

Lance laughed at himself. Then he pointed at the ground. "Drop down and give me fifty!"

After he said that, somebody giggled at him.

He turned around. It was the high-pitched giggle of a child. "Hello?" Lance said.

This wasn't a hallucination. It couldn't have been. The giggle was as clear as day and sounded as if it had come from somebody standing immediately behind him. At first, Lance wondered if somebody was just fucking with him. Lauren's voice was high-pitched enough to giggle like a child.

He went back the way he came and shined his light into the passageway. Nobody was in there. Dean probably wasn't even halfway to the others yet. There was no way Lauren would have been anywhere near this section of the cave yet.

Whispers echoed through the stalagmite forest. They were loud and much clearer than they were in the snake passage, yet he couldn't make out any of the words. It sounded as if they were speaking Spanish.

"Hello?" Lance asked.

He wondered if it were possible that other people might be in the cave with him. There could have been other entrances to this cavern all over the mountain. Just because the entrance Trent knew about was unknown to the public doesn't mean the whole cave system was unknown.

The whispers grew louder.

Lance followed them, stepping through the rock formations. As the light on his helmet moved, so did all the shadows around him, creating the illusion of movement. In the corners of his eyes, he kept seeing people walking toward him or ducking behind rocks. When he'd turn around, they'd be gone.

"Anybody out there?" he asked again.

The ceiling lowered as he travelled further into the cave. The only exit that he could find was straight ahead, toward the whispers.

When he was close enough so that his light hit the far wall, he noticed the rock face was covered in several holes the size of windows.

He shined his light through these windows; each one of them seemed to lead to new passageways.

The whispers stopped the second he shined his light against the wall.

"Hello?" he said.

Then a raspy voice answered back.

Hello.

Lance jerked his light in the direction of the voice and saw two young girls staring back at him from one of the window-like openings. They wore tattered colorless dresses covered in dirt. Their hair was gray and ratty. Dead expressions on their faces. Their eyes were two blank balls of white.

The shock of seeing them caused Lance to lose balance. He wasn't looking where he was going and stepped on a rock at an awkward angle. He stumbled and fell forward, catching himself on a large stone that slammed into his chest, knocking the wind out of him.

As he coughed and choked, he stared into a deep black abyss. Only a few feet in front him, hiding in the shadows, was a massive chasm that cut through the chamber. Had he stepped only a couple of feet further he would have fallen to his death.

Lance crawled away from the edge and looked back up at the wall of windows on the other side of the chasm. He shined his light through each of the holes, but he didn't see anyone staring back. The little girls, if they were ever there to begin with, were gone.

CHAPTER THREE
LAUREN

THE BRO CODE #145
A bro never touches another bro's muscles,
no matter how impressive.

The three girls were so cold, muddy, and banged up by the time they made it through the snake-like passageway that they hardly cared about the beauty of the rock formations in the massive chamber Dean and Lance discovered. They huddled together for warmth, trying to squeeze the water out of their clothes and wipe all the grit out of their hair.

"Why didn't you tell us we shouldn't wear cotton?" Selena asked Trent, showing him her ripped up soaking wet shirt. "We would have brought something waterproof had you warned us."

"Must have slipped my mind," Trent said. He was more interested in checking out the new section of the cave than dealing with their whining.

"We could've gotten hypothermia," Selena said.

"If you want I can keep you warm." He rubbed his chest in her direction. "I've got plenty of body heat right here."

Selena rolled her eyes. "Fuck off."

Lauren interjected with a squirrely smile on her face, "You can warm *me* up if you want."

Trent looked at her for a second and then turned and walked away. Lauren could tell what he was thinking. His body language was saying *Been there, done that.* He already fucked her the other night and didn't care to fuck her again, not with Selena in his sights.

Trent leaned against a rock and blew a rocket of snot from his left nostril. Gravy passed him the pipe.

"Well, that failed," Trent said, upset that his plan to give the girls hypothermia wasn't going to get him laid.

He frowned at the girls. They now looked disgusting to him—all muddy and shivering, snot dripping from their noses. And the worst part was that they huddled together to warm themselves up rather than warming against the bros. What a bunch of bitches.

"I'm still going to fuck that brunette," Trent said. "You wait and see."

"Totally, bro," Gravy said. "Hit that shit."

"Hell yeah."

Trent gave him a fist-bump for his support. However, he had no idea how easily voices carried in the cave. Selena was looking back at him with a face that said *in your dreams, asshole.*

"I'm telling you," Lance said to Dean. "There were two kids in that cave over there."

They were following the edge of the chasm, shining their lights at the wall full of windows.

"They were just staring at me with these horrible dead-white faces," Lance continued.

Dean didn't seem to care. He was more interested in exploring the cavern.

"Maybe they were vampires, bro," Dean said.

"I'm serious."

Dean changed the subject. "You sure there's no way across?"

"This chasm? We're not getting over this. Look at how deep it is. I can't even see the bottom."

"There aren't any other ways out of this chamber?"

Lance shrugged and said, "I searched it twice." He pointed at the windows. "The only exits are the way we came in and through that cave across the chasm. But there's no way I'm going that way."

"Don't worry about it, bro," Dean said. Then he finished the can of beer in his hand. "You can wait back at base camp with the flap if you don't want to go further."

"Base camp?"

"Yeah, we're making this room base camp, bro. For when we spend the night."

"So we're really going to sleep in the cave?"

"Hells yeah," Dean said.

He pointed at Trent and Gravy across the cave. They just returned from a trip to the canoes, carrying a lot of their equipment. There were sleeping bags, climbing gear, food, and plenty of Natty Ice.

"Dude, the beer's here," Dean yelled. "Let's get wasted."

He crushed the empty can in his hand, tossed it over his shoulder into the black pit, and then ran to the others. Lance waited behind. He listened for the can to hit bottom, but it just silently disappeared into the abyss.

An oil log was lit and the girls warmed themselves by the fire.

"Are you sure it's safe to burn a fire down here?" Lauren asked. "I thought fire burns up oxygen."

"Look at how big this room is, bra," Gravy said, wrapping his arm around her waist. "There's plenty of oxygen in here. Nothing to worry about."

Lauren looked over at Gravy and smiled, then laid her head on his shoulder. When she knew that Trent was looking, she kissed Gravy on the neck.

"Dudes, check this out," Dean said.

He tossed batteries into the fire, one at a time.

"What the hell are you doing?" Selena said.

"I'm trying to see if they'll explode," Dean said.

"Are you fucking stupid?" Selena said. "We need those."

"Just watch." Dean tossed more of them into the fire. "This is going to be awesome."

Lauren paid close attention to Trent's body language as she rubbed up against his best friend. She wanted to make him jealous. She'd already given Gravy a blowjob when they were back at the canoes, after Lance climbed up into the cavern and the two of them were alone. He used his not-very-smooth pickup line, "Want to see why they call me *Gravy?*" and she shoved his dick down her throat, knowing that it would come back to Trent eventually.

But, despite all efforts, Trent didn't seem bothered by any of her jealousy attempts. He was too obsessed with Selena to care.

"If we run out of light down here we're going to be fucked," Selena said to Dean as he continued to throw away their extra batteries. "Do you know how difficult it would be trying to find our way out of here in the dark? We'd have to hold hands and feel our way out, hoping we don't accidentally fall into that giant chasm back there."

"I'm not holding anyone's hand," Dean said. "That'd be gay."

When Lauren realized Trent wasn't in the slightest bit jealous of what she was doing with his best friend, she became so enraged that she bit into Gravy's neck.

"*Ow*, bitch," Gravy yelled, pushing her off of him.

She rubbed his blood from her lips.

"What do you think you are?" he asked. "Some kind of vampire?"

"Sorry," she said.

He pushed her away from him and went to the other side of the fire, holding his wound as blood trickled down his shoulder.

"I hate crazy bitches," Gravy said, not looking at anyone in particular.

"It was just a joke," Lauren said.

She turned to Trent and smiled. Her teeth were red with Gravy's blood.

"I'm not crazy," she told him.

There was a long awkward pause.

"*Any*way…" Trent said, turning away from her to look at the rest of the group. "We'll set up camp and rest here for a bit. Then explore other parts of the cavern. Not everyone's capable of making it across the ravine over there, so some of you can stay here until we get back."

"How are you going to get across?" Selena asked.

"Somebody will have to climb across the ceiling to get to one of the cave openings on the other side. He'll tie off the rope. It won't be difficult getting across after that."

"But which of you are going to climb across? It would take an expert to climb that thing."

"I *am* an expert," Trent said. "I've been doing this shit since I was a kid."

"You hardly made it up the free-climb back there," Selena said.

"It was slippery," he said. "Climbing across the ceiling won't be slippery."

Selena shook her head. "You're going to get yourself killed, idiot."

"I'll do it. You'll see."

"It's going to be so fucking extreme, bro," Dean said, getting between them. "You should let me do it. I'll be like Sylvester Stallone in Cliffhanger, climbing freehanded while fighting terrorists at the same time. It'll be fucking *awesome*."

"No way," Gravy said. "I should be the one to do it. You ever see me palm a basketball? My hands are like machines, bro. I could hang from a fifty story balcony with just one hand and never fall, even if I was there for hours."

"Hell yeah, bro," Dean said, high-fiving Gravy and then Trent. "We should all go together."

Selena just shook her head at them. "You're all going to die. You guys know that right? You're not as badass as you all think you are."

"No, we're even *more* badass than that," Dean said, then pumped his fist. "Booya!"

"Who wants lunch?" Lauren asked.

She dug into her pack and pulled out plastic bags filled with cookies and meat pies.

"I made everything myself." She passed them out to everyone. "There's enough for everyone."

Dean tore into a bag of cookies and ate two at once, holding his open can of beer between his breasts.

"I cook all the time," Lauren said. "It's kind of my thing. I make the *best* food."

She went to Trent and gave him a meat pie.

"What's this?" he asked, busy organizing the equipment.

She smiled and flirted with her eyes. "It's kind of like a hot pocket only homemade. I made this one special for you. It's delicious."

Trent took one bite, then spit it on the ground.

"It tastes like shit," he said.

Then he tossed it over his shoulder and walked away.

"I'm sorry..." she said.

She looked at her food on the ground and wanted to cry. She worked so hard on that pie. What Trent thought about her food was really important to her. She really wanted him to like it.

He said that it tasted like shit. That's because he actually was tasting shit. Lauren's shit. A few tablespoons of Lauren's feces were cooked inside of the food.

Lauren was obsessed with cooking for other people. She loved to see people enjoy something that she created with her own hands. But after a while, she wanted more. She wanted her food to be more special, more personal, more *intimate*. She wanted to put a piece of herself into everything she made.

At first, she just spit into the food she cooked. It wasn't much, just a little saliva. Nobody ever noticed. Then she started putting more of her body fluids into her recipes. Sometimes she cooked with her sweat or her tears. Eventually she grew brave enough to cook with her blood and vaginal fluids. It took a while before she could prepare food using her urine, vomit, and feces. This was mostly because it required skill to mask such pungent flavors.

"What do you all think?" Lauren asked the others as they consumed her food.

They nodded their heads, scarfing down the cold meat pies and oatmeal cookies.

Only Trent's food was cooked with her feces. She considered that the most intimate thing that she could cook with. There was so much warmth and soul inside of human shit. She only fed it to men she was passionately in love with. For the rest of the food, she cooked with her vomit. Because she was bulimic, this was the easiest ingredient she had on hand.

"Dude, there's spaghetti noodles in mine!" Dean said as he chowed down on his oatmeal cookies. "These cookies are fucking *awesome.*"

Lauren had spaghetti the night before she made the cookies. Her favorite part of cooking with vomit was when large chunks made it into the food, like noodles or tomato or chunks of meatball. Combining her vomit with other ingredients made cooking a challenge.

She never knew how successful a dish would turn out until she saw other people enjoying it. This was because she never ate her own food. The idea of eating food with her own sweat, vomit, and feces grossed her out. It was important that nobody ever found out how she prepared her food or they probably wouldn't eat it either.

"*Mmmmm...* These are *so* good," Selena said, eating the cold stew pie. "It tastes like Indian food."

Lauren smiled. "That's the curry sauce."

"It's so tangy and rich," Selena said.

As they ate her food, Lauren's eyes widened. Her tongue curled into the corner of her lips. Her fingernails dug into her thighs. She had no idea that she was getting sexually stimulated as she watched them eat. There was something about watching them consume fluids that came from her body. It was like they were consuming a part of her. It was her body being put into their mouths, rubbing against their tongues. It was her body going down their throats and satisfying their hunger.

"Dude, you have to try a cookie," Dean said, holding a cookie to Trent. "They're fucking *extreme*."

Trent took it and said, "Fine."

He placed it in his mouth and took the smallest bite.

"Awesome, right?"

"Yeah, it's good, whatever."

Trent didn't speak as if he enjoyed it, but judging by his body language Lauren could tell he really liked it. She watched carefully as he ate the cookie. He took tiny bites, eating around the outside until only the gooey center remained. Then he sucked out the moist, creamy insides.

Lauren couldn't take her eyes off of his mouth as he consumed the doughy, tender folds of the cookie. When Selena and Marta saw the expression on her face, it was as if some invisible person was giving her oral sex and she was on the verge of having an orgasm. At that moment, Lauren felt as if Trent was all hers. He just didn't realize it yet.

The seven college kids cracked open the warm Natty Ice and decided to get drunk. They're not sure if it was because of the altitude or because the campfire was burning up all of the oxygen in the cave, but the alcohol hit all of them really hard. It didn't take them long until they were all trashed. Dean, having been drinking all day, was especially hammered.

"*Raawr!*" Dean yelled. He was walking around shirtless in his boxer shorts, lifting large rocks over his head. "I'm a caveman!"

He threw the boulder at a rock formation, breaking it in half. The stalagmite fell over in three pieces.

"Caveman smash!" Dean roared. As he pounded his chest, his women's breasts slapped back and forth.

The other guys diverted their eyes away from Dean's breasts, but the girls couldn't take their eyes off of him. Lauren felt a little upset that his breasts were larger than hers.

"Don't break those," Selena said. "Do you know how many centuries it takes for those things to form?"

He kicked two thinner stalagmites, breaking them in half. "Caveman no understand abstract concept of time. Caveman only know sexing and smashing."

He picked up the tip of a broken stalagmite and held it in front of his crotch. "Who will sex with caveman? Caveman cock *huge*."

The others laughed at him, even though they didn't find it funny. They were drunk enough to laugh at anything.

"Caveman need cavewoman to sex!" Dean said.

"You've got Giant Gonzales over there," Trent yelled, pointing at Marta. "She's a Neanderthal. Go fuck her."

"She not Neanderthal," Dean said. "She woolly mammoth."

He went to Marta and shoved his rock-penis into her face.

"Caveman slay woolly mammoth with rock cock!"

"Suck it, Giant Gonzales!" Trent yelled, giggling. "Suck that rock cock!"

"Leave her alone," Selena told them.

Dean didn't stop. Marta moved her face away, but Dean just rubbed the rock against the side of her head.

"Caveman cock hard and ready!"

"You guys don't understand," Selena said. "You need to leave her alone."

But they didn't leave her alone.

Dean continued poking at her with the pointy rock. "Caveman stab! Caveman stab!"

"Seriously," Selena said. "You *don't* want to piss her off."

"Why not?" Trent asked.

Selena saw the fuming look in Marta's eyes. "Because she will…" She'd seen that look a dozen times before. "Fuck…" A look of burning rage. "You…" A look that would make Satan himself shit his pants. "Up…"

Marta grabbed the rock cock before it could poke her another time in the face. Then her flaming eyes looked up at Dean. The stupid smile dropped from the frat boy's face as she crushed the rock penis with her bare hand.

"Back when she was in high school," Selena said. "Her nickname wasn't Giant Gonzales. It was *She-Hulk*."

The frat boys shrank at the sight of her. Dean gulped in fear.

"She's normally the sweetest girl you'll ever meet," Selena continued. "Unless you make her angry. You wouldn't like her when she's angry."

Marta got to her feet, still holding the crushed rock in her hands.

"You want play caveman?" Marta said, her voice deeper, stronger, imitating Dean's caveman language. "I'll be the caveman."

"No, I don't want to play caveman anymore..." Dean whimpered in a mousy high-pitched voice.

She grabbed him by his female tits. "You look more like cave*woman* to me."

She squeezed her fingers into a fist and then clubbed him on top of the head. He blacked out and fell into her arms.

"I claim mate now," Marta said.

She picked Dean up and threw him over her shoulder, then stomped away from the camp further into the darkness.

"I'll make mate pregnant with my young," Marta said as she stomped off into the darkness.

The others laughed their asses off.

"Holy shit!" Trent laughed, high-fiving Gravy. "Giant Gonzales just made Dean her bitch!"

"Giant Gonzales is the bomb!" Gravy said.

Trent turned to Selena. "Why didn't you tell us Giant Gonzales was so badass?"

Selena shook her head. "You're lucky she's just fucking around. If he *really* pissed her off she would have put him in the hospital."

"No shit?" Trent said.

"She was born with a massive frame and unnatural amount of muscle," Selena said. "She was by far the toughest person in our school. They even let her wrestle on the men's wrestling team due to her size and she went undefeated. The only match where she even came close to losing was versus this guy who was almost her size, but he was mostly fat and she was mostly muscle. She ended up breaking both of his legs before the match was over."

"She should rush Sig Alp," Gravy said. "We could use another wrestler."

Both of them nodded, completely dismissing the fact that she was not male.

Marta didn't actually rape Dean after she took him behind the rocks into the shadows, but she made it seem as if she did. She pulled his pants down and made grunting and huffing noises. When Dean regained consciousness, she pretended as if she had just finished. It was all just a way to humiliate him in front of his friends in the same way that she was humiliated in front of hers.

"You were a fine piece of flap," Marta said to him, imitating the mannerisms of a frat boy. She grabbed one of his breasts and jiggled it. "Let's do this again sometime, Sweet Tits."

He had no idea that the act never happened.

When they returned to the camp, everyone laughed and cheered. Gravy and Trent gave Marta the high-fives instead of their frat brother. Dean walked meekly into the corner, covering his breasts with his shirt.

"Hell yeah, Giant Gonzales *got some!*" Trent yelled, high-fiving Marta for a second time.

"Yeah, you wrecked that shit," Gravy said. "You are *the man!*"

After giving her mad props, they laughed their asses off at Dean. There was no way they were ever going to let him live this one down. There was also no way they were going to make fun of Marta's weight ever again. They were now kind of terrified of the massive woman.

After a few more beers, Trent and Gravy took Dean aside

and asked, "So how was it?"

Dean shrugged. "How was what?"

"How was Giant Gonzales?" Trent said, chuckling. "Did she make you eat her out?"

"Did she make you toss her salad?" Gravy said.

"Was it good?"

"How was it?"

"I don't know…" Dean said. "I was knocked out so it was all pretty blurry. But I think it was kind of… *extreme*." Dean nodded his head as he thought about it. "Yeah, it was THE MOST FUCKING EXTREME THING I'VE EVER DONE IN MY LIFE." Then he pumped his fist and yelled, "BOOM!"

The other guys laughed and patted him on the back. They couldn't help but give him props for actually being proud of doing Giant Gonzales. The rest of the frat was going to flip out when they heard about it the next day.

But Dean was serious. Although he had no idea that he didn't actually have sex with Marta, he now realized just how awesome the woman really was. She had giant breasts, she wasn't afraid to get what she wanted, she could kick ass like nobody's business, and best of all she used to be on the wrestling team. Dean was all about wrestling. He never thought he'd actually find a girl who was not only into wrestling but was a wrestling team champion.

He wondered if he was falling in love.

The frat boys were getting drunker and drunker. They didn't notice all the water leaking into the cavern through cracks in the walls. They noticed the puddles forming as they stepped through them, but assumed they were all new.

"Check that out," Trent said, pointing at movement on the walls.

They all turned to see dozens of white salamanders climbing

up the rocks toward the ceiling.

"Where'd they all come from?" Lauren asked.

"Lots of animals live in caves like these," Trent said. "They spend their whole lives down here without ever seeing the surface. Most of them were born without any eyes."

"Where are they all going?" Lauren asked.

"It's not *where*," Selena said. "The question should be *why* are they all going? It looks like they're all running away."

"Maybe they're trying to escape something," Lance said. "Something that scared them."

"Animals act weird to disasters," Selena said. "Like tornadoes and earthquakes."

"If an earthquake hit now we'd be so fucked," Dean said, laughing. "We'd be buried alive down here."

Selena didn't think it was anything to laugh about. She turned to Trent and said, "If an earthquake hits while we're down here I'm so going to kill you."

"Don't worry," Trent said, opening another beer. "There hasn't been an earthquake here for over a hundred years."

They watched the salamanders as they crawled up to a hole in the rocks high above.

Lance, Selena, and Marta were in their sleeping bags next to the burning embers that remained of their campfire. It was impossible to get comfortable with the rocky ground beneath them, not to mention the noise of Dean and Trent rapping Jay-Z songs on the other side of the cave which seemed to echo right into their ears. Marta, however, had no problem falling to sleep.

"They say you have your own yacht," Selena said to Lance. She was bored of lying there and wanted to start up a conversation. "Is that true or were your friends just fucking with me?"

"It's kind of true," Lance said. "My dad gave me his old yacht for my sixteenth birthday, but I'm not really allowed to use it. He doesn't trust me with it yet."

"That's still awesome," Selena said. "I wish my dad gave me a nice boat for my birthday."

"I rather would have gotten a car," Lance said. "At least I could go places with a car."

"You don't have a car?"

"I don't even have a license," Lance said. "In high school, my dad didn't trust me driving. A chauffeur drove me wherever I needed to go. Of course the driver was under orders not to take me to things like parties or rock concerts, so it was a pain in the ass."

"Sucks being rich," Selena said.

"Tell me about it," Lance said, with no idea she was being sarcastic.

Before they could fall asleep, Lance and Selena heard the others laughing and cheering on the other side of the cave. Then they began chanting.

"GRAY-VEE. GRAY-VEE. GRAY-VEE."

"What're they doing over there?" Lance asked.

"I don't know," Selena said, getting out of her sleeping bag. "I'm going to check it out."

"GRAY-VEE. GRAY-VEE. GRAY-VEE."

They went to the other side of the cave and saw Gravy hanging from the rock ceiling, climbing effortlessly across like a child on monkey bars.

"Holy shit, bro!" Dean yelled. "You're doing it! You're really doing it!"

Gravy gripped the hanging rocks like handles, moving across the ceiling one rock at a time. Dean and Trent gave each other high-fives. Lauren clapped for him, jumping up and down like a giddy cheerleader. They were all incredibly trashed, leaving beer cans scattered all across the rocky ground by the chasm's edge.

"How the hell are you pulling that off?" Trent asked him. "I could barely hang up there for ten seconds."

"I couldn't even do it for *one* second!" Dean laughed.

"I told you," Gravy said, continuing to move forward. "I've got a grip like a vice. I could hang up here all day."

"Think you'd be able to climb across the chasm to the other side?" Trent yelled at him.

"I don't know," Gravy said. "Let me see."

The frat boy turned and climbed toward the wall of windows on the far side of the chasm, moving slowly, one handhold at a time.

"What the hell are you thinking?" Selena said. "You're going to get yourself killed."

"Hell no," Trent said. "My boy's a pro. Just watch him work his magic."

"But he's drunk," Selena yelled. "At least wait until he's sober."

"Yo, he's *better* at climbing when he's drunk," Dean said.

"Bullshit."

"Just shut up," Trent said. "You'll mess up his mojo."

Dean jumped up and down, pumping his fists.

"He's fucking doing it," Dean yelled. "This is SO FUCKING EXTREME. You are the man, Gravy. You are THE MAN."

Then they went back to chanting.

"GRAY-VEE. GRAY-VEE."

It was just Dean and Trent chanting at first, then Lauren joined in. Lance and Selena even found themselves chanting Gravy's name by the time he got halfway across. It was just too damned impressive not to.

"GRAY-VEE. GRAY-VEE. GRAY-VEE. GRAY-VEE."

The frat boy made it look easy. Just one hand over the other, his legs dangling in the air. He didn't even bother looking down at the chasm below, just stared forward, his eyes locked on his target.

"GRAY-VEE. GRAY-VEE. GRAY-VEE."

"I can't believe he's fucking doing it," Dean whispered to Lance as the others continued chanting. "This is so extreme."

"GRAY-VEE. GRAY-VEE. GRAY-VEE."

Gravy couldn't believe it himself as he climbed past the halfway point, closing in on the cave opening on the other side. Despite what he said earlier in the day, he'd never actually gone climbing or caving before.

"GRAY-VEE. GRAY-VEE. GRAY-VEE."

This was his first time, and with his powerful grip and upper body strength he was a natural.

"GRAY-VEE. GRAY-VEE. GRAY-VEE."

Dean opened another beer and took a chug. Then he turned to the others and said, "I'm totally going next."

"GRAY-VEE. GRAY—"

Then Gravy lost his grip and fell.

He didn't cry out. He didn't whip his arms around as he dropped. Gravy just quietly disappeared into the abyss of darkness below.

It happened so calmly that nobody believed it was actually real. It seemed like he did it on purpose, like it was just a joke he was playing on them, like he was just fucking around and was going to suddenly appear behind them laughing and slapping his knee, saying *Got you good, ya buncha wooks!*

But it wasn't a joke. It was real.

"Where'd he go?" Dean said with a nervous laugh. "Did he make it across?"

"Dude, he fell…" Trent said, looking over the edge.

"Oh my god…" Lauren cried.

Selena held her hand over her mouth. She knew this was going to happen, she *told them* this was going to happen, but she blamed herself for allowing it to continue. Being the only sober person there, she should have done more to reason with them. But it was too late.

"He couldn't have fallen…" Lauren said, her voice fast and frantic. "This isn't happening. It isn't real."

Selena looked over the edge.

"Gravy?" she called down below.

Lauren and Dean also called out, yelling as loudly as they could, "Gravy? You down there? Are you okay?"

But there was no response.

"We need to go down there," Selena said.

"Are you crazy?" Trent said. "Who knows how far down that goes? I can't see the bottom, can you?"

"I didn't even hear him hit the bottom," Lance said.

"He could still be alive down there," Selena said. "He could need our help."

"No way," Trent said. "There's no surviving a fall like that."

"Maybe there's water down there," Lauren said. "He might survive if he landed in water."

Trent shook his head. "We would have heard a splash. We would have heard *something*."

"Get the rope," Selena said. "We're going down."

"Fuck that, I'm not going down there," Trent said.

"Then stay up here," Selena said.

"I'll go with you," Lance said.

Selena nodded at him. Trent couldn't believe the wimpy nib actually grew a set of balls.

"I'll go, too, bra," Dean said.

Selena turned to Lauren. "Get the climbing equipment and wake up Marta. We need to act fast."

"Do you even know how to climb down something like that?" Trent said.

"I go to the rock climbing gym every Sunday," Selena said. "I'm probably a better climber than you are."

Trent just shook his head, saying *whatever*, and trying not to let her see that his hands were visibly shaking.

"Gravy? Are you down there?"

Lauren stood over the edge, continuing to call out for their friend as the others suited up for the climb. Dean and Selena were ready to go. Selena leaned back over the abyss, holding the rope, looking over the edge. They didn't bother to wait up for Lance who had never done any climbing in his life.

"So how does this work?" Lance asked Trent, trying to hide his anxiety.

Trent grabbed the metal ring on his harness. "This is your locking carbine." Then he took the rope. "You want to weave the rope through here and then…" Trent stopped. He saw the expression on Lance's face. He was too nervous to even pay attention.

Trent looked him in the eyes, trying to figure out what he was thinking.

"You're only doing this because you want to fuck her, don't you?" Trent whispered at him.

"What?" Lance said.

"The hot bitch," Trent said, nodding toward Selena as she began her descent. "You think just because she's nice to you that she gives a fuck about a scrawny nib like you, who can't get laid to save his life?"

"Of course not, what the hell are you talking about?" Lance said. "I want to help Gravy."

"Bullshit," Trent said. "Give me the rope." He pulled the rope away from Lance. "I'm going down. You stay up here."

"But I want to help," Lance said.

"You can help by staying away from my bitch," Trent said, then he rapelled over the edge after Dean, giving Lance a look that said *don't you dare cock-block me, asshole.* As if getting laid meant more to him than saving his best friend, Gravy.

Lance went over to Marta and Lauren. They leaned over the edge, shining their lights into the abyss. It seemed as if there was some kind of fog down there, covering up where their friends were going, reflecting their light back at them. It didn't take long before Trent and the others were swallowed by the darkness.

Selena rapelled as fast as she could to the bottom, but she was hardly able to see where she was going. The fog was thick down there, and freezing cold, turning her skin purple through the tears in her shirt. The chasm was deep but it wasn't as deep as they were expecting.

When Selena reached hard ground, she was disappointed to hit rock instead of water. She was hoping to find a lake down there, for Gravy's sake. It was incredibly wet and muddy at the bottom, nothing but sharp rocks and puddles, but there wasn't enough water to break Gravy's fall.

"Do you see him?" Dean asked as he came down behind Selena.

Selena removed the rope from her harness and scanned the chasm floor. It was all rocks and shadows.

"I don't see anything," she said.

When Trent reached the bottom, they searched the cavern floor.

"He should have been right here," Selena said, shining her light in the area where he'd fallen. "He's gone…"

"Do you think he's still alive?" Dean said, shining his light at the walls, looking for an exit. "Maybe he crawled away, trying to find his way out."

"But why wouldn't he have tried calling up to us?" Trent asked.

"Maybe his throat got fucked up," Dean said. "Maybe he was delirious."

"Dude, he's dead. If his body's not here it's because some animal dragged it off."

"What animal?"

Selena stayed out of the conversation. She had her light shined on some movement in the shadows.

"What's that?" Selena asked.

The bros stopped arguing and followed her toward the movement.

"It's him," Dean said.

They saw Gravy's leg sticking out from behind a rock. They couldn't see the rest of him.

"He's still alive!" Dean cried.

They rushed over to the leg and shined their lights over the rocks.

Dean said, "Bro, you had us so fucking worried that—" But once he saw what was beyond the rocks, he froze up.

The rest of Gravy's body wasn't there. It was just his leg, still twitching, severed at the thigh.

"Where the hell's the rest of him?" Trent asked.

Selena pointed her light to a small blood-splattered hole in the ground next to the twitching leg. "Down there."

"Down there?" Dean cried. "How could he even fit? That hole's barely big enough for a groundhog."

Selena couldn't believe it herself, but she knew it was true.

"In accidents, sometimes a car will be going so fast when it crashes that the person in the backseat ends up stuffed underneath the front seat," she said. "Their bodies get smashed and folded up, forcing an entire grown man's body into a tight space hardly big enough for a pair of shoes." She pointed at the hole. "Gravy must have fallen at such a velocity that it forced his body down there, tearing his leg off along the way."

"You've got to be kidding me…" Trent said.

Dean went to the hole and looked inside. He couldn't see anything.

"How far down do you think it goes?" Dean asked.

"I don't know," Selena said.

Dean took a rock and held it over the hole, then dropped it. He listened as the rock fell down the well and landed on something with a dull thud.

Owww… they heard a voice echo from down below.

"Holy shit…" Selena said.

"Did he just talk?" Dean asked.

Selena nodded. She couldn't believe it. None of them could believe it. Gravy was still alive down there.

CHAPTER FOUR
GRAVY

THE BRO CODE #134
A Bro never leaves a Bro behind.

"We need to get him out of there," Selena said.

Trent went to the hole and yelled down to his friend. "Gravy? Are you okay, man? Can you hear me?"

The only response was a soft echoing moan.

"How the hell did he survive that fall?" Dean said.

"The walls of the hole must have been tight enough to slow him down before he hit the bottom," Selena said. "It was a one in a million shot."

"That's my boy," Trent said, laughing out loud and slapping his hands together. "Only Gravy could survive a fall like that."

Selena grabbed him by the wrist.

"It's not time to celebrate yet," she said. "He's stuck so far down there that I have no idea if it's possible to get him out. The pressure of the walls against him might also be the only thing keeping him alive."

"So what should we do?" Trent asked.

"We need to get help," Selena said. "Climb back up and go into town. Take Lance or Lauren with you. Dean and I will stay with Gravy."

"But we're not supposed to be down here," Trent said. "We'll get arrested and fined."

"Do you want your friend to die?"

Trent had to think about it for a moment.

"Okay," Trent said, taking deep breaths. "Okay, I'll get help."

"Hurry," Selena said. "He might be bleeding to death down there."

Trent nodded. He knew that Gravy's survival was entirely up to him. He couldn't let his best friend down.

Before Trent could grab hold of the rope, the earth rumbled. The rocks shook and thundered around them.

Trent looked around. He couldn't believe what was actually happening. "What the fuck..."

"An earthquake?" Dean asked, trying to balance.

"Get back," Selena yelled as rocks fell from the ceiling.

The three of them ran for cover, ducking under a ledge as rocks and stalactites fell from the ceiling. It only lasted a moment and then everything went quiet.

"I thought you said there hasn't been an earthquake here in a hundred years?" Selena said.

"There hasn't..." Trent was just as surprised as she was. "I guess it was overdue."

"We have to do this fast," Selena said. "There might be aftershocks."

She didn't have to tell Trent. He was already at the ropes, beginning to make his ascent.

Dean and Selena went to the hole by Gravy's severed leg. They hoped none of the rocks from the ceiling fell into the hole, burying Gravy alive.

"Are you okay down there, Gravy?" Selena yelled. "Trent's going to get help. You need to just hang on, okay?"

She listened. There were moaning sounds, but she couldn't understand any of the words. He must have been delirious.

"Shit," Dean said, looking at his shoes. "My socks are getting soaked..."

Selena looked over and noticed Dean was standing in a large puddle. The puddle wasn't there before.

"The water..." Selena said.

The sound of rushing water echoed through the chasm. It

leaked down the cliff walls, filling the areas between the rocks, creating rivers and pools around them. It flowed into the hole where Gravy was trapped.

Selena looked up at Trent as he climbed up the cliff wall and yelled, "The cave is flooding."

"Hurry, bro," Dean cried. "Hurry!"

"He's going to drown," Selena said to Dean. "We have to get him out of there."

"How?" Dean said.

"I don't know, but we have to try."

Gravy opened his eyes.

At first, he had no idea where he was. The light on his helmet flickered on and off. It took him a few minutes to realize he was upside-down and couldn't move anything but his head. Water leaked past his neck, trickling down the walls. Blood dribbled from his mouth and forehead.

He saw a light down below. At first, he thought somebody was at the bottom staring up at him, but then he realized that it was his own reflection in the water. The hole was flooding.

"Hello?" he said, as a warm stone dangled in front of his face, connected to a strip of fabric from his shirt, rocking back and forth.

His voice was soft and raspy. He could hardly speak. His ribcage was crushed, squeezing all of the air out of his lungs.

"Anybody there?"

If anybody was there, they couldn't hear him. The sound of the rushing water drowned out his voice.

It was like he was in Lance's nightmare, the one where he imagined being trapped upside-down in a well. Only this was much worse. His body was mangled and broken. One arm was popped out of the socket and bent backward behind him.

When he wiggled his fingers he could feel them tickle the back of his neck. The other arm snapped off at the shoulder and was now connected by only a thin strand of meat.

He couldn't feel either of his legs, but one of them was folded in front of him, the steel toe of the boot resting on his chin. It was like he'd fallen into a trash compactor, crushing him into a form one-third his original size.

"Motherfucker…" Gravy said, leaking blood from his mouth.

Another thing that made this different from Lance's nightmare was that the walls weren't made of soft mud, they were made of jagged rocks. Gravy could feel his flesh tearing against the rocks. The water trickling into the hole lubricated his flesh, causing him to slip deeper into the tight space. It felt as if he was being peeled as he descended.

He heard a scraping noise like nails on a chalkboard every time he slipped further downward. Every time he heard the noise, a shooting pain rippled through his body. It reminded him of the pain his dentist administered every time he drilled into tooth cavities all the way to his nerves—only this pain tore through his entire body. He listened to the sound for a few more minutes until he realized it was coming from his own bones. All the flesh on his arms and ribs had been torn away, exposing the bone which was now grinding against the rock walls as he slipped further into the hole.

With the tiny amount of air moving in his lungs, he screamed.

When Trent reached the top of the chasm, nobody was there to greet him.

"Lance?" Trent called out.

There was no response.

He followed the sound of voices until he made it back to the camp. Marta was on her knees, a thin stalactite was stuck in her back.

"What happened?" Trent asked.

Lance and Lauren tended to her wound.

"It fell from the ceiling during the earthquake," Lauren said.

"Shit…" Trent said.

"I'll be alright." Marta nodded at him calmly. "It's nothing."

Trent fist-bumped her for being such a tough son of a bitch.

"I'm going to town to get help," Trent said. "I'll be back soon." He turned to his frat brother. "Lance, come with me."

"How's Gravy?" Lance asked. "Is he still alive?"

"He won't be if we don't hurry."

"Fuck me…"

Gravy had no idea how he was going to get out of that hole, but he wasn't one to give up so easily. He'd told Lance that if he were ever in such a situation he wouldn't be afraid. He would crawl up backwards and force his way out of that hole no matter what.

"Okay, motherfucker," Gravy said. "Let's do this."

He wiggled his fingers, reaching for the sides of the well. One of his arms couldn't move at all—the nerves were no longer attached. But on the other hand, he could move two fingers. They poked at the rock wall near his face.

Even though he only had two fingers to work with, Gravy knew there was still hope. When he told his friends he could climb a rock face with only his index fingers, he wasn't lying. He knew he could do that for real. But could he do it while his arm was dislocated?

With his index finger, he stabbed into the rock and shoved off with all the strength he could muster. His body moved slightly upward. Only by a centimeter, but it was a start. His finger shivered under the massive pressure of his body weight. He tried again, pushing off against the rock. Another centimeter.

"Fuck yeah, baby." Gravy wheezed. "I'm not dying here. No fucking way."

But water was filling the hole faster than he could move.

"Come on, Gravy. Pick up the pace."

He tried moving faster, putting both fingers to work. He shoved off against the rocks, gaining almost an inch at a time.

"Yeah, fucker," Gravy cried. "Fuck yeah."

A cracking sound echoed in his ear as his finger bent backward, the joint snapping in half underneath his weight. His scream was like the hiss of a dying rat as the rock peeled away the flesh and bone of his only functioning limb. But before his body could slip any further he caught himself with his forehead.

"Motherfucker…" His voice grew soft and weak. "Mother-fucker…"

Then he tried climbing up the rocks with his teeth.

Selena and Dean were frantic. They tried building a dam around the hole to keep the water out, packing rocks and mud around the hole, creating a foot-high wall to keep out the water pooling around them.

"Is this going to work?" Dean asked.

"I don't know," Selena said. "It might buy us some time."

But no matter how tightly they packed the dam, water still managed to find a way through the soil and into the hole. Their only consolation was that the water only trickled into the hole when it would have been gushing.

"Hang on, Gravy," Selena said. "Just hang on."

But Gravy, down below, could hear nothing but the sound of his own teeth grinding against rock as he tried to climb in the most difficult and desperate method imaginable.

Lance found himself in the tight squeeze again, following Trent out of the cave. It wasn't as difficult going up as it was going down, but a creeping fear grew a lump of tension in his chest.

"What if another earthquake hits when we're in here?" Lance asked. "We'll be buried alive."

"Yeah, that could happen," Trent said, pushing his way forward on his hands and knees. "But if we hurry up and stop hesitating we might get out of here *before* that happens."

The further up the snake they went the more wet and muddy it became. Water leaked into the passageway, freezing their fingers and knees even through the waterproof gloves and kneepads. They knew it must have been raining hard outside.

"I think we chose the wrong time of year to do this," Lance said.

"You think? I thought November would have been perfect…"

Lance had no idea where Trent's bitter sarcasm was directed. It was Trent's idea to go caving in this location at this time of year.

The water was pouring in by the gallons by the time they got to the exit of the snake-like tunnel. It was so slippery Lance had to boost Trent out of the hole, then Trent had to pull him up. The waterfall was twice as loud as it had been earlier that day and it was running at least three times as hard. They had to climb down along the sides, using the walls as support, or else they would have been carried away with the current.

"We're almost out," Trent said.

He crawled down the tube as quickly as he could. If Lance didn't catch up soon, he planned to leave him behind.

"Hang on, Gravy," Trent said to himself. "We're almost out. Just hang on a little longer…"

Gravy's jaw lost its grip on the rock and he slid, his teeth scraping down the rock like a blade down a sharpening stone, ripping open his lips and chin, falling all the way back to where he started.

"Fuck this," Gravy said, spitting blood.

The water level was now so high that he could see his reflection clearly in the water. It was only a foot away.

"Fuck *you*," he said to his reflection.

But then he looked more carefully at his reflection. He could clearly see how mangled his body was. It was even worse than he realized. His face was skinless, the nose torn off. His clothes were completely shredded and his neck was split open down the middle. But that wasn't the worst of it.

"How the hell…" Gravy said, as he saw it swinging there in front of him.

Before, he thought it was some kind of stone dangling from cloth in front of him. It wasn't a stone. In the reflection of the water he could see it clearly. His chest had been split open and his heart had fallen out. The organ was dangling by its arteries in front of Gravy's face, just swinging back and forth, still beating blood into his body at a slow and steady pace.

"How the hell am I still alive?" he said, as the water level continued to rise.

When Trent and Lance got to the edge of the waterfall, they saw the canoes floating in front of them. At first it appeared as if they were floating in midair, but Trent quickly realized it was because the water level had risen.

"Fuck…" Trent screamed.

"What?" Lance couldn't get a good enough view of the chamber to see what was going on.

"The tunnel is under water," Trent said.

He pointed at the tunnel beneath the surface. The canoes could no longer get through. They floated on the water like rubber ducks in a bathtub, bumping into each other and rubbing against the cavern walls.

"What are we going to do?" Lance asked. "Swim for it? We'd never make it."

"Yeah we will," Trent said.

He jumped into the water, swam toward one of the canoes and climbed inside.

"Here," Trent said, tossing Lance a wetsuit. "Put this on."

"A wetsuit?"

"I've got two of them," Trent said, balancing in the canoe as he removed his boots. "Plus oxygen tanks. We'll swim out of here."

"Are you sure? Have you ever used these before?"

"Never," Trent said. "We'll figure it out."

They suited up and then dove into the water. Trent went first. He focused on breathing slowly under the water before he went too deep, just to test how the equipment worked. Once he felt confident he knew what he was doing, he swam down into the tunnel. Lance followed after.

As he went into the black watery pit, Trent thought of his best friend. Gravy was the man. He was one of the most awesome bros he'd ever hung out with. He also had the biggest pair of balls in the whole frat.

Ever since they were first-year nibs, Trent and Gravy were best buds. He respected the man more than anyone else at Sig Alp. It all started during their first month. Gravy passed out at their frat party when he was baked out of his mind. This was something you never do at a frat party, especially when you're a nib, especially when you're the first one out. While out cold on the couch, their frat brothers went to work on him. They put shaving cream on his hand and in his boxers. They took off his shirt and strapped some sorositute's bra to his chest. Then they drew all over him with a sharpie. They drew penises on his chest and face, drew a mustache under his nose, and wrote *cum on me* and *big fat faggot* on his stomach and ass.

Had his frat brothers known what kind of guy Gravy was, they never would have done that to him. When he woke up, he didn't whine or complain. He looked at himself in the mirror and nodded his head. As everyone pointed and laughed at him, he calmly left the frat house and bought himself a tattoo gun. Then he got his revenge on his frat brothers, tenfold.

Whenever any of them passed out early at parties, Gravy didn't use a mere sharpie to draw on their skin. He permanently tattooed their bodies with drawings of boners and vaginas and crude sayings like *fuck my butt* or *virgin* or *two inch dick*.

The victims of his tattooing were not happy about it one bit, nor were their parents who had to spend craploads of money to get them removed, but Trent thought it was hilarious. Many of his frat brothers thought it was hilarious until they found themselves victims of the drunken tattooing.

The problem was that Gravy didn't know when to quit. He didn't stop at just getting revenge on those who messed with him during his first year; he turned it into a regular thing. For four years, Gravy continued tattooing those who fell asleep early at parties. He even got Trent once, by tattooing little vaginas on the skin between his toes.

Eventually, Gravy had tattooed almost every guy in the frat house. By then, it was no longer funny. They knew they had to get their revenge on him. And the revenge was sweet.

Gravy had a birth defect. He was born with a misshapen heart. It was a bit too large for his body and needed to be reconstructed. During open heart surgery, Trent and a bunch of his frat brothers paid the scumbag doctor a shit-ton of money to let them sneak into the operating room right before they sewed him back up. Then they all took turns getting their revenge, passing the tattoo gun back and forth.

As Trent swam through the tunnel, he laughed out loud at the thought of that moment. Bubbles sprayed from his mouthpiece. He shook his head. It was the funniest prank they'd ever pulled on another human being.

Gravy saw something reflecting in the water. It was on the other side of his heart that dangled in the air. He shifted to one side and the thumping organ turned around, facing him.

There was something drawn on the side of his heart. Tattooed with black ink, there was a crudely drawn picture of a giant boner and a giant butt. With each beat of his heart, it looked as if the boner was going in and out of the butt. In sloppy handwriting, above the picture, were the words *buttfucking faggot*. And the picture was even signed, *With love, your Sig Alp bros.*

When he first read it, Gravy was in shock. But then a smile crept onto his face and he found himself chuckling. His laughter grew until the walls quaked around him.

"Nice, bros," he said. "You totally got me."

He continued laughing as the water level reached his face.

Trent swam until he reached the end of the tunnel, but it didn't let out into the lake. He pressed his hands against a pile of dirt so tightly packed it might as well have been solid rock.

Lance came up behind him and punched his fist against the wall with him. They yelled through their bubbles, feeling their way across. The exit was gone, buried.

They looked at each other. Lance's eyes filled with fright. Trent's filled with remorse. They weren't able to get out the way they came in.

When they swam back to the canoes, Lance removed his mask and said, "What the hell was that? Did the tunnel cave in during the earthquake?"

Trent shook his head. "That was no earthquake. It was a landslide."

"A landslide?"

"The rain must have loosened the soil."

"Can we dig our way out?"

Trent just stared at him with a somber face. "Half the mountain just fell into the lake, burying the entrance to the cave. There's no way we're getting through there."

"We could try," Lance said, shaking uncontrollably.

"Look, we don't have time to argue," Trent said. "All this water is supposed to empty out into the lake outside. But now that the tunnel is plugged up, all this water has nowhere to go. It's going to fill the cave like a plugged kitchen sink."

"So what's that mean?" Lance asked.

"It means that if we don't go through the snake right this second it's going to be under water," Trent said. "And we might not be able to get through that squeeze wearing scuba gear."

Lance nodded. "Fine…"

"Take whatever you can carry from the boats," Trent said. "We're going to need as much of this as possible. Batteries, food, rope. Get everything you can."

The two of them took the last of their equipment and climbed back up the waterfall, which was now flowing as strong as a river. The snake was flooding, almost half-filled with black water that gushed through it like a sewer pipe. When Lance saw the flooded hole, he began to panic.

"I can't go in there," he said.

"You have to," Trent said.

"Fuck no." Lance was shaking his head. "There's no way."

"If you stay here you die," Trent said. "You go first."

Trent shoved him headfirst toward the hole. Lance resisted, pushing off against the edge, running water up to his knees.

"Fuck this," Lance cried. "Fuck this, fuck this."

He felt as if he were being flushed down a toilet bowl as Trent shoved him in headfirst. Lance had no other choice but to crawl forward and keep crawling. He moved as quickly as he could, pushing his oxygen tank in front of him. The water made it easier to move—it felt like a pitch black tube-slide at a water park—but Lance's panic attack increased the deeper into the snake he went.

"Keep going," Trent said, crawling behind Lance, pushing him forward.

Lance coughed and screamed as the water splashed in his mouth. The water became deeper the further into the snake they traveled. If it got any deeper they'd have to use the oxygen tanks in order to breathe.

"Almost there…" Trent said, even though they weren't even close to being almost there.

Dean and Selena continued building the dam around the hole, even though they knew it was no use. The dam was two feet high, but the water level was quickly becoming even higher, spilling over the dam into the well.

"Gravy!" Dean cried. "Gravy…"

They didn't stop working on the dam until they saw the water level reach the top of the well. It overflowed like a glass left under the faucet for too long.

When Selena looked around, she realized the entire chasm was flooded. There was no longer any solid ground to stand on. It had become a pool.

"We need to go," Selena said.

She grabbed Dean by the arm, but he jerked it away.

"No, we can't leave him," Dean cried. "Gravy! Come on, bro. Come on!"

But they couldn't even see the hole anymore. All they saw were their lights reflecting off the water as it rose up to their waists.

Before Selena and Dean could get to the ropes, somebody else was climbing down. He was wearing scuba gear.

"What the hell are you doing?" Selena called. "We're coming up."

"Stay there," said the climber. It was Trent's voice. "We're coming down."

"Trent? Why the hell are you still here?"

He didn't answer until he reached the bottom.

"There was a landslide blocking the exit." Trent had to speak loudly over the sound of rushing water. "We're trapped in here."

"What?" Selena cried.

Trent looked in the direction of the hole Gravy had fallen into. He didn't have to ask what happened to him. With all the water flooding the chasm, it was obvious.

"We have to find another way out," Trent said.

"Are you fucking kidding me?"

Lance and Lauren came down the rope after him, splashing into the freezing water, looking around for an escape.

"Why are you all coming down here?" Selena said.

"We have to climb up the other side," Trent said, pointing up at the wall of windows. "One of those tunnels has to lead somewhere."

Marta came slowly down the rope toward them, carrying most of their supplies on her back like a mule. Her wound was bandaged up and she moved as if she weren't in any pain at all.

"Let's go," Trent said, wading through the water toward the far wall.

Selena grabbed him by the arm. "I'll do it. Wait for me to send down the rope."

She swam across the chasm and climbed up the rock face. Her fingers were stiff from the frigid temperature and her teeth chattered, but the climb was just what she needed to get her heart pounding enough to raise her body temperature.

"Hurry," Lauren cried as she shivered below.

Selena moved as quickly as she could, climbing freehand up the rock face. Each window she reached, she peered inside. Most of them were not tunnels, just holes that didn't go very deep. They gave her a short rest from the climb, but she had to go further up.

As she passed some of the windows, she heard a whispering sound. At first she thought it was just the sound of the rushing water, but then it sounded like children. Whispering children.

When Selena dropped down the rope, the others were able to climb up with relative ease. All of them except for Marta, whose open wound was still bleeding and making it difficult for her to use her left arm. It didn't help that she was carrying most of the supplies.

"Come on, you can do it," Selena yelled down to her sister. "Just take your time."

But halfway up, Marta just stopped. She couldn't move another inch, just dangling there as water rained down on her from the ceiling.

"Come on, Giant Gonzales!" Dean yelled. "You can do it. You're badass!"

But Marta just rested her head on a jagged rock.

"Come on, we have to pull her up," Selena said.

Dean, Selena and Lauren all helped pull the woman up, but Giant Gonzales was heavy. Even with all of their strength combined, they could hardly move her up another foot.

"You bunch of wimps," Trent said, taking the end of the rope and pulling with all his frat boy strength.

As he tugged, the large pack on Marta's back became lodged under a sharp rock. Trent didn't notice, still pulling with all his strength.

"Wait..." Selena said. "She's caught on something."

"We don't have time," Trent said.

As he yanked on the rope, trying to free Marta from whatever had her caught, the strap on her pack broke.

"The supplies!" Lauren cried.

They watched as the backpack carrying most of their equipment plunged into the black water below and washed away.

"Shit…" Trent said. He peered down at Marta. "Giant Gonzales, you have to climb back down and get that stuff. We need it."

Marta looked down at the chasm floor.

"Fuck no," Selena said. She yelled down to her sister. "Don't worry about it, Marta. Keep coming."

"That pack had all of our flares, glow sticks, and extra flashlights," Trent said. "Not to mention food, water and extra rope. Somebody has to go back for it."

Selena shook her head. "Forget it. It's gone."

"Do you want to be lost in the dark down here?"

"No, but we're not getting that stuff back." Selena pointed her light at the other side of the chasm. "Look."

The water disappeared into a cleft in the rocks on the far end of the chasm. Anything caught in the current was swallowed into the earth. Trent watched as the pack went under.

"It's gone," Selena said. "We'll have to make do with the supplies we have."

Trent knew she was right. He hated when bitches were right. Without saying another word, he helped the others pull Marta up the cliff.

"So now what do we fucking do?" Trent said.

They were crowded inside of the tunnel above the chasm, resting after the climb. It was much more difficult climbing up than it was going down. Lauren curled around Marta for warmth.

"What do you mean *now what do we do?*" Selena said. "You're the caving expert. You tell us what we need to do."

Lance kept his light locked on the passageway behind them. They were inside the same tunnel where he'd seen the two little girls earlier. He was worried that they were inside of there with them, hiding somewhere in the shadows, just staring at him and giggling with their whispery voices.

Trent didn't say anything. He looked the other way, ignoring Selena's comment.

"You *are* an expert, aren't you?" Selena asked.

Trent still didn't respond.

Dean looked over at him. "Go on, bro. Tell her how awesome you are at caving. You've been doing it since you were a kid."

"Fuck off, Dean," Trent said, shoving his friend.

"You're not an expert, are you?" Selena said.

Trent looked at her, but still didn't respond.

"Have you ever even gone caving before?" she asked.

Trent shrugged.

"I have," Trent said. "Kind of…"

"What do you mean *kind of?*" Selena was fuming.

"Well, when I was a kid my dad used to take me caving," Trent said. "But he never let me go very far into the cave. I usually stayed at the camp with my mom."

"And that's the extent of your expertise?"

Trent shrugged.

"Just great…" Selena turned to Dean. "What about you? Were you also bullshitting?"

Dean raised a beer into the air and said, "Hells no, bra. I've been caving since—"

Trent gave Dean the evil eye, as if telling him to cut the bullshit and come clean. Dean looked down for a moment before continuing.

"All I know about caving was from what I saw on MTV's Extreme Caves documentary," Dean said. "But I totally learned a lot from it."

Selena glared at them.

"So let me get this straight…" she said. "You assholes brought us down here, claiming to be experts, yet not a single one of you have any fucking clue what you're doing. And now we're trapped down here without any chance of rescue. Is that what you're saying?"

Trent looked away.

"I think Gravy might have known what he was doing…" Dean said.

"I can't believe I came here with you morons," Selena said, shaking her head. "You threw half the batteries for our lights into the fire, drank enough beer to make you clumsy and useless, and didn't even tell us to bring the right kind of clothes for caving. We're practically dead already."

"But somebody will figure out we're missing and come find us eventually," Lauren said. "Won't they?"

"Nobody knows we're down here," Selena said, then she pointed at Trent. "King Dumbass over there made sure of that. It'll probably be a couple years before his vehicle is even found."

"But there's got to be another way out," Lauren said. "There's got to be."

Everyone looked down for a moment, silent in their worried thoughts.

"She's right," Marta said. Everyone looked over at the large woman, surprised she actually spoke. "This is a large cave system. There are probably several ways out if we can find them."

"Listen to Giant Gonzales," Dean said, getting to his feet. "We're way too badass to die here. We need to get moving, find another exit out of the cave, and then go home to do keg-stands until we puke."

"Sounds good to me," Trent said.

Everyone but Lance was anxious to move on. He knew they had no other choice, but the last thing he wanted to do was go deeper into that cave.

"Are you sure you weren't hallucinating?" Trent asked Lance, as they stepped carefully through the tunnel.

The passageway only allowed one person to walk through at a time, but it was dry and tall enough for them to stand up in.

They hiked far away from the sound of rushing water, heading toward an unmoving silence.

"No way," Lance said. "I saw them as clear as day. Two little girls, whispering and giggling."

"Did you say whispering?" Selena asked.

Lance nodded. He told her all about what he'd seen.

"While I was climbing I thought I heard something," Selena said. "It sounded like children."

"You see," Lance said. "They're here. I swear it."

"Well, if they're real maybe they can lead us out of here," Trent said.

"Hell no, I'm not going anywhere near them," Lance said. "They didn't look right. They looked…"

"Dead?" Lauren asked.

"Yeah, dead."

"They're probably ghosts," Lauren said.

Trent whistled the *X-Files* theme as she said that.

"Seriously," Lauren said. "I heard that when people die in caves their ghosts get trapped and can't find their way out. They roam through the caverns for all eternity. Those two girls probably went into this cave and got lost. Their bodies are probably still down here somewhere."

Lance nodded. He wasn't sure if he believed in ghosts, but it was exactly the same conclusion he'd come to.

"You guys actually believe in ghosts?" Trent said. "Can you hear yourselves?"

"I don't know, bro," Dean said. "I've seen mad ghosts. Like one time I had my foot grabbed when I was trying to go to sleep and it freaked me out so much that I kicked it in its face."

"Did it punch you back?" Trent asked.

"Yeah, right in the head. So hard it knocked me out."

"Dude, that was just Gravy fucking with you," Trent said. "He does that to people all the time."

"Really?"

"Yeah."

"What a dick. I'm so getting him back for that when we get back to the frat house."

After Dean said that, everyone went silent. They had no idea if Dean wasn't aware Gravy was dead, had already forgotten Gravy was dead, or was trying to make a bad joke about his death. Either way, they didn't comment.

CHAPTER FIVE
TRENT

THE BRO CODE #52
If a Bro should fail at anything during sporting
activities or games, he is required to make an
excuse for himself, it is always the ball, bat, racket,
shoes, glove, controller or equipment's fault.

Trent was an asshole, but it wasn't really his fault. He was raised to be an asshole. It was what his parents always wanted for him.

"Being a nice guy gets you nowhere in life," Trent's mother always told him. "You can't be afraid to screw people over in order to get ahead. In this world, assholes finish first."

When Trent was young, he didn't like the idea of being an asshole. He wanted to have friends and he thought he needed to be nice in order to have friends.

"You don't need to be nice," she would always say. "You just need to be confident. Confidence is what makes people respect you. Confidence is what attracts careers, friends, and women. Being nice just makes you appear weak and insecure."

When he got older, Trent became more and more indoctrinated into his parents' way of thinking.

"Most Americans refuse to admit it, but success involves screwing people over," Trent told his seventh grade social studies class, reading from the essay his mom helped him write. "This country was built upon screwing people over. We wouldn't have electricity in our homes or gas in our cars if there weren't people on the other side of the ocean getting screwed over for the sake of our happiness. Businesses wouldn't make any money unless they figured out a way to screw people out of their hard-earned cash. Wars wouldn't be won unless our government screwed people out of their lives or their freedom."

His liberal teacher gave him an A+ on that paper, thinking he was making a statement against corporate greed. The teacher had no idea he was trying to promote this behavior.

"Nothing in this world is fair, my love," said his mother, a week before she died. "You have to do everything in your power to make sure you aren't the one holding the short end of the stick. You have to ask yourself: do you want to be the person doing the screwing or do you want to be the person getting screwed? There is no middle ground."

By the time he was in high school, Trent was happy he was raised to be an asshole. He was the most popular guy in his class and had more girlfriends than he could even remember. People feared and respected him. They loved him like the god of the Old Testament. That's how he wanted to be seen: as a *god*. He wanted to be nothing less than that. But for some reason he felt like he was missing something. Something *real*. He wondered if he was missing a real relationship with another human being.

As he walked through the cave behind Selena, Trent wondered if *she* was what he was missing. A woman he could love. A woman who could love him back. A *real* love. He was so used to getting women by manipulating them, physically or psychologically overpowering them, making them appear small and insignificant compared to him, using them for nothing but sex. But it was getting old. He needed something more than that. He needed somebody like Selena.

"Bats…"

Dean didn't have to point them out to everyone. They could all see for themselves. There were hundreds of them on the ceiling. Maybe thousands.

"Oh, gross," Lauren said. "I hate bats."

"No, this is good," Selena said. "Bats are a good sign."

"Why's that?" Lauren said.

"It means there's an exit nearby. These bats have to get out of here somewhere."

They couldn't even see the ceiling there were so many bats up there, crowding together, making noises that sounded like a cloud of locusts.

"Let's go," Trent said. "Let's find the exit as soon as we can."

"We can't go through there," Lauren said. "We're going to get rabies."

"It's actually pretty rare that a bat will carry rabies," Selena said. "And even if you're bit there's only a one in a hundred chance you'll catch the disease. Don't worry about it."

The ground was lumpy and thick with bat shit. There were black oily mountains of the stuff. Their shoes sunk in it all the way to their ankles.

"Isn't this stuff toxic?" Lance asked. "Should we be walking in it?"

"Dude, we should try smoking it," Dean said. "That would be *extreme*."

"Let's just get through here as fast as we can," Selena said. "Look for exits."

They shined their lights around the room and found tunnels branching out in many directions. There were exits, but too many of them. At least seven.

"Which one is it?" Trent asked. "It'll take forever figuring out which direction to take."

"Just watch them until they leave," Selena said. "If we see which direction they fly we'll know where to go."

They stared up at the ceiling for a moment. None of the bats seemed to be going anywhere.

Trent said, "We don't have the battery power to wait that long."

"Then let's try to scare them off," Selena said. "Throw rocks at them."

They looked at the ground. There were no rocks in sight, just the swamp of bat droppings.

"I'm not sticking my hand in that shit," Trent said.

"Just do it," Selena said. "At least you're wearing gloves."

Selena shoved her hand into the sludge, feeling around for something hard.

"What the…" she said.

The others stuck their hands in and helped her. Dean used both hands, moving quickly through, as if it were a competition to see who could find a rock first.

"Got one!" Dean said.

He pulled it out and raised it over his head. But it was not a rock. It flapped and squirmed in his hand.

"Bat!" Lauren said, yelling at the creature Dean held.

Dean threw the sludge-covered bat away, but the bat turned around and flew back at him, slamming into his chest.

"Rabies! Rabies!" Dean cried, slapping his arms at his chest, trying to get the creature away.

"Why was there a bat buried in that stuff?" Lauren asked.

Selena wondered what was moving against her hands. She felt them. It wasn't just one bat that was inside the sludge.

"They're everywhere," Selena said.

They scanned their lights across the swamp. The ground churned. Beneath the layer of bat droppings, thousands of bats were lying there, piled on top of each other, squirming.

"What the hell's going on?" Lance said, as soggy bats climbed up his boots.

He kicked them away. Everyone kicked and jumped, trying to get out of the pile of bats. But there was no escape. The creatures were everywhere.

"Why are they just lying here like this?" Lauren asked, kicking the slime from her shoes.

"They might be sick," Selena said.

"With rabies?" Lauren cried.

"With anything." Selena watched the creatures squirming on top of each other like a bucket of night crawlers. "They'd only be lying here if they were sick, dying or dead."

"Let's get out of here," Lance said, moving toward a random exit.

"Not yet," Selena said. "This could be our only chance of getting out of here." She turned to her sister and nodded toward a pointed mound of sludge.

Marta nodded back. She stepped through the black slime toward the mound, then kicked it with all her strength. The mound broke in half. Beneath all of the bat shit was a stalagmite. Marta took the half she broke off, aimed it at the ceiling, and then threw it.

Although it didn't hit the ceiling, it was enough to startle some of the bats. And those bats startled the rest of the bats. The swarm took off.

"Nailed it, bro," Dean said, raising his sludgy hand to Marta for a high-five.

The bats all flew through three different tunnels on the other end of the room.

"So…" Trent said. "Which tunnel is it?"

"That one." Selena pointed at the middle tunnel. It was the largest of them and more bats flew through it than the other two. "They probably all lead to the same place."

The bats squirming in the muck did not seem capable of flying away. They crawled and squealed in the mire, attacking boots and ankles as Selena led them through the swamp and into the next tunnel.

The bats were gone. There wasn't any sign of them or where they went.

"Are you sure they came through here?" Lance asked.

"Positive," Selena said. "There's got to be a way out up here somewhere. Just keep moving."

They followed the tunnel, but it sloped downward instead of up. If it were leading toward the surface you'd think it would be going up, not down.

Lance heard the whispering again.

"Wait…" Lance said, stopping everyone in their tracks.

They all looked at him.

"Do you hear it?" he asked.

Lauren looked around. "Hear what?"

"The whispering. Can't you hear it? The sound of little girls…"

"God damn it, nib," Trent said. "This shit again?"

Lance saw a white face at the end of the tunnel staring back at him.

"There," he said, pointing at the face.

They all looked in the direction he was pointing.

"What the hell is that?" Selena asked.

They all saw it, too. It was a pale eyeless white face, just staring at them.

"You see it, right?" Lance cried. "I told you. I wasn't lying."

Trent moved forward, heading toward the ghostly face.

"Where are you going?" Lance said.

Trent kept moving. He pulled out the machete strapped to his thigh. "I want to check it out."

"What are you going to do with that thing?" Lauren pointed at the machete. "It's a ghost. You can't kill a ghost."

Trent didn't care. He didn't believe in ghosts.

They closed in on the white face, moving slowly, stalking. It turned away once they were close enough to see it, oinking and growling at them.

"What is it?" Lauren said.

"That's not a ghost." Trent held up his machete, ready to strike if it came near.

"It's some kind of pig…" Selena couldn't believe her eyes. It was an animal species she'd never seen before. As somebody who had a passion for studying animals and animal behavior, she knew this was something nobody had ever seen before.

"Yeah, it's just a cave pig," Dean said, as if pigs in caves were a normal everyday thing.

They stepped forward into the cavern. There wasn't only

one of them. There were dozens. The animals were fat and white. Like the salamanders, they didn't have any eyes. The skin on their backs was hard, almost like an armadillo shell, and their tusks looked strong enough to break through stone.

"We've just discovered a new species," Selena said. "Subterranean Pigs. I can't believe it…"

The pigs snorted and squealed like bats, eating a purple fungus that grew on the walls around them, drinking from a small lake on the far side of the room.

"Anybody want any pork chops?" Trent said, moving toward one of them with his machete.

"Stay away from them," Selena said.

Trent didn't listen to her. "Why? Because they're a beautiful rare species that should be protected and not killed?"

He crept up behind a fat one, stuffed full of meat.

"No…" Selena said, backing away. "Because wild pigs are fucking dangerous."

As Trent raised his machete, the pig turned and charged him.

"Fuck!" Trent screamed.

He turned and ran. The pig snorted and snarled after him. He jumped onto boulder, out of the pig's reach. It hopped and snapped at the rock, baring its teeth like a mad dog.

"I told you," Selena said, laughing at Trent as he nearly crapped his pants on top of the boulder. She turned to the others. "Let's leave the pigs alone. When we get out of here, this is going to be huge."

"Are we going to be rich?" Dean asked.

"I don't know if we'll be rich. Famous, maybe. We might be able to name them. Either way, this is huge."

"I think we should name them Tankjaws," Dean said.

"Why Tankjaws?"

"Because it sounds AWESOME," Dean said.

The pig leapt up in the air, snapping at Trent, trying to rip out his throat. He tried to climb down the back of the boulder, but the pig circled around. It wasn't going to let him escape.

"You really pissed that thing off, Trent," Selena said. "You should have listened to me."

Trent didn't care. He poked at the thing with his machete, but couldn't do any damage.

"Can somebody help me." Trent sounded annoyed. "*Please.*"

A loud banging noise vibrated through the walls. It sounded like a cross between thunder and the slamming of a door. The noise startled the pigs, causing them to take off down a side passage, squealing and oinking with panic.

"What the fuck was that?" Trent asked, jumping down from the boulder and scurrying toward them.

"I don't know," Selena said. "Let's see where they're going."

She took the passage the pigs entered, stepping carefully through the slippery patches of fungus.

There was light up ahead. They stepped into a massive cavern that looked almost like a forest of vines and roots. Far above, three holes punctured the ceiling, letting in beams of light.

"What the hell is that?" Lauren asked.

There was a small building in the center of the cave, resting silently in the moonlight.

The white bulbous bodies of the pigs scampered through the beams, curving around the small building and quietly disappearing into the shadows beyond.

"It's a house," Selena said.

They stepped closer to the wooden shack. It was old. Very old. The wood was warped and curved, the roof sinking under the weight of fallen dirt and rocks, and the windows sagged downward like two droopy eyes. Just looking at the building caused a deep sense of sorrow and loneliness to wash over them.

Selena went to the window and shined her light inside.

"It's an old schoolhouse," Selena said.

They all peeked through the windows and saw rows of desks. A chalkboard hung from the far wall.

"Why is it here?" Lauren said. "Why is there a school underground like this?"

Trent tried the door. It wouldn't open. The frame was buried in the mud. He stepped back and slammed his way inside, breaking the door from its hinges.

"It looks like it's from the pioneer days," Selena said, stepping down the aisle and examining each of the desks. "It must be a hundred years old."

"This is fucked up, bro," Dean said. "There shouldn't be no fucking school underground like this. Unless it's some kind of Satan school for demon kids."

The room was covered in dust and cobwebs. Roots from trees grew through one of the walls, digging deep into the wooden floor. It smelled cold and ancient.

"It's pretty well-preserved for being a hundred years old," Lance said, feeling the sturdiness of one of the desks.

"Being sealed underground like this would have kept it intact," Selena said. "Like canning food."

"But I still don't understand," Lauren said. "Did somebody build this here? Underground?"

"No," Trent said. "I'm pretty sure I know why it's here."

They all looked at him.

"Remember I said the last earthquake here happened a hundred years ago?" Trent continued. "I knew that because it's a story my dad used to tell. It's kind of local legend."

He sat down on one of the little kid chairs to tell the story.

"It happened more like a hundred and twenty years ago," he said. "There was a mining company up here owned by the Turtle family. That's where the mountains got their name. They were supposedly into some weird shit. Black magic shit. No, not black magic…"

Trent thought about it.

"Alchemy!" Trent raised his finger as he remembered the

word. "That's it. They were alchemists. You know, those ancient scientists who tried to figure out a way to turn lead into gold? Well, these alchemists were trying to find the chemical recipe for immortality. That's what the Turtle family was supposedly working on out here. They believed there was some kind of powerful mineral that could only be found in these mountains. A mineral which could be used in a recipe for immortality. As you can guess, they were complete psychopaths."

"Are you fucking with us?" Lauren said. "Don't fuck with us."

"You actually believe that story?" Selena asked.

"I never said I believed it," Trent said. "That's not the point. The point is that during an earthquake one day, the entire town disappeared. The ground opened up and just swallowed the town whole. Nobody ever heard from the Turtle family again. *That* is the part I believe."

Lance looked out of the window, up at the ceiling of the cave. "So you think that's where this schoolhouse came from? It was swallowed up in an earthquake?"

"It makes sense to me," Trent said.

"But why is it in such good shape?" Selena asked. "If it fell down here during an earthquake it would be nothing but pieces of wood."

"You never know." Trent stood up and looked around. "Tornados, tidal waves, hurricanes—they've all been known to carry structures away without damaging them. It's not impossible."

"Then where are all the bodies?" Selena asked. "Wouldn't there be dead people all over this room?"

"Not if it happened while the school was closed," Trent said.

Lance saw bones in one corner of the room.

"Guys," Lance said, pointing at the remains. "I think we should get out of here."

They were small skeletons, the remains of children. The bones were scattered. None of them were whole skeletons. It was as if animals had gotten to them a long time ago.

Lance backed away, heading for the exit.

"Yeah, this is creeping me out, bro," Dean said, following Lance.

Before he exited the schoolhouse, something made him freeze in his tracks. The outside of the building suddenly seemed a lot more terrifying than the inside, as a chirping of whispers echoed across the dimly lit cavern.

"Did you hear that?" Lance asked.

Everyone looked around, listening. The sound of giggling children echoed across the walls. They all heard it.

"*That's* the sound I heard earlier," Lance whispered.

"It's exactly what I heard, too," Selena said.

Nobody spoke. They couldn't speak. They just stared out the schoolhouse door.

A little girl giggled. There was a sound of footsteps running across the ground outside, like children playing hide and seek. Shadows moved across the schoolhouse doorway, but they didn't see anything out there. Trent tried to peek out a window, but his helmet light just reflected his own image back at him.

They didn't know what to do, just standing still, listening to the children outside. Then, eventually, the voices faded. Whatever they were, they were gone.

"Shit…" Trent said, breaking the silence.

"I told you," Lance said. "I wasn't hallucinating."

"They must be the ghosts of the children who died down here," Lauren said. "They were in school when the earthquake buried them alive." She pointed at the bones in the corner. "Those could be their remains right there."

"They're not ghosts," Trent said.

"Then what are they?"

"I don't know," he said, pushing his way past her. "A group delusion. Our minds playing tricks. Let's just get out of here."

Selena saw Dean standing perfectly still, frozen in his place, a terrified expression on his face. One of his breasts dangled out of his shirt, milk leaking out of the nipple.

"Are you lactating?" Selena asked, looking more carefully at his breast.

Dean looked down and wiped the milk away, shaking his head and chuckling nervously. "No, no. Of course not."

Everyone looked over at him.

Dean explained, "Sometimes when things get too intense my awesome pecs get all creamy."

Trent cringed at the sight of his bro's milk. "Creamy?"

"You know," Dean rubbed the milk into his chest hairs, "thick manly sweat leaks out of my nipples and shit."

"So you lactate when you're scared?" Selena asked.

"No, no. I'm not scared. Why would I be scared? Ghosts won't fuck with me. I can handle it."

Milk drizzled from his nipple onto his shoe. He looked down, put his breast back in his shirt, then zipped it up.

"I work out a lot," he said, trying to look cool and relaxed as warm cream dripped down his belly.

Outside of the schoolhouse, they looked up at the holes in the ceiling. Even if they were capable of climbing all the way up there, none of them were small enough to fit through those holes.

"You think that's where the bats came in?" Trent asked Selena.

She just nodded.

"So what should we do?" he asked.

She just shrugged.

The light from the holes went black as clouds moved in and blocked out the moon. Thunder rumbled the cavern walls. It was still raining out there.

"What about the rest of the town?" Dean asked.

They looked at him.

"You said that the earthquake swallowed up the whole mining town," Dean continued. "If this is the town's school, where are the other buildings?"

Trent and Selena looked at each other.

Selena raised an eyebrow. "If they exist, they're probably close by."

Trent agreed. "Let's go find them."

"Shouldn't we just be trying to find a way out?" Lance asked. "We only have a limited amount of light."

"Maybe they'll lead us to a way out," Trent said, though everyone knew it was just curiosity that was motivating him.

The rest of the town wasn't too far away, just as Selena predicted. It was the largest section of the cave they'd seen, almost canyon-like. They walked through a flat open area, surrounded by mountainous peaks and crevices. Their helmet lights revealed the faces of buildings lining the hills around them—quiet ancient structures, splintered wooden walls, windows that were cracked or clouded with dust.

"What a ghost town…" Selena said, examining the structures. It was like a graveyard of houses.

"They look so lonely…" Lauren said.

"What does?"

"The houses. They're so colorless and old. So alone down here. It's kind of sad."

"Don't worry about it," Trent said. "The people who lived down here died a very long time ago."

"Why are all the buildings intact?" Selena asked.

Trent wasn't following her. He shined his lights across a row of small rickety buildings. "What do you mean?"

"If this town was swallowed by an earthquake these buildings would have been demolished," she said. "I could believe one or two might have survived the fall. But *all* of them? It's not plausible."

"Maybe somebody put them back together," Lauren said.
"Who?"

Lauren shrugged. "The ones who survived the earthquake. I'm sure some of the townspeople weren't around when the ground swallowed the buildings. Maybe they came down here and built this as a memorial to the people they lost."

"If this was a memorial then how come nobody's ever heard of it before?" Selena said. "You'd think this would be a huge part of the local legend. It would also be a pretty big tourist attraction."

"Maybe the people who constructed it wanted to keep it a secret," Lauren said.

Trent stepped between them to end the conversation.

"We should search the buildings," he said. "See if there's anything useful here."

"Like what?" Selena said.

"Anything we can use," he said. "Maps, ropes, fuel, weapons."

"Weapons?"

"If we're down here long enough we might have to start hunting pig," Trent said. Then he turned to the others. "Split up. I don't want to spend all day here."

They went in three different directions.

Lance and Selena stuck close to the ground level, while the other two groups took trails leading up the hills heading west and east. The first couple of shacks reeked like feces.

"Oh, man…" Selena said. "We're not going in those."

"Are those outhouses?" Lance asked. "Why do they still smell like shit?"

"Who knows…"

The next shack was a tool shed.

"Here we go," Selena said. "Tools and weapons."

They stepped forward and examined the ancient tools on the walls. Everything was nicely organized and in good condition.

Selena took a pickaxe off the wall and tested its strength. It was still strong enough to break through solid rock.

"How old is this stuff, really?" Selena asked. "Without anyone maintaining equipment like this it should have crumbled in my hands."

"Maybe it's like you said. Being buried in this cave has preserved it like food in a can."

"You actually believed that bullshit?" Selena fingered the blade of a small axe. It was still sharp. "I think somebody must have constructed this place much more recently than a century ago."

"How recent do you think?"

A crying sound echoed from the next shack over, the crying of a man. Selena handed Lance the hatchet and kept the pickaxe for herself. Then she communicated with her eyes *let's check it out.*

The next shack was a slaughterhouse. Subterranean pigs lined the walls on hooks. A blood-stained cutting block centered the shack. Piles of pig bones lay scattered across the floor.

"Oh, shit…" Selena said.

The pigs on hooks were not only still fresh, they were still alive. They wiggled and cried, squealing, trying to escape. Meat was stripped from their bones. One was cut in half. Another was gutted, completely hollow inside. Yet they were still alive.

"Somebody lives down here…" Selena said.

She turned to Lance. He just stared at the squealing half-butchered animals, unable to speak.

"We need to get out of this place," she said. "People are still living down here."

Dean and Marta hiked up the trail toward the church in the center of town.

"So, you know," Dean said to her, walking backwards in front of her, flexing his abs with a cool-guy expression on his face, "after we get out of here, I was thinking… Maybe the two of us should go out sometime. Like go see some pro-wrestling event or something."

Marta ignored him, more interested in the buildings around her.

"We could get some cheeseburgers, maybe play a little *extreme* air hockey," Dean said. "Go back to the frat house, slam some beers, and see what happens. You know. It'd be pretty sweet."

Marta peered into the windows of a house. There seemed to be movement inside, but the light reflecting off the glass made it difficult to see within.

"So, what do you think?" Dean asked, bulging his muscles at her. She shook her head. "No thanks."

Dean's mouth dropped open. "What do you mean, *no thanks?*"

"I'm sorry, but you're not really my type," she said.

"What?" Dean was shocked. "Why? How?"

"It's not that I find you ugly, per say," she said. "It's just... you're kind of a dork."

Dean didn't know how to react to that. Nobody's ever called him a dork before. He was Extreme Fucking Dean. He was *the man.*

"What? A dork? How can I possibly be a dork? I'm in a fraternity. That automatically means I'm fucking awesome."

She laughed and shook her head.

"No, it doesn't. I'm surprised a frat would even let you in."

"But..." Dean said.

He stopped in his tracks, just watching Marta as she walked away. He couldn't believe he was just rejected by Giant Gonzales.

"But I'm extreme..." Dean said, frowning at the ground, too softly for anyone else to hear.

Marta opened the doors to the old church and stepped inside. It was charred and warped, but surprisingly clean. A crucifix was on the far end of the chapel. Stained glass windows lined the walls, only one of them cracked.

Marta stepped down the aisle and kneeled in front of the crucifix.

"What are you doing?" Dean asked from the doorway.

"Praying," she said, her eyes closed, her fingers pressed together.

"Why?"

"I think we could use a little help getting out of this mess, don't you?"

Dean shrugged.

"So you're religious?" he asked.

"Can you fuck off and let me pray?"

He groaned quietly, but shut up about it. At least he understood why Marta wanted to investigate the church first.

While pacing in the back row, listening to Marta's whispery chants, he realized his buzz was starting to wear off and the hangover was taking its place. No hangover was worse than a Natty Ice hangover. He wished his friends didn't leave his beer back at the camp. It would have come in handy at about this time.

"I wonder if this place has some old whiskey stored in a pantry somewhere," he said aloud.

When Marta turned around to give him the evil eye, something caught her attention. Her eyes were locked onto dozens of objects above Dean's head.

"What?" he said. "What are you looking at?"

She pointed above him.

Dean had to step over to where she was kneeling to see what she was pointing at. Above the door, lining the walls, three dozen human heads grew from wooden shelves like wild mushrooms.

"Oh, fuck…" Dean said. "Are those real?"

One of the heads opened its mouth as if trying to talk. The other heads moved their eyes in their sockets, looking frantically around the room.

"Holy shit, bro," Dean said. "They're alive. The heads are alive."

Gargling noises rose from their bodiless throats as the severed heads tried to scream.

"Trent, I think I'm pregnant," Lauren said, as they entered one of the mansions on top of the hill.

Trent turned to her. "Are you fucking with me?"

"It's okay," she said. "Don't worry about it. I *want* to be pregnant."

Trent looked around the room. It was a Victorian style home, old red carpet covered the wooden floors. A gray spiral staircase twisted into the ceiling toward the second floor. The mansion must have been owned by members of the Turtle family, whereas the miners must have lived in the shacks on the other side of town.

"But how is it possible?" Trent said.

"We didn't use a condom, remember? You didn't want to."

"No, I mean we just had sex the other day. Only once. How do you know you're pregnant already?"

"I just know," Lauren said. She looked at him with a smile and rubbed her stomach. "I can feel your essence growing inside of me."

Trent looked at her as she lifted her muddy shirt and exposed her belly to him. The last thing he wanted to do was have a child with the psycho chick, but imagining his child inside of her turned him on.

"I want you to put another in me," she whispered.

She went to him and rubbed her hand on his penis, outside of his wetsuit. It was already erect before she touched it.

"And another," she said. "And another, and another. Fuck me again. I want my belly to be swollen with your babies."

Trent breathed heavily as she rubbed his penis. If he wasn't still wearing his scuba gear he would have fucked her right there.

"Let's find a room upstairs," he said.

She smiled wildly as she nodded.

Lauren was lying about being pregnant. She told him that because she knew it would turn him on. Getting Trent was all she cared about, even if she had to lie and cheat in order to make him hers.

Because Lauren was so gifted at reading body language, she always knew what turned people on. She could tell a person's darkest kink, deepest desire, strangest fetish, just by paying attention to the way they cough or clean their fingernails. And what she knew about Trent was that the only thing that could get him off was the idea of impregnating women.

Trent never wore a condom when having sex. He had no interest in that. He also wouldn't have sex with women if he knew they weren't ovulating or capable of having children. If there wasn't a good chance of getting the girl pregnant then he couldn't even get a hard on. He *needed* to believe he was getting the woman pregnant while having sex.

He didn't want babies, he didn't want to get married, he just wanted to impregnate as many women as possible. And if he found a woman he was attracted to, that became his mission: do whatever it took to get her pregnant. Even if he had to get her drunk or slip her a roofie when she wasn't looking, he would impregnate the woman. He would put his baby in her whether she wanted it or not. Then he would move on to the next girl, spreading his seed to every womb he could find—as long as it was fertile, and inside a girl beautiful enough to breed with.

"My womb is hungry for your baby," Lauren said, licking her lips as she pulled him up the stairs. "Grow it inside of me. Give me twins. Triplets. Make my belly so big that I can't even walk."

Trent had no idea how hot Lauren was until she started talking in this way. He really hoped she was pregnant. And if she wasn't yet, he wanted to make sure she would be.

In high school, he was responsible for five pregnancies. Three resulted in abortions, one resulted in a baby that was put up for adoption, and one resulted in a baby whose mother wanted nothing to do with Trent. He had far more sexual encounters in college than he did in high school, but since he rarely remembered the names or faces of the women he slept with he was unaware of how many pregnancies might have resulted.

"I hope there's still a bed in this place," Lauren said, as she opened the door to the master bedroom.

Because her back was to the room as she pulled Trent forward, she didn't see what was behind her. But she heard the whispering sounds. Trent's eyes widened, he jerked her hands away and pulled out his machete.

"What is it?" Lauren asked, her voice soft and panicked.

She turned around and saw them. They were just standing there, in the dark, huddled together. Motionless like mannequins.

"Children..." she said.

About seven little girls in torn colorless dresses turned to face them. Their hair was scraggly and gray, like the hair of corpses, what little of it was left on their scalps covered their faces.

Trent backed away, the machete shaking in his hand.

"Let's get out of here," he cried.

Lauren didn't follow him. She stepped forward, into the room with the girls.

"Hello?" she asked.

They didn't move. Just standing there whispering to each other. She couldn't understand what they were saying. She couldn't even see their lips move.

"Are you okay? What are you doing down here in the dark?"

"Get away from them," Trent said as he stepped down the stairs.

"They're not going to hurt you," Lauren said. "They're just children."

Lauren kneeled down and brushed the hair out of one girl's face. Then she jumped back at what she saw. There was nothing there. No eyes, no nose. It looked like the child had eyes at one time, but the skin had grown over her eye sockets. Her nose looked as if it melted off her face. And her mouth was just a lipless slit across her face.

The child stepped forward, reaching out its arms. Raspy breaths emptied from the slit. Lauren turned and ran down the steps after Trent.

"They're not human," she cried.

In the living room, more children came out of the rooms, stepping silently toward them with their hands outstretched. Before Trent and Lauren could react, the children grabbed them.

"Get away from me," Trent yelled, jerking their hands off.

But there were too many of them. The children held him close to their bodies, touching his skin and hugging his legs. They weaved their fingers through Lauren's hair, held her by the hand, and kissed her on her belly.

"Get off," Trent yelled.

A little girl wrapped her warms around his waist, rubbing her eyeless sockets into his stomach.

"I said *get off!*" Trent screamed.

He raised his machete and lowered it into the girl's skull. The child screamed like a dying bird. Even with the machete splitting her brain in half, the child was able to scream. He pulled the machete out and hacked off another girl's arm. Then he slashed the blade across another's throat.

"Stop it," Lauren cried, trying to hold his arm in place. "They're not trying to hurt you."

But Trent couldn't help it. The sight of the withered ghostly children caused something in his brain to crack. He sliced into their flesh, chopped open their faces, cut them all apart. Some of them continued to try to hug him, others ran away.

"They're only children!" Lauren cried.

The children squealed and hissed, whispering in such an alien way. Their cries sounded as if their throats were filled with sand.

He dismembered their arms so that they couldn't touch him anymore. Then he chased after the ones that fled.

"Leave them alone!" Lauren followed, but she couldn't do anything to stop him.

He ran through the front door and raced down the hill after the creatures. He slashed them across their backs, hacked into their skulls and necks. They fell over, crumpling to the ground, spasming in the dirt.

When he got to the bottom of the hill, there was just one left. Trent jumped on top of her and hacked at her back. He forced the blade through her ribcage, through her heart, stabbing her over and over again. The girl didn't die. She just hissed and screamed like a crazed animal.

"Why won't it die?" Trent cried as he stabbed her. "Why can't I kill it?"

Trent stood up and decapitated the child. But it still didn't die. The head wiggled on the ground, opening and closing the slit-like mouth on its face.

"You fucking demon!" Trent yelled.

Then he kicked the head across the dirt.

Selena and Lance ran across the cavern, trying to warn the others the town was still inhabited, but it was too late. They could tell the others already knew. Marta and Dean were racing down the hill toward them. Lauren was holding her hand over her mouth, stepping slowly away from the buildings. And Trent was standing over the body of a little girl.

After Trent kicked the child's head, it rolled across the dirt into the hands of an old woman. Selena stopped running. Everybody stopped.

The old woman was missing the right side of her face. The left side was wrinkled inward like a rotting peach. The eyeball in the remaining socket was a blank white orb. She lifted the severed head up from the ground and cradled it in her arms like a baby, petting its hair and stroking its cheeks as if rubbing tears from its eyes.

"I'm sorry," Lauren said, stepping up behind Trent. "He didn't know what he was doing. He was only scared."

The old woman sniffed at the air, cocking her head to listen. The moans and cries of the other wounded children echoed through the cavern. A look of anger curled into the woman's face. Then she screamed. It was the scream of a banshee, ripping through the cavern.

Others heard her call. They stepped out of their rickety homes. All of them were deformed, blind monsters. Their clothes were in tatters. Their faces melted and bulbous. If they had eyes in their head they were white blank balls, but most them had their eyes sewn shut or removed from the sockets entirely.

"Blind monsters," Selena said when she saw them, as if reciting a poem. "Living down in the dark…"

The creatures stepped forward. Selena and Lance met up with all the others in the center of the cavern, as the creatures closed in on them. Selena held up her pickaxe. Lance raised his hatchet. The monsters were out for blood.

"This is fucked up, bros," Dean said. "This is really fucked up."

"What are they?" Lance cried. "What do we do?"

"We run," Trent said.

Without waiting for anyone, Trent took off running, shoving Lauren out of his way as he went.

"Wait," Lauren cried, as Lance and Dean ran after him. "We can reason with them. It was just an accident…"

Selena and Marta grabbed Lauren, then ran after the guys.

The creatures lined up outside the tunnel, staring in the direction the college kids ran. There were eight of them. Each one of them a hunter, their tools melded into their flesh.

A man with a turtle-like head poking out of his shriveled neck, two sickles growing out of the flesh of his arms, screamed into the cavern. Then he charged forward, racing through the dark after his prey.

They were running so fast they almost didn't see the edge of the cliff in time.

"Dudes!" Dean yelled as he skid across the dirt, stopping himself just in time before he fell over into the chasm below. "Look out."

This one was ten times the size of the last one. Their lights couldn't even reach the other side. It was just an ocean of blackness.

"This way," Selena yelled, pointing them in the other direction.

Sickle Arms caught up to them quickly. He was used to hunting pigs in the dark. He knew every tunnel, every cliff, every rock in the cave system, and could run across it with no fear of ever tripping on anything in his path.

"He's coming," Lance yelled. "Hurry."

But the college students were new to this cave and their lights barely lit their path for them. They had no way of moving at their fastest speed without falling into a pit or breaking both their legs.

"Just keep going," Trent said. "Don't look back."

Selena grabbed him by the arm.

"He's too fast," she said. "We should stay and fight."

"Fuck no," Trent said. "That thing's not human."

"There's only one of them," she said.

Trent wiggled out of her grip and kept running. He knew he couldn't outrun the blind monster, but that didn't worry him. All he had to do was outrun the rest of his friends.

They dashed along the edge of the cliff, looking for an escape. There was no light or air current ahead of them. They seemed to just be fleeing deeper and deeper into the netherworld.

Marta was oddly the fastest runner of the group. Her leg muscles were strong and her lungs even stronger. She led the way, searching for a tunnel they could escape into.

Lauren, on the other hand, was the slowest runner. Being thin and bulimic was hard on her heart, bad for her muscles. She lagged behind, trying to catch her breath.

"Lauren!" Selena cried, as Sickle Arms closed in.

Lauren turned around just in time to see the sickle-shaped blade pierce her belly, just below the belly button, through her womb. The turtle-headed mutant growled in her face, twisting his sickle blade deeper into her body.

"Trent…" she cried, looking back at her friends as blood leaked from her mouth. "Help me…"

Trent stopped and turned around, staring back at Lauren. He saw the blade in her abdomen. If she had really been pregnant she wasn't anymore.

"I love you…" Lauren said, choking on her words, as Sickle Arms hissed in her face.

Trent gripped his machete. It wasn't too late to save her. Selena was by his side, holding the pickaxe over her shoulder. They could take him. Trent *knew* they could take him.

"But I don't like being mean," Trent said to his mother when he was seven years old. "I want to be a good guy."

His mother leaned down to him and stared him in the eyes.

"I don't care what you want," she said. "You're going to be a winner, my love. You're going to care about no one but yourself."

She reached into his pocket and pulled out a wad of dollars, stuffing them down the front of her shirt.

"I'm not giving you lunch money from now on," she said. "If you want lunch you have to get it from the weaker children."

"You want me to borrow it?"

"No, I want you to beat it out of them," she said.

"I can't do that," he said. "I'll get in trouble."

"Then tell the kid you take the money from to hold his tongue. Threaten to beat him up again if he tells anyone you took his money. That's what the best bullies do."

"But I don't want to be a bully. I don't want to be the bad guy."

"There is no good and bad. That's all made up nonsense. There are only winners and losers. And you, my love, are a winner."

At school, Trent looked for the wimpiest loser he could find. He knew the perfect kid—the scrawny Indian kid with the crutches, Beni. But by the time he found Beni, another bully had beat him to the punch. The bully was a grade older than Trent. A real jerk. Everyone hated the guy. He was exactly the kind of kid Trent's mom wanted him to become.

The bully took the money and pushed Beni to the ground. After he left, Trent helped the kid up.

"He took my lunch money," Beni said. "It's the third time this week."

"I'll get it back for you," Trent said.

Trent wanted to help people and his mother wanted him to screw people over. So he figured the best option would be to try to do both. He could help the Indian kid by screwing over the bully.

It wasn't difficult getting the money back from the bully. Although the guy was much larger than Trent, he wasn't as clever. Trent's mother had taught him how to pick pockets by the time he was old enough to walk. She thought it was an important skill to have as a child, especially if anything were to happen to her and he found himself in desperate times.

Trent pretended to bump into the bully on the way into the bathroom. As he slammed against him, Trent slipped his hand into the boy's pocket and pulled out the cash.

"Watch where you're going, butt-pipe," the bully said, pushing him to the ground.

When the boy left, Trent counted the money. There wasn't just the Indian kid's lunch money in his hands. He was holding enough to buy lunches for at least five children, all of which was surely stolen from weaker kids.

Trent did it. He was a hero. He could return the money to all of the kids the bully robbed and become their savior. Trent liked that feeling more than anything he ever felt. He wasn't a bad guy. He was a good guy. He was *the best* guy. At that moment, he vowed to always be the hero when the situation arose. He vowed always to save people when they needed saving.

"Please, Trent," Lauren cried. "Save me…"

Trent charged. He yelled at the top of his lungs—a fierce battle cry. Running away wasn't the solution. Selena was right about that. He needed to be brave. He needed to stand and fight. He had to be a hero. A savior. Trent was going to kill the mutant with the sickle arms and save everyone. Well, everyone except for Lauren, that is…

Trent ran at Lauren and shoved her off the cliff.

"Trent?" she cried, her face in shock as she found herself falling backward into the abyss.

The mutant tried pulling his sickle out of Lauren's abdomen, but it was hooked too deep inside of her. The weight of her body pulled Sickle Arms off of his feet and he fell into the abyss with her, hissing in a terror.

Selena glared at Trent as Lauren's screams echoed into the chasm below.

"What the fuck is wrong with you?" she cried.

But Trent just smirked back at her, strolling away from the cliff's edge with a satisfied expression on his face. Now there were only seven mutants they had to deal with.

Beni hopped into the cafeteria on his crutches. When he saw Trent eating lunch at one of the tables, he came over to him with a smile on his face.

"So did you do it?" Beni asked. "Did you get my lunch money back?"

Trent shook his head. "Sorry. He was way too tough. You might want to start carrying your money in your shoe or something."

"But what am I supposed to do about lunch?" Beni asked.

"Here," Trent said. "You can have my lima beans. I fucking hate lima beans."

Trent took the slice of pizza and slid the tray over to the Indian kid. Then he stood up and walked out of the cafeteria toward the playground, chewing on long string of cheese.

He had planned to give the money back to Beni and the other kids that had gone without lunch that day, but then he realized just how much money he had in his hands. He had at least twenty-five dollars. He could eat lunch and still have enough money left over to buy a few G. I. Joe action figures after school that day.

The idea of being a hero sounded great at first, but his mom was right. Fuck being a hero. Getting new toys was way better.

CHAPTER SIX
GIANT GONZALES

THE BRO CODE #76
A bro always has his bro's back, especially when being
hunted by subterranean cannibal mutants.

Marta and Selena were not sisters by blood. They were both adopted into a family in their pre-teens. Before that, they each had very different childhoods.

Marta was raised by Satanists. She lived in a nice middle-class suburb, went to a good school, wore pretty dresses with flowers on them, volunteered at the homeless shelter on weekends, and behind closed doors, she worshipped Satan.

"Did you brush your teeth?" Her mother asked, baking cinnamon cookies in the kitchen.

"Yes," young Marta said.

"Did you finish all your homework?"

Marta nodded.

"Did you sacrifice Mr. Floppy Ears to the dark lord?"

Marta frowned and looked away.

Her mother groaned. "You didn't, did you?"

Marta shook her head. "I don't want to kill Mr. Floppy Ears. I love him."

The mother rolled her eyes at her daughter.

"Every month we buy you a pet bunny to sacrifice to the dark lord and every month it's always the same thing with you," she said. "When are you ever going to learn? Satan needs the blood of the innocent so that one day he'll be able to rise up from the bowels of Hell and turn the Earth into his sadistic unholy playground." The mother patted Marta on the butt. "Now go upstairs and do as Satan commands or you won't be getting Mermaid Princess Barbie for your birthday."

Marta moped all the way up the stairs.

"She gets that attitude from *your* mother, ya know," her mom said to her father.

"Whatever you say," the father said, not really listening.

He was more focused on piecing together a pentagram out of rat bones, macaroni and Sculpey clay as *Dharma & Greg* played in the background. It was kind of a hobby of his. He gave them away in a raffle at the monthly Satanic picnic.

Marta went to her room, removed her white bunny from the cage on her Hello Kitty nightstand and looked him in the eyes.

"I'll miss you, Mr. Floppy Ears," Marta said, tears running down her cheeks.

She put the bunny on the sacrificial alter on the shelf between her Barbie Dreamhouse and Easy-Bake Oven. Black candles were placed on each point of the blood-red pentagram, as well as the one on top of the goat skull in the center.

As she raised the sacrificial snake-handled blade, she looked down at her rabbit and said, "Satan better be worth it."

Then she offered the sacrifice to the dark lord.

Marta slowed to a stop. She turned around, caught her breath, waiting until her friends to catch up.

She noticed they were short one person. "Where's Lauren?"

Selena glared at Trent, waiting for him to explain, but he didn't say anything. It was obvious Lauren wasn't coming.

"Where are the other creatures?" Lance cried. "Are they coming? Are they following us?"

"What the fuck is going on, bro?" Dean yelled. "What the fuck were those things, bro? This is getting too extreme, bro. Too extreme!"

"It's the Turtle family," Trent explained, out of breath. "Just like the legend said. They were looking for the key to immortality. Sometime before their town was buried alive, they must have found it."

"So they're not ghosts?" Lance cried. "They're the same people from the mining town? They've been down here a hundred and twenty years?"

"Yeah, that's what I'm saying," Trent said.

"How is that possible?" Lance cried.

"How the fuck should I know? I stabbed those kids a hundred times and they didn't die. I cut that chick's head off and she didn't die! None of them can die!"

An army of footsteps vibrated through the cave.

"They're coming," Marta said, turning to run.

"Let's go!" Dean cried.

Marta followed the edge of the cliff until she hit the far wall. There were only two paths she could take. One was a thin ledge going down into the chasm, which was barely six inches wide in some areas, the other was a tight passageway that she'd barely fit through even lying down. Neither option seemed safe.

"Shit…" she said.

She decided to take the tight passageway.

"This way," she called out to the others, as she squeezed her massive body inside.

Lance was behind her, trembling in his wetsuit as he saw Marta leading them into the tiny hole in the rock.

"We can't go in there," he cried. "No fucking way. What if it doesn't go through? What if we get trapped?"

Marta didn't argue with him, she crawled in, shining her light ahead.

Tears were falling from Lance's eyes, but he didn't have a choice. He climbed in after her, crying, pushing her in the ass.

"I'm going as fast as I can," she said.

Lance looked back to see Dean coming in behind him. That was his worst case scenario—being trapped between the two largest people in a tight squeeze.

"Hurry up, bro," Dean said. "We need to get the fuck out of here."

"Give me room," Lance cried. "Don't crowd me."

Over Dean's shoulder, Lance saw Selena and Trent stumbling over the rocky ground. And behind them, in the distance, three figures were racing through the shadows toward them.

Dean looked back and saw the creatures. The one leading the way was a female carrying a shovel. She was nearly naked, her rubbery muscled white flesh wrapped in bandages that only covered her crotch and nipples. She wailed like a banshee through the oily black hair that covered her face and neck.

"Let's go, bro, she's coming," Dean said.

Lance crawled in, catching up to Marta, trying not to get his oxygen tank stuck on the rocks. Dean pushed him forward.

"Come on," Dean yelled. "Come on!"

Trent entered the crawl space next. Then Selena.

"Hurry up," Selena cried, knowing she was in the most danger being in the back.

The tunnel became tighter the further up they went. Marta's pace slowed drastically.

"Please, Jesus, see us through this," Marta whispered. "Let the path lead to the other side."

Then she kissed a crucifix that dangled from her neck.

"What in the world are you doing with *this?*" Marta's biological mother said as she found a crucifix in her FernGully lunchbox. "You can't bring a rightside-up cross into this household!"

"It's not mine." Marta shook her head. "I was just holding it for a friend."

"Likely story," said the mother. "You better not be thinking about converting to Christianity. I won't have a Jesus-worshipper in my house."

"But all my friends at school worship Jesus," Marta said. "They always laugh at me because of my beliefs."

"Don't let that bother you," said the mother. "One day the dark lord will rise from the pits of hell and swallow the world in fire and darkness. We'll see who'll be laughing at who when that day comes."

"But Christianity seems fun and cool."

"Well, Christianity is responsible for the Dark Ages, the Crusades, homosexual persecution, overpopulation, censorship, and general close-minded bigotry. Do you think that's *fun* and *cool?*"

"No..."

"Now go up to your room and pray to Satan for forgiveness."

Marta nodded and went upstairs. But it wasn't Satan she prayed to. Beneath her bed, she retrieved a rosary and a statuette of the Virgin Mary. Then, when she was sure her mother couldn't hear, she prayed to the one she truly worshipped—Jesus, the anti-devil.

When Marta heard water up ahead, she knew it was a blessing from her true savior. There was a way out.

"Hurry," Lance cried, the cave walls closing in on him. "Get me out of here."

"I see an opening," Marta said.

The female mutant crawled into the passage after Selena, hissing and wailing through her black teeth. She was shorter and thinner than the college kids and could move much faster through the crawl space.

The blade of her shovel had a razor-sharp jagged edge with a pointed tip. Barbed wire was wrapped around the shaft. The steel shovel had been modified so that it could be used as a spear, saw, and axe all at the same time.

Selena screamed. A sharp pain shot through her ankle as the mutant hacked at her with the edge of the shovel. Looking back, Selena saw the creature's white featureless face behind the oily locks of black hair. The woman still had eyes, but they were inhuman—far too wide for a human face and flat, as if painted on with makeup, with long unnatural eyelashes. The centers of the eyes were just tiny black pinholes. Selena thought her eyes made her resemble something between a spider and a mad clown.

The mutant squirmed through the tunnel, her shovel-weapon leading the way. She continued to poke and stab at Selena's legs, hooking her flesh with the barbed wire. Selena cried out, kicking at the spider-eyed woman. The pickaxe was useless in that tight space, otherwise she would have fought back. Instead she had no choice but to keep crawling.

"Fucking bitch," Selena yelled.

Then the point of the shovel stabbed through the bottom of Selena's boot, digging into the arch of her foot. Selena screamed.

"Hurry," Selena yelled to the others. "I'm getting torn apart back here."

But they were no longer moving. At the front of the line Marta had stopped, unable to continue.

"What's going on?" Selena cried. She kicked at the mutant's face, but the woman was too fast. She ducked and dodged, then drove her shovel deep into Selena's crotch, cutting a gash into her inner thigh.

"Come on, come on," Lance cried, suffering in the confined space as they stopped moving. "Get me out."

But he didn't see what Marta was seeing. Nobody did.

Marta crouched at the end of the tunnel, peering out at the massive chasm below. She was on the edge of a cliff, next to a roaring waterfall. The only way out of there was a sixty foot drop or back the way they came.

Dean shoved at Lance's back, squeezing him tighter against Marta's ass.

"Move it, bro," Dean yelled.

Lance couldn't tell him what was going on. He couldn't even speak. His eyes closed tight. Panic squeezed all of his muscles together into tight knots.

"Tell them we're on the edge of a cliff," Marta yelled at Lance. "Tell them we have to go back."

But Lance was in too much shock to speak and the waterfall was too loud for anybody else to hear her. Dean continued pushing and Marta was forced to lean further and further over the edge.

The sound of Selena's screams echoed through the crawl space. There was also the sound of her clothes and flesh tearing against the jagged edge of the shovel, and the sound of her kicking and struggling in a futile attempt to fight back.

"Hurry, bro," Dean cried. "What's the hold up?"

Lance blocked the outside world from his consciousness, trying to escape to another place in his mind. But the feeling of human bodies pressed against him in the confined space overwhelmed his senses. He felt as though he were a child again, trapped in a sleeping bag with his older brothers, rolling over each other across the floor.

But as he thought back on those times, he remembered something else, something he'd forgotten a long time ago. It wasn't just his brothers who liked to play *Time Machine*. Sometimes their Uncle Manny would play with them. That was where Lance's phobia really came from. His Uncle Manny would unzip the sleeping bag, then crawl inside with them. Lance was so small and Uncle Manny was so big. He kicked and screamed as he was crushed against his uncle's bare chest, unable to breathe anything but the sweat from his greasy chest hairs.

As the memory of Uncle Manny flashed in Lance's head, he started kicking and screamed. Somehow he forgot where he was. Marta became Lance's uncle and he kicked and shoved her until he finally left the sleeping bag.

Marta shrieked as she fell off the ledge into the chasm.

"Dude!" Dean said, when he saw the cliff in front of them.

Lance was still in a panic, still out of his mind. He climbed right out of the tunnel, without thinking, focused solely on escaping the confined space. Before he knew it, he was falling off the cliff right behind Marta.

Dean looked over the edge, wondering if they were okay. He saw the lights from their helmets moving across the floor of the cavern. He heard them yelling and crying out. They were still alive.

"I think there's a river down there," Dean said to Trent.

"Jump," Trent said. "We don't have a choice."

Dean nodded. Then he took a deep breath and leapt from the cliff.

Trent looked back before following him down. Selena was still trying to defend herself against the woman with the shovel.

"Come on," Trent said.

She turned and saw the path was clear.

"Fucking bitch," Selena yelled, kicking the woman's shovel away. The blade hooked on the rocky ceiling, buying Selena some time. She crawled forward and caught up to Trent.

"We have to jump," Trent said.

"Not yet," Selena said. "I'm going to decapitate that bitch."

Selena wanted revenge. Her legs and feet were pierced, slashed, and covered in blood. The bitch with the shovel wasn't going to get away with that.

"Climb out," Selena said.

The two of them climbed out of the opening and scaled the wall. Selena went to the left, Trent to the right. Selena was good enough at rock climbing that she only needed one hand. The other gripped the steel pickaxe. Trent made sure he had a good handhold before he drew his machete.

Selena and Trent nodded at each other once they were

ready. Then they raised their weapons, waiting for Shovel Bitch to peek her head. But the creature didn't show herself. She probably knew exactly where they were and what they were planning. She was used to lurking in the dark. Her hearing was probably so strong that she could sense the sweat dripping from their fingers as they gripped the rocks.

"She's not coming," Trent said. "We should go."

"Not yet," Selena said.

Then something flew through the air and pierced the rock between them. It fizzed and sparkled in the dark.

"What's that?" Trent cried.

Selena examined it more closely. It was an arrow. Attached to the shaft, just below the arrowhead, was a small explosive similar to a stick of dynamite.

"It's..." Selena's eyes widened. "A bomb!"

Trent looked back. Across the chasm, an archer was aiming a crossbow at them. He was a short, hunchbacked creature with a nose so long it looked like a beak. His skull was lumpy and bald. A crooked toothy smile stretched up the sides of his face like that of a porcelain jester doll.

"Jump," Trent shouted.

But there wasn't enough time. The fuse ignited and the explosion blew Trent off the side of the cliff. Selena turned in time and took most of the shrapnel in her back. She fell a couple feet, but caught herself with the pickaxe.

"Not giving up...*bitch*," Selena growled, trying to hold on as her legs dangled beneath her.

She didn't see The Shovel Bitch until the blade came down on her. Selena felt the sudden sting of cold gritty metal inside her throat. Then, a split second later, it was gone. The shovel was ripped out leaving a geyser of blood in its wake, spraying across Selena's shoulders, drenching her cleavage.

Selena fell. Holding her neck, gurgling blood, her body tumbled into the chasm below.

The river was deep and the current strong. Trent was carried away by the water. The rapids thrashed his body around, slamming him into rocks and against the steep walls of the chasm.

"Trent!" he heard his friends calling out. "Grab on!"

He saw the others off to the side, clutching onto the rock wall, trying to climb out of the water. Trent reached out his arm and Dean seized him by the wrist, swinging him over toward them.

"Where does this go?" Trent yelled, freezing water splashing him in the face and neck.

Dean pointed behind him. At the end of the chasm, the water emptied into a black hole in the rock.

"The water goes in there," Dean said, yelling over the turbulent water. "No way we're going that way, bro. That's a fucking deathtrap."

Marta and Lance were already trying to climb the rock face, but it was too steep, too wet.

A fizzling arrow pierced the rock near Marta, the fuse burning quickly.

"Look out," Trent yelled. "It's going to blow."

But the fuse was too short from them to react in time. The wall exploded. Rocks the size of boulders came loose. Everyone went in the water.

The river swept them through the hole at the end of the chasm, sucking them deep into a black abyss.

It was like a waterslide. The river pulled them down a smooth rock slope, descending deeper into the earth. Marta was in the front and all she could see was darkness ahead of them. She tried to grab onto the walls to stop her descent, but they were too slippery.

Lance was behind her, thrashing his limbs around. He clawed at the walls, trying to stop, breaking off his nails, slicing open his fingertips, bruising his knuckles. When he tried using the hatchet, it only created sparks as it grazed against the rock.

"Too extreme, bro," Dean cried behind him. "Too extreme!"

The walls squeezed tighter the further down they went and the ceiling lowered, as if trying to crush them. Thousands of thin stalactites hung above like icicles.

"Look out for the spikes," Trent yelled, pointing at the ceiling.

Dean was sitting up as the ceiling lowered. A stalactite grazed his forehead, cutting open the skin. He cried out and was thrown back.

"Fuck, bro," Dean yelled, holding his bleeding face as he slid.

They flattened themselves as much as they could and the passageway narrowed even further. The stalactites flashed by, only inches away from their faces. Lance cried out, imagining his flesh shredding against the spiky rocks as he flew down the slide at a speed he couldn't even fathom.

Then the passage became even tighter and Marta got stuck. She became lodged halfway beneath a low-hanging rock, blocking the water tube like a plug. The others traveled at such a high velocity that it created a pileup. The layer of stalactites on the ceiling was shattered to pieces as Dean was thrown on top of Lance. Trent squeezed alongside them and Selena's body toppled into their heads.

When he realized he was trapped and smothered by other people, Lance screamed at the top of his lungs.

"Fuck," Dean cried, shifting his weight on top of Lance. "I can't move." His knee was twisted sideways, stuffed into an awkward position.

Lance thrashed his arms, punching and kicking, having the worst panic attack he'd ever had in his life.

"Dude, cut it out," Dean yelled. "You're making it worse."

But Lance couldn't stop. He shrieked in Dean's face, elbowing Trent and stomping on Marta's shoulder.

"We have to climb back out," Trent yelled, trying to push Selena's body out of the way. "It's the only way."

But before he could even separate himself from Dean and

Lance, he saw something else coming down the tube behind them. The boulders that had loosened from the chasm wall in the explosion were flying toward them, thrust by the torrent.

"Look out," Trent cried.

He held his arm out like a shield as a giant boulder soared down the slide toward them. But as the passageway tightened, the boulder locked into place. The other boulders piled up behind it.

"We're blocked in," Trent said.

He clambered past Selena and slammed his fist on the rock. It was fastened tightly. They weren't going to get through that way.

With Trent no longer squeezed alongside the others, Lance was able to have a bit of wiggle room. But he used it only to kick and thrash even harder. Dean tried to hold him down so that he wouldn't hurt himself.

"What the fuck, bro?" Dean cried, his mouth less than an inch from the ceiling. "What do we do? We're stuck."

Then Dean realized the water level was rising. Because Marta was plugging up the passageway, the water had nowhere to go. The confined area they were trapped within was quickly flooding.

"Giant Gonzales!" Dean cried, as he watched the water level rise to Marta's head. She was seconds away from going under. "She's going to drown! Somebody do something!"

Lance shoved and kicked at the others. He was unable to breathe. Even though he wasn't yet underwater, his mind told him he was unable to breathe. Trent and Dean were pressed against his body. Even though they were fully clothed, his mind saw them as completely naked. Their erections rubbed against his chest and neck.

Uncle Manny didn't have any pants on when he wanted to play *Time Machine* with Lance. He was putting oil all over his body, wearing nothing but a pair of purple flip-flops.

"Put it on," his uncle said, tossing him the bottle of oil. "It's more fun that way. More slippy-slidey."

Lance didn't want to put it on. He just stood there in his Spiderman underpants, trying not to look directly at his greased up uncle.

"I don't want to play Time Machine, Uncle Manny," Lance said. "I don't like that game. Can't I just go to bed?"

His voice was soft, as if he was ashamed to admit this to his uncle.

"What do you mean you don't like that game?" he asked. "All your brothers like to play it. Don't you want to be like your big brothers?"

Lance shrugged.

"Of course you do," said Uncle Manny. "All kids like traveling through time." He took off his glasses and flip-flops. "Now get into the Time Machine and I'll be there in a minute."

Lance looked back at the sleeping bag.

"And take these," his uncle said, tossing him a stack of tissue paper. "You know, for cleaning up the time juice."

"Get away from me!" Lance cried, pushing against Dean's chest. "I don't want to play Time Machine! I don't want to play Time Machine!"

Dean tried to restrain him. "What the fuck are you talking about, bro?"

"Let me out," Lance yelled. "I don't want to play anymore."

"Calm him the fuck down," Trent said.

Dean shook his head. "How?"

Lance raised the hatchet and brought it down into Dean's chest. Dean cried out. Due to the awkward angle of Lance's blow, the axe blade didn't even break through his clothing. But it still hurt like hell.

"Get away from me," Lance cried.

Dean wiggled away from Lance, squeezing between Trent and Selena. "He's lost it, yo."

With the extra room, Lance leaned up and attacked Marta.

He swung the hatchet, cutting into her shoulders and chest. With her arms trapped beneath her, she wasn't able to defend herself. All she could do was take the pain. The water level was rising and she could hardly breathe through the one nostril that was not submerged.

"Get me out of here," Lance cried. "I want to get out of here!"

It was like he was trying to cut his way out through the fat girl. He chopped into Marta's scalp and forehead, breaking open her skin. Blood sprayed into her eyes. Lance still couldn't maneuver a good enough angle in the confined space to do any major damage, but that didn't stop him from trying.

"Cut it out, bro," Dean said, grabbing at Lance's wrist. "What the hell's wrong with you?"

Trent and Dean both tried to catch the hatchet as Lance brought it up for an attack, but it slipped from their fingers each time.

"I don't want to be a time traveler!"

Marta squeezed through the rocks and slipped free before Lance could strike her again. All the water that pooled up on top of her created enough pressure to force her out of the constricted space. The passage opened up and they slid free. But Lance was still delirious.

"I hate traveling through time," he cried.

At the end of the tunnel, there was a drop off. Marta tumbled down the waterfall into a subterranean lake below, clutching her hacked up face as she dropped.

But Lance did not fall behind her. He fell into a massive man-made spider web of hooks and wires. At first, he had no idea what had happened to him. He felt like he was floating, flying through the black abyss. Then the pain hit him and he saw all the hooks digging into his skin.

"I'll never travel through time with you ever again..." Lance said, suspended high above the lake, watching as his friends plunged into the dark waters below.

Marta carried her sister to the shore, unfazed by the open wounds covering her upper body. Her sister was limp and cold in her arms, still dragging the pickaxe behind them in a death grip. She climbed up onto the rocks, crossed the cavern, and lay Selena down in a dry less-rocky corner. When she examined the wound on her sister's neck, she saw that the jugular had been cut. She bled out several minutes ago. Marta didn't even get a chance to say goodbye.

"Dude," Dean called up to Lance, standing in a shallow area of the water. "Lance! Are you alright?"

"What's going on?" Trent asked Dean. "Why is he stuck up there?"

They couldn't see anything, not the wires, not even Lance. All they saw was the light from his helmet moving around up there.

"It's like he fell into some kind of trap," Dean said.

"Why would there be a trap up there?" Trent asked.

"I don't know. For hunting or something."

They shouted and called up to Lance, but their friend wasn't going anywhere. He was stuck up there, at least fifty feet above them. Nobody could hear him over the roaring sound of the waterfall.

Lance didn't know there was a hook in his left eye until he tried to close his eyelids and couldn't get one of them all the way shut. The hook was the size of a finger. It went in through his temple and out through the eye socket, piercing the white of his eyeball. He couldn't blink in that eye, but he was still able to see through it—though all he saw were blurry smears of light. The pain had more to do with the pressure of his weight hanging from the hooks than the stabbing sensation. He wondered if it

147

would've been more painful if he wasn't in shock.

There were also hooks pierced through his arms and legs, some in his chest, two on his back, and one deep in the side of his neck. Each hook was attached to a wire that went up into the darkness above him somewhere.

"Dude! Lance! Are you alright?" he heard his friends calling from below.

His skin stretched at least an inch off of his body where the hooks were embedded in the flesh. Gravity hooked them in deeper and caused a tearing sensation as the holes widened around the metal.

"Are you alive?" his friends called. "Are you coming down?"

Movement in the wires caused pain to shoot through his body. Something was trapped up there with him. He shined his light above him and saw a subterranean pig hanging by hooks next to him. It squealed, wiggled and struggled, pulling on the hooks and wires, whipping Lance around by his wounds.

Lance cried out, trying to hold himself steady. He wondered what the pig was doing up there. He guessed that it had also gone through the waterslide and fell into this trap. Lance wondered if that was the point of the hooked wires—to catch pigs. The mutant hunters could have herded the pigs into the chasm above, forcing them to jump into the river and be swept down the water tube. Then the livestock would get hooked in the trap and reeled in like fish on a line.

Is that what they were doing to us? Lance wondered. *Scaring us into the chasm? Herding us like wild pigs?*

"Try cutting yourself down, bro," his friends yelled beneath him. They shined their lights up at him so he could see better. "The water will break your fall."

Lance looked down and saw it wasn't too far of a drop. He still had the hatchet in his hand. He wondered if it were possible to cut himself free.

The first swing did nothing but send waves of agony vibrating through his muscles. The axe could not cut the wire. He wasn't sure what it was made of, but it was strong. It could even have been made of steel, like the g-strings on an electric guitar. He hacked again with the same results. What hurt the most were the wires attached to his forearm as he did the hacking.

His movement startled the pig and caused the animal to thrash harder, wiggling and jerking. Lance cried out. The pig's leg twisted around the wire that was connected to Lance's left eyeball. It kicked and pulled, sending explosions of pain into his eye socket. He felt fluids leaking down his cheek, but it wasn't blood or tears. Some kind of fluid was leaking from his eyeball as the hook tore it further open.

Lance used the blade of his axe like a saw to cut one wire. Instead of a hacking at it, he sliced the wire until it snapped. His left arm was free. He sawed through two more wires until both of his arms were free. But the more wires he cut, the more weight was distributed to the remaining hooks. The extra pressure swelled in his eyeball. His throat skin stretched with the hook in his neck, causing him to feel as if he were being strangled by it. The hooks on his chest, which held the most weight, felt as if they were about to tear off large hunks of meat at any second.

Lance whimpered, grinding his teeth. He had to cut the wires in his neck and eye next. The pressure would just be too much if any more weight was put on them. He brought the axe to the wire in his eye, but just grazing the line was too great a pain. He brought it to the wire in his neck, but when he tried to cut, blood sprayed out of the hole. It'd pierced a major artery. If he removed the hook it would probably kill him.

"Bro, look out," his friends called from below. "Someone's coming."

Lance looked around. He didn't see anyone. Then the pig was pulled up toward a ledge high above him. The animal squealed and thrashed harder than ever, yanking on the wire in Lance's eye. He screamed as his eye was pulled and ripped. He cut the wire in one quick hack and his eye was free, dangling out of its socket on the edge of the hook.

The pig disappeared somewhere up above. Lance could no longer hear the squealing. Though he couldn't see anyone, he could sense somebody up there. Somebody massive.

"Look out, bro! Look out!"

Lance shrieked as the person high above pulled on the wires connected to his flesh. His body was raised a few feet at a time along the cliff wall. Lance had to act faster. He cut another wire free, one connected to his chest. Then he cut the other one.

"Hurry, bro!"

As his weight fell onto the remaining hooks, he could hear the tearing of his flesh. The hook in his neck ripped open his throat, causing blood to erupt from the hole. He tried cutting the wire attached to the neck hook, but every time he touched it the hole tore wider. If he cut anymore wires the hook in his throat would kill him.

"You have to hurry!"

Lance had only one option left. He had to wait until he was pulled up to the ledge above, kill the mutant with his hatchet, then with his feet on the ground he could safely cut the wires and remove the hooks. That was, as long as the hole in his neck didn't stretch any further and bleed him to death.

Lance saw the monster at the top of the ledge. The deformed man stood there, pulling on the lines like a fisherman reeling in a fish. He wore a gore-stained butcher's apron and a surgical mask across his face. His white arms bulged in an almost unnatural way, as if he possessed muscles that don't normally exist on the human body.

With his hatchet at the ready, Lance kept his eyes on the monster's head. He endured the pain of being pulled up by his neck and back, just holding out until he was within striking distance. The agony swelled to such an extent that Lance weakened. He knew he only had one chance. He'd have to put everything into the first swing.

When the ledge was in reach, Lance grabbed it with his

free hand, then swung the axe. The blade cleaved through The Butcher's surgical mask, crushing his face.

"How'd ya like that, asshole?" Lance yelled at the mutant.

But even with the hatchet buried deep in his face, The Butcher wasn't fazed. He grabbed Lance's wrist and snapped it in half, then lifted him up into the air.

Lance shrieked as The Butcher held him by his broken arm, ripping the hooks out of his flesh. An explosion of blood splattered across The Butcher's apron as the monster ripped the hook out of Lance's neck.

Before his blood drained out, Lance saw The Butcher remove his surgical mask. The hatchet hadn't crushed the mutant's face. The hatchet hadn't done any damage to his features at all. There were no eyes, nose, or mouth behind the surgical mask. His entire face was hollow from the eyebrows down, as if scooped out with a shovel. There was a brain pulsing behind a thick layer of skin, and ears for hearing in the dark, but otherwise The Butcher's head was just an empty skull.

The light on Dean's helmet flickered. He smacked it as he stepped out of the water onto the rocks. They saw Lance's body as it was dragged away. There was nothing they could do about it. Only three of them were left now.

"My batteries are dying," Dean said. "Got any extras?"

"You burned them all, dumbass," Trent said.

"Think we're safe down here?" Dean asked. "Those things can't follow after us, can they? Those rocks blocked up the waterslide."

"There are probably other ways to get down here," Trent said. "We should hurry."

"Do you think there's another way out of these caves?" Dean asked.

Trent shrugged. "We keep going deeper. We're not going to find a way out if we keep going deeper."

They looked at Marta. She was still holding her dead sister in her arms, cradling her pale limp body.

"We should give her a minute," Dean said.

Trent shook his head. "We don't have time." He turned to Marta. "Giant Gonzales, let's go. We need to get out of here."

"I'm not leaving her," Marta said, blood leaking down her cheeks and forehead.

"She's dead." He walked over to her and kicked the corpse's floppy leg. "Leave her."

"You go if you want to. I'm staying."

Trent put his finger in her face. "Listen, you fat fuck. You can't do anything for her. She's dead and she's not coming back. Now come with us before those fucking things get down here and slaughter the rest of us."

"Get lost," she said, slapping his finger away. "This is all your fault. If you didn't bring us here none of this would have happened." Marta was in tears, rubbing her chin against Selena's shoulder.

"Nobody forced you to come along," Trent said. "If I knew Lauren was friends with any fat bitches I would have told her not to bother bringing you."

"Guys…" Dean said.

"Your fat ass nearly drowned us all back there," Trent continued.

"Hey, guys…" Dean said.

"Why don't you have any goddamned respect for yourself?" Trent said. "You fat bitches think I'm an asshole when I criticize your weight, but if you actually cared about your appearance you wouldn't be so fat and disgusting in the first place."

Marta just glared at him, but said nothing.

Dean was jumping up and down behind them. "Guys, seriously…"

"Do you fat chicks really think you should be treated equally to attractive people like me?" Trent continued. "Do you know how much hard work it takes to maintain my looks? Do you know how many hours I spend in the gym each week, while you lazy fat asses sit around eating deep dish meat-lovers pizza and watching *Family Guy*? You deserve all the shit you get. You deserve to be mocked and ridiculed. It offends me if you think you could ever be my equal."

"Guys!" Dean yelled.

Trent turned to him. "What?"

"We have company…" Dean said.

Trent saw them stepping out of the caves toward them. Three mutants. Each of the hunters moved slowly, brandishing their weapons, closing in for the kill. There was nowhere they could run. The frat boys were going to have to fight.

Trent and Dean went back to back, but Marta didn't move. She refused to leave Selena's side.

The hunters circled them. The Shovel Bitch hissed and slithered across the rocks. There was also a thick, stocky gorilla-like male with what looked like axe blades running down the front of his face. The hunchbacked archer stood in the back, loading his crossbow which was sewn into his left arm.

"Do you see the size of the tits on that chick with the shovel?" Dean whispered to Trent. "They're fucking sweet, bro."

Trent shot him a look of disgust. "Dude. Ew."

"Just saying, bro." Dean said.

Trent held up his machete. Dean raised his fists.

"Let's do this, bro," Dean said. "Let's show these wooks how Sig Alp throws down."

Trent nodded. Then he took off running.

"Bro, what the fuck?" Dean yelled.

"Sorry, bro," Trent yelled as he ran. "I'm not dying here. Not me. No way."

He jumped into the water and put his oxygen mask over his face.

"But bros stick together," Dean cried. "That's the bro code."

"Fuck the bro code," Trent said.

The words struck Dean like a knife in his back. He didn't know what to say. He just stared at his bro with his mouth dangling open. Then Trent turned away and dove under the water, swimming toward an underwater cavern to make his escape.

"Fuck the bro code?" Dean was dumbfounded by those words.

A harpoon whizzed past Dean's face and splashed into the water.

The man with the axe blades in his face charged to the shore of the lake, grabbed the handle of the harpoon, and lifted Trent out of the water like a fish on the end of a pike. The frat boy cried out, clutching at the shaft of the pole that was skewered through his upper thigh. Water rained from his soggy blond hair.

"Bro," Dean yelled. "See what happens when you diss the bro code?"

"Fuck you, Dean," Trent said as he hung in the air, grabbing at his leg in agony.

Axe Face threw his harpoon aside, tossing Trent into the rocks. Then he unraveled a chain from his muscled arms. The Shovel Bitch and The Hunchback kept their distance, blocking the exits and allowing their older brother to take his prey single-handedly. Axe Face dropped what appeared to be a bear trap on the ground, attached to the end of the chain. Then he swung the trap in a circle next to him like a morning star, aiming the weapon's jaws at Trent's face.

A rock hit the mutant in the back of the head. Axe Face dropped the chained bear trap and turned around, glaring at Dean with his sewn up eyes.

"Over here, bitch," Dean yelled.

Axe Face turned away from Trent to face the other frat boy. He growled like a lion, dragging his trap over the rocks toward his new opponent.

Dean didn't cower at the massive figure before him. He stood his ground, giving the monster the most intense expression he had in reserve. It was Extreme Dean's signature throwdown face.

"You might not care about the bro code, Trent," Dean said, getting all intense and serious. "But it's something *I* happen to live by. And the bro code says that if somebody messes with my bro he messes with me, too."

Dean took off his shirt, threw it on the ground, then roared and flexed his muscles.

When Trent saw Dean's hairy jiggling breasts, he whined, "Ah, dude, not with the shirt again…"

Dean paced back and forth, staring down his opponent, his pecs getting all creamy.

"You see, being a bro *means* something," Dean said. "Sure, it might mean being badass at every sport imaginable, totally getting any chick you want without even trying, and being the embodiment of pure awesome at all times. But it means even more than that. It means *loyalty*. It means *devotion*."

Dean's breasts slapped against his chest. The sound made the blind monsters cock their heads, confused by what could cause such an odd noise.

"I've *always* got my bros' backs, even when they don't got mine," Dean said, pointing at the beast. "So if you want Trent, you'll first have to go through me."

Milk squirted rapidly from Dean's nipples, splashing in Axe Face's direction. Even the hundred and fifty year old subterranean immortal mutants were disturbed by the frat boy's lactating breasts.

"They call me Extreme Dean. That's because I'm the most *extreme* motherfucker you've ever seen."

"Yeah, Dean!" Trent yelled, pumping his fist while lying on the ground with the harpoon stuck in his leg. "You are *the man!*"

Dean raised his fists, spraying milk across the rocks. "Let's do this, bitch!" Then he charged the mutant.

The bear trap flew through the air and chomped onto Dean's forearm. The jaws dug into his flesh, blood spraying through its metal teeth. Before the frat boy could even scream, Axe Face pulled on the chain, lifting him off of his feet.

Dean's body was tossed in a circle over the mutant's head,

then thrown into the side of the cave. The back of his skull cracked against the rocks, blood and brain spraying in a geyser. The milky discharge continued leaking down Dean's chest as his limp body rolled into the lake.

"Ah, bro," Trent said. "You went out like a bitch…"

The mutant pulled the body out of the water and pried open the massive bear trap. Then he twirled it over his head again, aiming at Trent.

"Don't go after me," Trent said. "What about her?"

He pointed at Marta in the corner.

"Go after the fat chick," Trent cried.

Axe Face didn't listen. He swung his weapon over his head, aiming for Trent's throat.

"Don't just sit there," Trent yelled at Marta. "You're supposed to be a badass wrestler. Kick his ass."

Marta just looked at him, her face red, her eyes glaring.

"Do something, you fat bitch!" Trent yelled. "There's no way I'm dying before a worthless fat fuck like you!"

Axe Face pulled back on his weapon, just about to launch it at Trent, when Marta stood up.

"Get away from him," she said, rage in her eyes.

The mutants all turned toward her.

"I won't let you kill any more of my friends. Not even an asshole like Trent."

She stepped forward. Her eyes glowed red.

"You are all going to die," she said. Her voice went deeper, stronger. It was the voice of a demon. "By the power of Satan, I will destroy you."

"Are you ready to become Satan's Little Princess?" asked Marta's mother. Her naked body was covered in black paint and red arcane symbols.

Marta was lying on the altar, her arms and legs bound.

"But I don't want to marry Satan," she cried.

The mother paused with an aggravated face, tapping her scepter sternly against the altar. She did not like hearing those words come from her daughter's mouth.

"I don't want any lip out of you, young lady," the mother said. "You're going to do as you're told and marry the dark lord and that's final."

"But *Mom...*"

"It's a great honor," said the mother. "I wish I was chosen when I was a little girl."

"But I want to marry somebody nice and handsome when I grow up," Marta said. "I want to have children and a normal family."

"You are permitted to date or even have kids with other boys if you wish. But you must never love another boy more than you love the dark lord. Remember, the spirit of Satan will become a part of your body after this wedding. He will see everything you do, think everything you think. He will know when you love someone more than him."

"Is that what marrying him means?" Marta asked. "I'll be possessed by the devil?"

"In a manner of speaking, yes," said the mother. "Satan's spirit will infuse you. You will share the same flesh and soul. Satan will take control of your body when you're angry, upset, or sexually aroused, and you'll get to control it at all other times. That's what it means to be the bride of our dark lord."

"Satan takes over whenever I become angry?"

"That's right."

"But what if Satan hurts people when he takes over? I don't want to hurt anyone."

Her mother laughed. "Satan won't just hurt people that make you angry. He will *destroy* them."

Tears slipped down Marta's eyes as her mother stepped back and pulled a goat mask over her face. A row of curtains opened, revealing a black church filled with a large crowd of masked naked cultists. They rocked from side to side, chanting a dark hymn, awaiting the ceremony that would drive the dark lord's spirit into Marta's body.

"He will obliterate them from the face of the planet," said her mother.

Marta's eyes flared red as the power of the dark lord took over her body. She stood like a bull ready to charge, air puffing fiercely from her nostrils, as the subterranean mutants circled her like sharks.

They did not strike immediately, almost as if they were intimidated by Marta. Perhaps they knew something dark had taken over her body.

The one with the axe blades in his face attacked first. He swung his chained bear trap and the jaws snapped onto Marta's shoulder, digging into her muscled flesh. The mutant pulled on his chain, attempting to toss her across the cave as he did with Dean. But nothing happened. Marta wouldn't budge.

Axe Face curled his arm around the chain and put more of his strength into it, but no matter how hard he yanked he couldn't move Marta even an inch.

Giant Gonzales just stared at the mutant as he desperately tried to throw her to the ground. She made not a sound, but looked at him as if he were a pathetic worm. As he continued tugging, Marta grabbed her end of the chain. She slowly twisted it around her wrist. Then she ripped the mutant's arm off at the fucking shoulder.

Axe Face roared as he heard his arm rolling across the ground, but he did not bleed. His blood dried up a long time ago. Only dust and slime fell from his open wound.

The Shovel Bitch charged Marta from behind, but was knocked to the ground by a limb hitting her in the side of the head. Marta used the severed arm at the end of the chain as a weapon. She swung it at Shovel Bitch twice, smacking her in the face and clubbing her in the chest. Then she aimed for the archer.

As The Hunchback loaded his crossbow, Marta slapped the arrow out of his hand, then tangled his legs in the chain and swept him off his feet. A cracking noise echoed through the cave as his skull connected with the rocks.

"Hell yeah, Giant Gonzales!" Trent yelled, dragging himself behind her for protection. "Kill those ugly fuckers!"

Marta stepped to Trent and ripped the harpoon out of his leg. Trent screamed, grabbing at his wound as blood spurted from the hole.

Before Shovel Bitch could get to her feet, Marta drove the harpoon through her stomach and into the rock beneath her. She tried to move, but Shovel Bitch was pinned to the spot.

The only one left standing was Axe Face.

"You're all alone now," the frat boy taunted the mutant. "No one left to back your bitch-ass up."

Axe Face turned to Marta. With his one remaining arm, he pulled out a rod that was strapped to his back, then he slammed it against the ground. Like a four-foot switchblade, a spearhead sprung from the tip, extending the rod into another harpoon.

When Axe Face threw the weapon at Marta, she just caught it in one hand, broke it in half like a twig and tossed it aside.

"Ah, man, you are *fucked!*" Trent yelled from the ground. "Giant Gonzales is gonna fuck all you bitches up!"

Axe Face stood there for a moment, as if staring Marta down. Then he stepped to the side, getting out of the way. Something big was coming through the tunnel behind him. Something unbelievably powerful. Axe Face moved far away from the tunnel entrance, bowing out of the fight.

Their ultimate warrior was about to arrive.

"What the fuck is that?" Trent cried. "What is that sound?"

It was the sound of a train. A roaring engine. The rocks vibrated beneath them as it came closer. The entire cavern shook. Waves rippled through the water. The sound pounded in Trent's ears.

When the thing entered the cave, Trent couldn't believe his eyes. It was a massive steam-powered machine made of black rock and steel. The thing was man-shaped, like a robot of stone. It walked on two legs and had four arms, each with its own power tool. One arm had a drill, the other a massive pickaxe, another had a deep shovel, and the last was a mechanical hand. The machine seemed built for mining, for digging holes, breaking apart rocks, and collecting minerals for the underworld community.

The driver was hardly a man at all. The lower half of his body was missing, his arms were just bone and nerves without any flesh, his face was flat and wide, with a long gray miner's beard that stretched down his shriveled belly. His flesh was fused into the machine, as if he hadn't left the driver's seat since the First World War.

The Miner came toward Marta and raised its four mechanical arms. Marta just stood there, holding her ground, not the slightest bit intimidated by the colossal machine in front of her.

"Don't, Giant Gonzales," Trent said, squirming away from the machine, trying to get to his feet. "You can't beat him. Run away. Help me up and let's run away."

Marta didn't listen to him. She eyed The Miner down.

Trent got to his feet and staggered across the cave.

"Run!" he yelled.

An arrow pierced his back and exited the front of his chest. He turned around and saw The Hunchback was back on his feet, loading his crossbow. When Marta looked back and saw the life fade out of Trent's eyes, she roared with fury. He was the last of her group. The last surviving friend. She wasn't going to allow the mutants to get away with it.

Marta charged The Miner. Like a bull barreling forward horns-first, Marta lunged at the machine. The pickaxe arm slammed into Marta, throwing her back before she could even reach him. She shook off the pain, blood leaking down her face. Then she charged again.

This time she grabbed the pickaxe arm, holding it in place before it could attack her. The center of her chest bruised against the weight of the stone-crushing tool, the engine vibrating through her body. Then the Miner swung its waist to the side and slammed the digging arm into her side, cracking two of her ribs. She lost her grip on the pickaxe and stumbled back.

The Hunchback hissed at The Miner. They were human words, but so distorted and raspy coming from his ancient lungs that they were hardly intelligible. It sounded as if he said *Finish her...*

Marta moved out of the way as the machine's drill plunged into the earth where she was standing. She pushed her way through The Miner's limbs and wrapped her muscled arms around its mechanical body.

Crush her skull...

The Miner swung his metal limbs at her, but she was in too close. He couldn't reach her. She tightened her muscles around the machine, crushing the pipes and levers. Steam shrieked out of the cracks, blowing into the driver's face.

Weakling...

Marta roared and flexed. With all of her strength, she lifted The Miner off of the ground. Like the machine was a wrestling opponent, she lifted it off of the ground, crushing it in a bear-hug. Its limbs thrashed and jerked, but they could not reach her. The driver squealed and howled through holes in his beard as the metal exoskeleton crumpled around him.

"Die, little insect..." Marta roared in her demonic voice.

An arrow hit her in the shoulder blade. She didn't see the dynamite attached to it, too focused on crushing The Miner's metal body. The sparkling fuse disappeared into the stick, then exploded.

161

Marta and The Miner were thrown apart. The machine tumbled over the rocks, trying to balance on its twisted legs. But Marta did not tumble. She stood exactly in the place she had been, the same burning anger flowing in her eyes.

End this now...

The left side of Marta's body was gone. Her left arm was in pieces on the floor. Meat from her ribs and shoulder fell in chunks beneath her. But she did not fall. She did not even cringe. She just stomped forward and grabbed the machine's driver by the throat.

The Hunchback fired another explosive arrow at Marta, but she just slapped it out of the way. It exploded in the lake. A geyser of water sprayed across them.

The Miner stabbed its drill into her chest, cutting a hole right through her ribcage and lungs, but it only pissed her off more. She crushed the driver's neck, cracking it in a hundred places, turning the bones to powder.

She was a wife of Satan. Nothing could stand up to her wrath.

Marta slept in her new home for the first time. She had a new family. A new sister and a new dad.

"It's a good thing we got her out of there when we did," said Steven Renwood, the new father. "Her parents really messed her up."

Steven was a journalist who had been writing a book on demonic possession in children. There were two cases that he came across that he took a strong interest in. He really felt for these girls, really cared about them—so much that he decided to adopt them and make them his family. He wanted to do everything he could to help them. The two children were named Marta and Selena.

"Can I be fiends with her?" little Selena asked, peeking into the room at Marta.

"Not *fiends*, you mean *friends*," said Steven. "Your language skills are still atrocious. You should study harder."

"Can I be friends with her?" Selena asked.

Steven nodded. "Of course you can be friends. She could really use one about now. Even though she was psychologically abused by her parents, she still loved them. They meant the world to her. She's going to be incredibly confused and lonely without them. I hope you'll be able to help her."

"I'll help her," Selena said, baring her fangs in a smile at her father.

"Good," he said. "You're a good girl."

Before Selena closed the door, she saw Marta growl and hiss in her sleep, talking in strange demonic tongues.

"Daddy?" Selena asked, a concerned look on her face.

"Yes?"

"Is she really possessed by the devil?" Selena asked.

Steven shook his head.

"No, Selena, the devil doesn't exist," he said. "Her parents brainwashed her to *think* she was possessed by the devil. She's just an ordinary girl."

"Not like me?"

"Not like you."

The Miner drilled through the side of Marta's chest and severed her remaining arm. Her hand dropped from the driver's throat and plopped onto the ground. She stumbled back, her body wobbling on her spine.

The Hunchback launched an arrow into the hole in her chest. Marta had no arms left to stop the fuse in time. When the fire reached the dynamite, her body exploded into thousands of bits of meat which rained across the subterranean lake like wet confetti.

CHAPTER SEVEN
SELENA

THE BRO CODE #23
If a Bro accidentally strikes another Bro's
crotch while walking, both silently agree
to act as if nothing happened.

Selena's eyes opened. Everything was black. Her body was cold and stiff against the wet rocky ground. She had no idea where she was or what the hell was going on. All she knew was that most of her body was numb except for the wound on her throat, which hurt like hell. The throbbing pain felt like a starving rat was trying to eat through her flesh.

The light on her helmet had burned out. She sat up and smacked it with the gritty palm of her hand, but the batteries were dead for good. The only light was in the distance, far ahead of her. It was just a tiny point of light, like a candle flickering in a vacant hotel room, moving slowly across the ground as if it were being dragged.

Selena narrowed her eyes. A one-armed mutant with axes in his head was dragging a limp body behind him. The light issued from the helmet that dangled from the corpse's head.

With the pickaxe in her hands, she crawled to her feet and moved through the darkness, careful to be as quiet as she could. When she was close enough to get a good look at the scene, she saw that it was Trent's body that was being dragged by the creature. There was no sign of any of her other friends or any of the other mutants. If Marta, Dean or Lance had been there they must have either fled or their bodies were already dragged away.

A moan emptied from Trent's lungs. He wasn't dead.

"The fuck is this shit..." Trent said in a weak, wheezing voice.

He was fading in and out of consciousness, unable to even

lift an arm in resistance as he was hauled away.

Selena crept up behind the mutant, moving only when Trent wheezed and moaned, covering the sound of her footsteps.

"Selena, what the hell…" Trent said when his rolling eyes saw her lifting the pickaxe over her head.

Axe Face roared as the spike of metal entered the back of his skull. He dropped Trent. Selena tore the pickaxe out of the creature's head. Black congealed blood dribbled down his spine. Before the mutant could turn to his attacker, she slammed the pickaxe into his head again, driving it through his temple. The monster cried out but he did not fall.

"He's immortal…" Trent said, trying to bring himself to full consciousness. "You can't kill him…"

Selena slammed all of her weight into the handle of the pickaxe as it was still lodged in the mutant's cranium, twisting it back. The force threw his head sideways and snapped his neck.

"Immortal, huh?" Selena said.

Axe Face's body lay on the ground. He was still alive, but was paralyzed from the neck down. Only his mouth opened and closed.

"How's this for immortal…" Then she crushed the mutant's skull with the back of the pickaxe.

She continued to sink the metal blade into the freak's head until all that remained were bits of bone, blood and black brain matter.

"Anything will die if you smash it into enough pieces."

Long white worms slithered through the mush at Selena's feet. She wasn't sure if the worms were already on the ground before she smashed up the mutant's skull or if they were a colony of brain parasites that had been living in the mutant's head for decades—something that would have killed a normal human, but an immortal would have had to just suffer with the pain as they dug through his neural tissue for all eternity.

"Actually, even destroying the brain didn't quite kill him," Trent said. "He's still alive."

Trent pointed to a piece of brain that was throbbing in the rocks.

"His body and brain no longer function, but he's still alive," Trent said.

Selena saw the twitchy meat on the ground. She wondered if he could still think, still feel with his brain turned into mush, or if his consciousness had become a thoughtless residue of life force left behind in the meat.

"Where's everyone else?" Selena asked.

"Dead. Taken. I don't know about your sister, though. She was still alive last time I saw her." He pulled on the arrow in his chest, but it wouldn't budge. He asked Selena for assistance. "Help me get this out."

"We shouldn't take it out," Selena said. "It could kill you."

Trent burst into laughter when she said that. "It won't *kill* me."

"Of course it could," she said. "That arrow held in place is probably the only thing keeping you alive. You shouldn't move it."

Trent laughed harder, causing a shooting pain through his chest. "You have no idea, do you?"

"About what?"

"Removing the arrow's not going to kill me because I'm already dead."

"What do you mean? Like *him?*" Selena pointed at Axe Face's corpse.

Trent nodded. "This arrow is in my heart. I don't have a pulse anymore. Neither do you."

"It can't be..." Selena said, feeling for a heartbeat in her wrist. She felt nothing.

"You died back there," Trent said. "Your throat was cut. You bled to death. The second I saw you still walking around I knew it was true. We're just as immortal as the Turtle family."

Selena thought about it and nodded her head.

"It makes sense," she said. "These mountains…"

Trent clenched his teeth as he tugged on the arrow, moving it a few inches. His fingers were too slimy with blood to get a good grip.

"Remember when Lauren told you about our friends who disappeared in these mountain when we were in high school?" Selena asked.

Trent nodded, but was more focused on the arrow than her story.

"There were all sorts of rumors about what happened to them, but one of them was so ridiculous I never gave it much thought until now."

Selena went to Trent and ripped the arrow out for him. He opened his mouth to scream but no air escaped his lungs, cradling his chest and rocking back and forth.

"A guy named Casey went up to these mountains to look for them a couple of weeks after it happened. He was related to one of them. Rick's brother, I think. Anyway, the story goes that Casey found them still alive, living in the mountains. But they weren't exactly alive. They were like walking corpses, the undead. Something in the area was keeping them alive, some unknown supernatural force."

Selena looked down at the arrow in her hand. The blood was warm against her cold, bloodless fingers.

She continued, "If they were ever to leave the area they would instantly drop dead, so all of them were cursed to live on in this backwoods community cut off from the rest of the world with others like them. Casey would go back and visit them from time to time. He'd bring them books, decent food, and news about their family and friends, but supposedly their immortality was hard and depressing. They all felt as if they would have been better off if they just died."

She tossed the arrow aside.

"I never thought it could have possibly been true," she said. "And now we're exactly like them. We can never leave these mountains again…"

She sat down, staring across the subterranean lake.

"Even if we escape the mutants," she said, "we can never go back home."

Trent crawled over and sat next to her.

"Yeah, but look on the bright side," he said.

"What bright side?"

"Nobody can die in these mountains," Trent said, wrapping his arm around her back. "That includes Lauren, Dean, Lance, and even Gravy. They're all still alive out there."

Trent shot her a smile.

"None of our friends are actually dead."

Lauren woke up at the bottom of a ravine. She should have been dead. She knew she should have been dead, but somehow she was still alive.

Rolling over, there was a mutant beneath her, the one with the sickles growing out of his arms. All of his bones were broken and twisted. Most of his insides were sprayed across the rock. Lauren landed on top of him and he must have absorbed some of the impact. It was a shock to her that Sickle Arms, even in his mangled state, wasn't dead, either.

"Hello?" Lauren called out, looking up at the ledge where she fell. "Trent? Selena?"

There wasn't anyone else around, just her and the mangled mutant.

It took Lauren a moment before she realized just how serious her condition was. When she lifted her arm to brush sweat from her brow, she saw the bone sticking out of the skin. Her hand dangled from her wrist like a limp glove. One of the mutant's sickle arms was severed and buried inside of her guts. The backs of her legs were missing several layers of skin, exposing tendons and muscle.

"Are you still trying to kill me?" Lauren asked the mutant.

Sickle Arms dragged himself toward her, trying to get himself to his feet, holding out his remaining sickle arm.

Lauren pulled his other sickle arm out of her stomach and held it out in a defensive stance. Because the weapon was embedded into the flesh, she had to hold the severed arm like a handle.

"Stay back," she said.

But the man could hardly move. He dropped his head onto the rock and breathed from a hole in his face that must have been a mouth at one time.

"Don't even try it," she said. "I know what you're trying to do."

Lauren read the mutant's body language. She could tell he was pretending to be a lot more injured than he really was. He was waiting for her to get closer and then he would attack.

"I'm not going to fall for it," she said.

Though she wasn't close enough, Sickle Arms lunged at her anyway. He swiped at her with his blade, but missed by at least two feet. She just stared at him, the air blowing against her eyelids. Then he fell to the ground and landed on a sharp boulder that broke his meatless spine in two.

"See," she said, pointing at his torso as his lower half rolled backward, limp and dead. "You're only hurting yourself more."

The mutant didn't give up, crawling with his last remaining limb, whining and hissing at her.

"I'm sorry that my boyfriend killed your children," Lauren said to the mutant. "Well, he's not my boyfriend yet, but he *will* be." She paused for a moment. The thought of Trent becoming her boyfriend put a smile on her face. "He was just scared. He didn't know what he was doing. Your people shouldn't have reacted so violently. We could have resolved this without anyone else getting hurt."

Sickle Arms continued toward her. Lauren just backed away.

"Look at you. You're a mess."

Lauren backed away even further. As she watched the

man's body language, she realized there was more to his violent behavior than she thought. He wasn't only trying to get revenge for what Trent did to the little girls. He was also trying to protect something.

"What is it?" Lauren asked. "What's so important that you'd want to kill me to prevent me from finding it?"

The creature faced her and moaned, dragging himself closer.

Lauren looked behind her. There was a path through the ravine that led to a small tunnel.

"You don't want me to go that way, do you?" she asked.

The mutant continued crawling and hissing.

"Something is over there that you want to protect," she said. "Something of incredible value. A treasure, maybe? A secret?"

Lauren looked back. It just seemed like a normal tunnel, but Sickle Arms definitely didn't want her to go that way. If he could he would have killed her to prevent her from going.

"I'm sorry, but I can't leave you here like this," Lauren told the mutant. "If your friends find you I'm sure you'll tell them where I'm going and I can't have that."

She lowered the severed sickle arm into the mutant's neck, decapitating him.

"I'll have to bring you with me." She picked up his severed head from the ground and placed it in her backpack. The head moaned and gurgled. "Don't worry. I'll let you go later, when it's safe."

Then she draped the backpack over her shoulder and headed in the direction of the tunnel, wondering what the mutant was trying to protect.

"Hello?" Dean said, the moment he awoke. "Is anybody there?"

He was in a dark room and couldn't see a thing. His arms and legs were bound by old itchy ropes. He was shirtless and he could feel droplets of warm fluid dripping from his nipples.

The last thing he remembered was getting knocked out after the fight with one of the mutants. He realized he must have been captured and taken prisoner.

"Hello?" he called out again.

There was movement in the room with him, the sound of somebody struggling against the wall. Then somebody moaned.

"Who's there?" Dean asked. "Is somebody in here with me?"

Another moan. Then a grunt. Dean recognized that grunt.

"Lance? Bro, is that you?"

Lance grunted again.

"Bro, wake up," Dean said. "Come on…"

It took a while for Lance to become conscious.

"What?" Lance asked. His voice was soft and weak. "Dean? What's going on? Where are we?"

"I don't know, bro. I think we've been taken prisoner by those deformed mutant dudes."

"Does anyone know we're here?" Lance was beginning to panic. "What are they going to do to us?"

"Bro, relax," Dean said. "We'll get through this. We're Sig Alp. We're fucking badass. These ropes can't hold us."

"How are we going to get out of here?" Lance cried.

"No worries, bro. We'll think of something. But first we need to get some light in here. Are you still wearing your helmet?"

"I don't know," Lance said. "I don't think so."

"I'm still wearing mine," Dean said. "But I think the batteries in the light are dead. Give me a second…"

Dean slammed his head against his arm tied above him. It flickered for a second. "Yeah, I think there's still some juice in it…"

He slammed again. Then again. Each time he hit, the light would come on a little more, revealing quick flashes of their surroundings. All he could make out were pigs. Lots of pigs.

When the light came on for good, Dean said, "About time…" And he could finally make out where they were.

They were in a shack that was being used as a slaughterhouse.

The bodies of subterranean pigs hung from meat hooks, gutted with their heads cut off. A head from one of the pigs lay on the cutting block in front of Dean. It wiggled its nose and licked its lips.

"Dude, that pig head is still moving..." Dean said.

Then he turned to Lance. When he saw the condition of his friend, Dean freaked the fuck out.

"HOLY FUCKING SHIT, BRO!" Dean cried.

Lance looked like one of the pigs on the meat hooks. He had been skinned. Most of the meat was stripped from his bone. His intestines were in a pile on the floor at his feet.

"What?" Lance asked, as if nothing were wrong.

"HOW THE FUCK ARE YOU STILL ALIVE?" Dean cried. "YOUR FUCKING ORGANS ARE SHOWING!"

Lance looked down and saw what was left of his body. He was mostly just a skeleton with lungs and a heart that was still beating. Only a small amount of muscle was left on his arms and shoulders.

"WHAT!" Lance cried, in complete shock at the sight of himself. "WHAT!"

"BRO, THEY ATE YOU! THEY'RE CANNIBALS AND THEY ATE YOU AND YOU'RE STILL FUCKING ALIVE!"

"It can't be..." Lance cried, shaking his head. "This can't be real..."

"IT'S REAL, BRO! IT'S WAY TOO FUCKING REAL! HOW THE HELL ARE YOU GOING TO GET LAID LOOKING LIKE THAT!"

They stared at each other, screaming at the tops of their lungs.

"WAY TOO EXTREME, BRO! WAY TOO EXTREME!"

When Selena found her sister's remains, she couldn't believe it. Marta was dead. Though she wasn't entirely dead... The top half of her head was still functioning, lying like half a watermelon in the corner of the cave. Everything below her eyes was missing. She was just a brain with eyes inside of a skullcap.

Selena couldn't deal with it. She couldn't accept the fact that her sister was still alive inside of that half a skull. She couldn't even say goodbye.

Trent took care of it for her. He removed the brain from the bone and burned it using fluid from his lighter. The meat fizzled and popped in the flames, filling the cave with a burnt gizzard-like smell. The fire went out before the organ completely burned away, but Trent decided not to tell Selena about it.

"They're all going to pay for this," Selena said, gripping the pickaxe in her lap. "I'm going to kill every last one of those fuckers."

Trent sat down behind her and rubbed her back, as if he was consoling her.

"We will," Trent said. "We'll get them together."

"We've got to rescue the others," Selena said. "Dean and Lance. And we have to find Lauren."

"Of course…" Trent said, rubbing his fingers along her neck. "But not just yet. We should get some rest first."

Trent handed Selena some water.

"Drink this," he said.

Selena took the water bottle and stared off into the subterranean lake, imaging what she was going to do to each and every one of those mutant freaks.

She brought the bottle up to her mouth and paused, then looked over at Trent. He was rubbing her arms, staring at the bottle with wet lips. Something weird was going on with him. She put the bottle aside.

"We need to come up with a game plan," she said. "I think we should try to go after them one at a time if we can. We wait until one separates from the others, then we strike. If we find any of the others they can help us. Eventually their numbers will decrease. Then we can finish them off."

"Of course," Trent said, rubbing her shoulders. "Just drink your water. You'll need to be hydrated before we go after them."

At the moment, Selena knew something was definitely up with the water. She lifted it to her nose and smelled.

"Did you put something in this?" she asked.

"Of course not. What are you talking about?"

There was definitely something in there.

"You tried to roofie me, didn't you?"

"What?" He rolled his eyes at her. He wasn't in the slightest bit convincing.

"You did," she said, pushing away from him. "You motherfucker! You tried to drug me and have your way with me!"

"Okay, fine," he said, annoyed by her tone of voice. "You got me. Big deal."

"Why the fuck would you do that at a time like this?" she cried.

"Well, you wouldn't put out. What do you expect me to do?"

"Those freaks are still out there," Selena said. "They could be back at any minute. I would've been fucking defenseless."

"So what. Just drink it." He grabbed the water bottle and tried to force it down her throat. "You'll be fine."

Selena smacked the water out of his hand. "Get the fuck away from me."

Trent tried to retrieve the bottle but most of the water had already dumped out.

"We don't have time for this," Selena said. "We've got to save our friends."

"You want me to help you with that, you're going to have to do something in exchange," Trent said.

"What? They're *your* fucking friends."

"I don't care about those assholes," Trent said. "I'm not doing shit for them unless you make it worth my while."

He grabbed for her pants and she backed away.

"Come on, bitch," Trent said.

He looked at her belly sticking out of her ripped up shirt. It pulsed with her breaths, shifting inward and outward. He imagined his baby inside of that stomach. He imagined it growing in her, stretching it bigger. He saw her bulging breasts hanging out of her shirt and imagined them filling with milk to feed his future baby. The thoughts were turning him on like crazy.

"This could be my last chance to fuck," Trent said. "I'm not going to miss it just because you're a stuck up bitch."

"What the hell is your problem?" she said.

He reached for her again and she backed away. She raised her pickaxe, threatening him not to come any closer.

Trent pulled out his machete. "You want to play it that way, slut?" He pointed the blade at her. "I'm not afraid to use force if I have to."

"You come near me and I'm putting this pickaxe right in your head," she told him. "Being immortal won't be very fun if you don't have a face."

"Yeah, well how about I chop off your arms and legs," Trent said. "I can just stash you in a cave and use you as my personal slam piece for as long as I want, then ditch you there once I get bored."

"You're such a fucking asshole. You probably would do that, wouldn't you?"

"I'll do whatever it takes to get what I want. You should remember that."

Trent reached for Selena's pickaxe and she slammed the handle against his knuckles. He pulled his hand back and shook his fingers at the pain.

"Fucking bitch," Trent said, raising his machete.

As the frat boy lunged at Selena, she lowered the pickaxe into his knee. It was his good leg, the one he was still able to walk on. Trent didn't realize his kneecap had been broken off until he tried to chase after her and crumpled to the ground.

Selena took off running deeper into the cave.

"Where do you think you're going, bitch?" Trent struggled to get back up. "You think you can survive out there without me?"

Selena ran into a side tunnel and hid behind the wall, holding out her pickaxe, ready to attack if the asshole tried to follow her.

"I've got the only light, bitch," Trent said. "How long do you think you can last wandering in the dark out there?"

Selena realized Trent was right. She wouldn't be able to help the others without a light. She wouldn't be able to take her revenge on the mutants. She would just be lost in the cave, wandering in the dark until she fell into a chasm or was captured by one of the freaks. She couldn't do it without Trent.

"You're fucked without me," Trent yelled.

But Selena didn't care. She continued running, deeper into the darkness, leaving the crippled frat boy behind.

The battery in Lauren's helmet light was running low on juice.

"No, come on…" she said to her lamp, smacking it as it flickered.

She picked up her pace, trying to explore as far as she could before the light went out. But she only made it another ten yards before the batteries died.

"Oh, shoot!"

However, it was dark for only a moment. Once her eyes adjusted, she could see a glow coming from off in the distance.

"What is that?" Lauren asked.

She moved carefully toward the light. When she turned a corner, it was even brighter—an orange glow coming from off in the distance. At first she thought it was a way out, but the glow was definitely not sunlight. It was created by something unnatural. Something alien.

"Is this what you were trying to hide from me?"

When she discovered where the light was coming from, she couldn't believe her eyes. There were radiant orange crystals all around her, glowing like neon lights. They leaked a fluid, also orange in color, which collected in a large pool in the center of the room.

"It's beautiful," Lauren said.

She pulled Sickle Arms' severed head out of her backpack and faced him toward the crystals.

"What are these?" she asked. "Is this what you wanted to protect from me?"

She watched the head's expressions. From what she got out of him, these crystals were definitely what Sickle Arms didn't want her to find. She wasn't sure what they were or where they came from, but she was able to ascertain that the crystals were responsible for keeping the mutants alive. They radiated some kind of energy that could keep the electrical currents in human brains flowing, even after the rest of the body was no longer functioning.

"I see why you'd want to protect this," Lauren said. "If this stuff were discovered, people would mine it and sell it. The world would never be the same after that."

Lauren reached out and touched a crystal. It burned her finger.

"Ow!" she cried, wondering why it was so hot.

She took a water bottle from her backpack and dunked it into the lake of glowing orange fluid. When the bottle was full, she tightened the cap and held it up over her head. The bottle was hot, but it did not melt. She took off her shirt and wrapped it around the bottle. The light was bright enough that it shined through the fabric. It created an excellent lamp.

"I don't care if it's dangerous," she said to the severed head in her arm. "I don't have a choice. I can't see in the dark without it."

Lauren continued into the cave, entering a labyrinth of passages, all made with walls of orange crystal. She hoped her friends found similar crystals once their lights burned out as hers did. The thought of Selena or Marta being lost in a dark cave somewhere filled her with trepidation. Selena, in particular, was always scared of the dark.

"What's it feel like, bro?" Dean asked Lance. "Being just a skeleton, I mean."

Lance couldn't answer. His brain was exhausted from the shock and stress of seeing his body in such a state. But he also couldn't answer because it was hard to describe how he felt. Without much meat left on his skeleton, he didn't have as many nerves. He shouldn't have been able to feel much of anything. But he could. He felt every bone in his body, every shred of meat still attached. Everything seemed raw and sensitive to the air, but he wasn't in much pain. The most discomforting part of his condition was how cold it was in there without any skin or muscle on his bones.

"Do you think you can walk on those legs?" Dean asked, looking at the skeletal bones that remained of Lance's limbs. "I don't know if I can carry you out of here if you can't."

Lance looked at himself. He didn't think he could even wiggle his legs let alone walk on them. His lower half was now useless. Perhaps his entire body was now useless.

The sound of slow, heavy footsteps grew outside the slaughter shack.

"Quiet, bro," Dean said. "I think someone's coming."

They didn't say a word when the massive mutant stepped through the door. Lance recognized him. It was The Butcher. The faceless man walked across the room carrying a rusty metal platter.

"Get away from him, bro," Dean said, as The Butcher approached his friend. "Leave him alone."

The Butcher took a serrated knife from the cutting block and sliced more meat from Lance's body. The frat boy screamed as the mutant cut him up—not from pain, but from the sight of seeing himself carved up like a Thanksgiving turkey. The Butcher placed the slices of meat onto the platter in his other hand, neatly arranging them as if they were cold cuts about to be served as appetizers at a dinner party.

"I'm warning you, bro," Dean said to The Butcher. "You don't want to see what I do to people who try to eat my friends."

As Dean said that, milk squirted from his nipples. The Butcher heard the noise. He turned around, set the platter of meat on the cutting block, and went to Dean.

"What the fuck are you looking at, ya wook?" Dean said.

The Butcher's faceless head cocked to the side as he felt the moistness on Dean's stomach. Her rubbed his wrinkled, rubbery fingers up his chest and squeezed one of Dean's breasts. The Butcher seemed intrigued as the fluid squirted across his hand.

"Don't touch my pecs like that, bro," Dean said. "Are you gay or something?"

The Butcher removed his apron and tossed it on the cutting block.

"What the fuck?" Dean cried, as he saw what had been hidden behind the apron.

The Butcher's body was hollowed out. And in the torso cavity, on what appeared to be shelves made of flesh, there were two rows of living human heads. Three in his chest and four in his belly. The heads had grown into the The Butcher's flesh, fused to him as well as fused to each other. It even appeared as if their nerves had grown together, as if all of their brains were connected together to form a hive mind.

"What's with all the heads, bro?" Dean asked the mutant. "Why are they in your stomach like that?"

Some of the heads still possessed eyes. They looked Dean's body up and down, examining his breasts. It was as if The Butcher could see what these heads were seeing.

The bug-eyed head on the top shelf of the chest cavity belonged to the patriarch of the Turtle family. He was their leader, their father, before their community went underground. He appeared to be the one in control of the body at that moment, even though the body belonged to the large man with the scooped out face.

"You want to fight or something?" Dean asked, staring down the head inside the mutant's chest. "Come on. Untie me and we'll go right now. Let's do it."

The Butcher leaned his body forward until the Patriarchal Head could reach Dean's breasts.

"Hey, wait a minute…" Dean said. "What are you doing?"

The old man's head opened its shriveled lips and took Dean's breast into his black hole of a mouth. Then it began to drink.

"Bro!" Dean cried. "That is not cool!"

Dean could feel his nipples becoming erect as he breastfed the old man's severed head. The creamy fluid disappeared into a working stomach deep inside The Butcher's body.

"A dude sucking on another dude's nipples is not cool, bro," Dean cried. "Not cool at all."

When the Patriarchal Head finished drinking from Dean's breast, milk dribbling down his wrinkled chin, The Butcher stepped back and wiped his milky mouth using a small yellow handkerchief.

"Don't even think about coming near my pecs again, yo," Dean said. "I'm a man. Only fine women get to stroke these bad boys."

The Butcher put a bucket beneath Dean, as though he were preparing to milk him like a cow. But instead of grabbing Dean's breasts, he grabbed the platter of Lance meat and took it out of the shack, leaving them alone in the dimly lit slaughterhouse.

"Dude, I think I just got molested by Man-E-Faces," Dean said.

Lance didn't care. He would have rather had his nipples sucked on than had all of his flesh removed.

Selena stepped slowly through the dark, traveling through an unknown tunnel, careful not to trip and fall off a cliff or into a bottomless pit. But after a while, her eyes began to adjust. She was able to see. At first, she thought it was some distant light aiding her vision, but then she realized there wasn't any other light. Her eyes were just changing, mutating. Her eyes were suddenly capable of seeing in the dark.

"No... you can't..." Selena said, touching her eyelids. Her fingernails seemed sharper against her skin.

She looked into a puddle of water near her feet. Her reflection revealed her eyes were no longer human. They had become narrow slits. The eyes of a cat.

"Don't wake up now," she said to her reflection. "You can't wake up now."

She put her finger in her mouth and felt her teeth stretching into fangs. Her ears became pointed.

"You fucking bitch," Selena said. "I won't let you take me again."

Selena looked around. She had to find more light. Even if she went back to Trent, she had to be in the light again. As soon as possible. Or else the darkness would consume her completely.

"What's her name?" Steven Renwood asked the Brazilian prison guard.

"We've been calling her Selena," the guard replied. "We have no idea what her real name is or where she came from."

They walked down the row of prison cells. A documentary film team followed them, recording every second of their conversation.

"Which one is she?" Steven asked, examining the wretched prisoners rotting in their cells.

"She's not being held in this block," said the guard. "We couldn't keep her with the normal prisoners. She ripped a woman's arm off the first day she arrived."

"And how old is she again?" Steven asked.

"Only six years old. The woman she attacked was a twenty-eight year old bodyguard that weighed about two hundred and thirty pounds."

"Is she really that strong?"

"Stronger. This girl's not human. She's a beast. They found her out in the jungle eating a small crocodile."

"Can she speak?"

"Not a word. We believe she's lived in the wild for most of her life."

They entered a door and took a flight of stairs down into the basement of the facility. The area was very dimly lit. The guard led the way with his flashlight.

"It's too dark down here," Steven said. "You should have more lighting. A lot more lighting."

The guard held out his flashlight. "Do you want to use my flashlight? I don't have a problem seeing in the dark."

"Not for me. For *her*."

"The girl? She doesn't need any light. She can see in the dark."

"Yeah, but if she is what I think she is the dark is making her condition a lot worse."

The guard laughed. "And what is it that you think she is?"

"Possessed," Steven said.

"Possessed by what? Demons?"

"Not demons. There are many other things that can possess human beings. Animals, for instance."

"Animals?" The guard smiled. "Seriously?"

The journalist nodded. "I have seen a few cases in the past. It is often referred to as Lycanthropy. The spirit of an animal takes control of a human's body. The possessed will even exhibit physical characteristics of the animal's spirit in extreme cases."

"Well, then this must be one of those extreme cases," said the guard. "She definitely has beast-like characteristics." Then he stopped and point at a cell in the corner of the basement. "See for yourself."

The journalist couldn't see anything but shadows beyond the bars of the cage. When he stepped closer, he heard the deep growling of a beast coming from the cell. It did not sound at all human. No human could make a noise like that. He paused for a moment.

"Film this," Steven told the documentary crew.

They came up behind him and aimed their cameras at the cage. The growls became louder as they moved in. Steven didn't make any sudden moves. He stepped toward the bars and kneeled down.

"Selena?" Steven asked the growling creature in the cell.

A beast leapt from the shadows and attacked, slamming its body against the cage, trying to get at Steven through the bars.

"My, you're a feisty one," Steven said to the beast, using a gentle tone.

It was a little girl. She was naked, covered in dirt, long knotty black hair grew to her waist. Her eyes and teeth were like those of a cat. Her fingers ended in claws that were sharp enough to rip Steven's throat out if he got too close.

"Give me some light," Steven said.

The guard handed him his flashlight. He pointed it in the girl's eyes as she clawed at him.

"You see that," Steven said, pointing at her face. "The eyes are returning to normal."

The camera zoomed in on the girl's face. Her pupils changed in the light, going from cat-like to human.

"You should keep her out of the dark," said the journalist. "The spirit's hold on her is far more powerful in the dark."

"So you were right?" the guard asked. "The girl has an animal spirit controlling her?"

The journalist nodded. "Selena here is possessed by the spirit of a jaguar. It's the worst case of Lycanthropy I've ever seen in person."

"And you think you can cure her? Make her human again?"

"There's no real cure," Steven said. "But if we can keep her in the light long enough, perhaps a few years, then the jaguar spirit, as well as her jaguar features, will eventually recede. As long as she doesn't spend an extended period of time in total darkness, she will likely be able to live a normal life."

When they finished their segment with the jaguar girl, they all left the basement and stepped outside. The cameraman packed up his equipment. Then he handed Steven a cigarette.

"Are you really going to adopt that thing?" the cameraman asked, lighting Steven's cigarette for him.

Steven took a drag. "That's my plan."

"Are you sure that's safe? She ripped a woman's arm off."

"She needs help and she needs a family. I can give her both. Deep down inside, she's just a frightened six-year-old girl."

"Yeah, a six-year-old who ripped a person's arm off. Imagine how dangerous she'll be when she's a full-grown adult."

The journalist took a long drag off his cigarette, thinking about what the cameraman just said.

"I'll just make sure the jaguar never takes over again," Steven said. "All she has to do is avoid the dark."

Selena didn't remember her childhood before she was adopted by Steven Renwood, when the jaguar was in control. But Selena always felt the beast inside, hiding in the back of her brain, waiting for a chance to come out. But she thought it would never happen. She didn't always have to sleep with the lights on, she could roam the streets at night, she could go to the movies. The darkness never brought out the jaguar. She thought she was safe.

But then she went into a cave and became lost in complete and total darkness. The jaguar decided it was time to come out.

"Don't..." Selena said, her claws stretching from her fingers. "I can't let you out."

She fought the jaguar with all her willpower, but the jaguar wouldn't give up. Selena didn't exactly want the beast to disappear completely. She needed her in order to see in the dark. She needed her in order to rescue her friends and take revenge on the mutants for what they did to her sister.

"I'll cut you a deal," Selena told the rising spirit. "Help me and you can keep this body. You can take over and run free forever."

The beast inside could sense her thoughts. They understood each other. The jaguar agreed to take only partial control. They would work together as one being, for now.

"Just let me get my revenge. That's all I want. Revenge."

Selena smiled. She was now the perfect killing machine. The jaguar knew how to hunt her prey in silence. The mutants wouldn't hear her coming; they wouldn't even hear her heartbeat now that she was dead. She would be completely imperceptible to them.

"Let's do it," Selena said to the cat in her head. "Let's slaughter them all."

The slaughterhouse door opened with a slow creak. Dean and Lance looked through the doorway. It wasn't The Butcher returning. There was just blackness outside of the shack.

"Who's there?" Dean called.

It was silent. They didn't see anything.

Dean said, "You scared of me kicking your ass or something?"

They heard whispering out there. Then a child's giggle.

"Oh fuck…"

Two little girls entered the shack, dragging their raggedy dresses behind them. Their frizzy gray hair covered their rubber white faces. They moved like a gust of wind through leaves.

"Little mutants…"

The girls went straight to Dean. They grabbed his breasts, sucked them into their lipless gaping mouths, and fed from him like little whispering leeches.

"Ah bro, not this shit again…"

Dean struggled against his ropes, but no matter how much he jerked or pulled he couldn't get the little creatures away from his bulging pecs.

Trent wasn't able to move very fast with two damaged legs. He could have stood up and limped on them if he had crutches or a cane, but there was nothing like that in the cavern. It was faster for him to crawl, grinding his open wounds against the jagged rocks.

He didn't care about the mutants. He just wanted to find that bitch Selena and get his revenge. That was all he cared about doing before he died. He didn't care about living forever. He didn't *want* to live forever. He just wanted to fuck that bitch and cut her fucking limbs off, and not necessarily in that order.

"Fucking cunt," Trent grumbled.

He crawled in the direction she had gone, hoping to find her cowering in a corner somewhere. She couldn't have gotten very far without any light to guide her. He should have been able to catch up to her by then, even crawling, but she was nowhere to be seen.

"Come out wherever you are," Trent called into the echoing cavern. "Bitch."

His light made a popping noise and went black. He paused for a moment.

"Fuck no," Trent said.

He banged his helmet. The light was dead. He was stuck in the dark.

"Where are you?" Trent yelled. "Speak, you fucking bitch!"

His voice echoed through the blackness.

"Answer me! Don't leave me in the fucking dark!"

But he was all alone. He listened, wondering if he could hear her breathing or stumbling somewhere up ahead, but all he heard was the sound of dripping water.

Selena's hearing was improved greatly with the power of the jaguar spirit. She could hear something off in the distance. A low rumbling sound. She followed the noise, going deeper into the caverns, traveling through a maze of tunnels.

A low growling noise came up from her throat when she saw what she was hunting. It was some kind of steam-powered machine, driven by one of the mutant men.

Foam sprayed from her lips as she growled louder. The jaguar in her was frightened of the machine.

"Don't worry," Selena told the beast inside her. "We just need to target the man inside of it."

The Miner drilled into the rock wall, breaking apart the stone to get to the minerals within. There was coal in these rocks. One of the most useful minerals The Miner collected was coal. With his mechanical shovel limb, he scooped up the rocks and dumped them into a cart for sorting.

Selena crept up behind the machine, gripping her pickaxe.

"Aim for the head..." she said to the jaguar.

When the jaguar leapt her body high into the air, The Miner stopped drilling. He heard something above him. Something like the sound of an air current. He raised his ear toward the sound.

"Die!" Selena's voice was more beast than human.

The Miner hissed in pain as the pickaxe pierced the top of his skull. Then Selena slithered into the machine with him and growled into his ears. He waved his mechanical limbs about, but they could not reach her. She was within his exoskeleton. It felt like a cat had just crawled inside of his skin.

Mercy... The Miner begged.

He could feel the heat of her breath against his wrinkled face as she growled.

Then the jaguar attacked. She dug into his ancient meat with her claws, bit into his neck, ripped his flesh to pieces. The Miner just hissed and squealed as he was eaten alive, his machine body twisting, shaking, and violently banging against the wall of the cave until nothing but scraps of bone and muscle lay in the driver's seat.

"Selena?" Lauren asked, walking through a tunnel, holding up her glowing orange shirt like a lantern.

She thought she just saw Selena run past her in the cavern, heading in another direction. But there was something different about her. Something animal-like. The person was fast, running on all fours, a wild look in her eyes.

"Is that you Selena?" Lauren called out again.

Then she shook her head. She decided she was just imagining things. If it were really Selena, she wouldn't be running around in the dark, nor would she be headed in that direction. That was the way back to the mutant's underground mining town. She didn't believe Selena would have gone back there.

"What the heck is that?" Lauren asked.

She saw some kind of machine lying at the end of the cage. It was smashed up, steam billowing out of the metal. When Lauren got a closer look, she realized there were the remains of a man lying in what was once a passenger seat. There were claw marks all over the seat and metal.

"What could have caused this?" she asked.

She decided not to linger. This attack happened only recently. Whatever did it was probably still in the area.

"How do I make them stop, bro?" Dean yelled at Lance, looking down at the monstrous little girls as they drank from his breasts.

Lance looked like he was ready to fall to pieces on the ground. "I don't fucking know, man…"

Dean glanced down at the freaks.

"Hey, little mutant things…" Dean told them. "You, uh… You think you can cut that out and maybe… untie us or something?"

The little girls didn't respond, sucking with all their strength.

They probably hadn't had milk in a very long time.

Dean raised his voice. "I'm serious. You better untie us right now and shit. You don't want to make Extreme Dean angry."

Milk dribbled down the girls' cheeks and dropped into the bucket below them. Dean waited for them to respond to his threat, but they just continued suckling.

"That's it, bro," Dean said. "Now I'm pissed…"

Dean raised his legs in the air and grabbed one of the girls with his thighs. Although his legs were tied at his ankles, he was able to get the girl's head between his knees, and put her in a wrestling hold. The girl choked and squealed as Dean tightened his grip around her throat.

"There, you like *THAT?*" Dean cried, getting way too intense as he strangled the mutant. "I told you bitches not to piss off EXTREME DEAN, THE MOST BADASS WRESTLER OF ALL FUCKING TIME!"

The other girl whimpered and hissed, tugging at Dean's legs, trying to get him to let her sister go.

"IT'S PAYBACK TIME, *BRO!*" Dean cried. Then he howled as he choked the girl. "I'M GONNA FUCK UP ALL YOU MUTHAFUCKAS, SIG ALP STYLE!"

Dean squeezed his legs, getting ready to snap the girl's neck.

"Don't do it," Lance said. "Just get them to untie us."

Dean agreed with the plan. He stared down the girls.

"Hey ugly chick," Dean said to the other mutant girl. "You don't want me to break her neck, you better untie me." He tightened his grip to make the girl squeal louder. "I'll do it, bra. I'll rip her fucking head off!"

The mutant girl seemed to understand him this time. She untied the ropes on his legs. Then she went around behind him and untied them from his wrists. Her hands were shaking, paranoid about losing her dear little sister.

When he was untied, Dean held onto the hook his ropes were hanging from so that he could keep the girl in his grappling hold without falling down.

"Thanks for freeing me, girls," Dean said. "I appreciate it."

Then he twisted his legs to the side and snapped the little girl's neck.

"BOOYA, *SLUT!*"

Her sister shrieked as she saw her limp body crumple to the ground. She covered her mouth and ran for the door.

"Not so fast," Dean said. "Extreme Dean comin' at ya!"

He jumped over the cutting table and grabbed the girl in a headlock, then twisted her head back until a cracking sound echoed through the slaughterhouse. Her body tumbled forward onto the blood-stained floor.

"HELL YEAH, BRO!" Dean cried, basking in triumph. "I AM SO FUCKING *BADASS!*" He shoved his finger in the girl's face. "THAT'S WHAT YOU GET FOR MESSIN' WITH EXTREME DEAN, THE ULTIMATE ASS-KICKIN' MACHINE!"

As Dean did a victory dance over their bodies, Lance stared at him with his mouth wide open.

"Dude, what the fuck?" Lance cried.

Dean turned to his bro, wondering what the problem was.

"They were only kids," Lance said.

Dean looked down at the tiny twitching bodies on the floor.

"What do you mean?" he asked.

"You just broke the necks of two little girls. Why the hell'd you do that? We could have just tied them up or something."

Dean looked down at the bodies again, then back at Lance. He had a confused look on his face. It was a common expression for him.

"Those were little girls? I thought they were just like midgets or something."

"No, they were children," Lance said.

"Yeah, but they were still mutants and shit."

"They were children. Seven-year-old children."

"But aren't they really like a hundred years old or something?

That would make them even older than me."

"It doesn't matter. They still had the minds of children. They were innocents."

Dean let out a sigh and then untied Lance's bonds.

"I still kicked ass though…" Dean said quietly to himself.

The Hunchback stepped outside the church and groaned. He had just spent the last ten minutes getting yelled at by the village matriarch. That old woman was always a pain in his ass. As the town's priest, he was always the one held responsible whenever anything bad happened. She thought he, in all his godly wisdom, should have been able to prevent any and all disasters that befell them.

Old cow… he said, in his hissing whispery voice.

She treated him as if he actually wanted their dear children to be attacked by those intruders.

You think I really wanted Sarah to get decapitated? he said to himself, reenacting the argument he had with The Elder.

The Hunchback pulled a sack of dried mushrooms out of his pocket. He took a pinch of them and stuffed it into his pipe.

I should blow that woman to bits… The Hunchback said, lighting up his pipe and inhaling the hallucinogenic mushrooms into his rotten hole of a mouth.

As he exhaled the mushroom smoke, he felt a current of air against the back of his neck. He turned around. He couldn't hear anything in the area. Everyone else was on the other side of town.

Hello? he called out. *Is anybody there?*

He pulled another hit from his pipe, then went around the side of the church to see what could have caused that movement. He wondered if one of the girls was playing a trick on him.

I'm not playing games with you today, Bethany...

There was another current of air behind his back. He turned around. He heard no footsteps. No breathing. No recognizable movements of any kind. The air didn't just move at random like that, not in that section of cave. He decided it must have been his imagination.

Selena peered down at her hunchbacked prey from the roof of the church, drool dripping from her fangs. When his back was turned, she leapt into the air and sunk her claws into his lumpy back.

Before The Hunchback was able to scream, Selena tore his throat out and ate his brain from the back of his head.

Trent saw a light in the tunnel up ahead. An echoing of footsteps. At first, he thought it was one of the mutants hunting him, so he ducked behind a rock. But it couldn't have been a mutant. They didn't need light.

"Lauren?" he said when he saw who was coming down the tunnel.

She was topless, walking around in her dirt-caked bra, holding some kind of orange light with her shirt.

"Trent?" she called. "Is that you?"

"Yeah," he said.

As Lauren came closer, Trent contemplated bashing in her head with a rock, stealing her light, then going after Selena and getting his revenge. But when he saw Lauren, he decided it would be best to let her carry the light.

"I can't believe it's you," she said with a wide smile. Three of her teeth were missing.

Whatever was glowing orange inside of her shirt seemed radioactive. The hand that was holding it was turning red and her fingertips were blackened. The light was discoloring large sections of her skin.

"What happened to you?" Trent asked.

"I fell off a cliff," Lauren said. "You pushed me, remember?"

She only smirked when she said that, as if it were merely annoying that he did that to her and obviously forgivable. Trent just ignored the comment.

"No, I mean the blisters spreading across your body," he said.

She held the light to her naked skin. Small burns bloomed on her flesh, especially the flesh closest to the glowing light.

"Huh…" Lauren said, not all that concerned. "Anyway, you have to come with me. I found a way out."

"A way out of the cave?"

She nodded excitedly.

"You mean we can get out of here?"

She nodded again, so fiercely that it caused another tooth to fall out of her mouth.

"Yeah, we can get out right now," she said. "Let me help you."

She wrapped her arm around his waist and assisted him to his feet.

"Lean on me," she said, using an almost seductive voice. "I'll help you."

Trent didn't want to touch her blistery skin, but he didn't have a choice. He couldn't move very fast without her support.

"What about the others?" Trent asked, as she helped him through the cave.

"We'll get help and come back for them later," she said. "It's the best we can do for them right now."

As they moved, Lauren made sure to rub against him as much as possible. Even though he was wearing a wetsuit, she liked the feeling of his body pressed against hers.

"Before we go, do you want to have some fun." She rubbed her fingers toward his crotch.

He looked down. One of her fingernails peeled off as she attempted to grab at his penis through the wetsuit.

"No thanks," he said, pulling her hand away. "Let's just focus on getting out of here. We can get to that later, once we're safe."

"Promise?" she asked.

"Promise," he said.

She could tell by his body language that he was completely lying. He hoped he'd never have to touch her ever again.

Shovel Bitch needed to get laid. She always needed to get laid after a hunt, especially one as fierce as the hunt they went on that day.

She knocked on the door of a shack.

Come on, let's go... she said outside the door.

Is it safe? asked a voice from within the shack. *Are they gone? Yes...*

Are you sure?

Just open the door, you yellow coward...

When the door opened, Shovel Bitch attacked the man inside. She wrapped her arms around his ass and kissed his throat with her goopy lipless mouth.

I want you...

The man was scrawny and thin. Though he was over a hundred years old, he had a youthful look to him. He must have been just barely out of his teens when he died.

Be a good doggy... she said to him, tugging on the chain around his neck. *Take off your clothes...*

The young man had a dog collar around his neck and was chained to a post in the room. He had enough slack to leave the house and walk around town, but not enough to venture out into the cave.

Get on the bed...

After he was stripped naked, Shovel Bitch pulled the chain, forcing him onto the stale mattress. He had been chained up for so long that his flesh had grown around the collar on his neck. The chain had become a part of him. When Shovel Bitch stroked it, it felt like she was stroking a part of his body. It gave him an erection.

Good doggy… she said, rubbing his erect penis as she took off her clothes.

Then she lowered herself on top of him, guiding his cold gray meat toward the ancient hairless pit in her crotch. When he was inside, she pulled on the chain, lifting his face to her breasts.

Suck on them, doggy…

Dog Boy was a prisoner they captured long ago. They would have decapitated him and put his head in the church with the other town pariahs, but he served as an excellent slave for the community. And for The Shovel Bitch, he served as an excellent sex slave.

I want to feel you cum in me…

She fucked Dog Boy slowly at first, then furiously, yanking on his chain when she wanted him to go faster. Her long black hair draped across his chest like a blanket as she fucked him, her clownish spider eyes staring into the ceiling.

Yes, yes…

She was already close to orgasm. She yanked the chain tighter.

Yes, harder…

But he stopped moving. She tugged on the chain. He didn't move.

Come on… I need to finish…

No matter how much she yanked on his chain, Dog Boy didn't respond, his body was limp beneath her.

She yanked one last time and the shackle fell free. She felt the end of the chain and discovered an empty collar covered in wet flesh. Then blood oozed down his body and chilled her inner thighs. She grasped his upper body. His neck was torn open. His head was missing.

Doggy…

Somebody did this, but she had no idea who. She heard nobody in the room. She felt nothing. It was like some kind of invisible presence.

Who's there?

Something slammed into her crotch. It was Dog Boy's severed head. His mouth opened and closed as if to speak.

She rolled off of him and grabbed her shovel, then swung it in a circle. Somebody was inside there with her. She couldn't feel them or hear them, but somebody had just decapitated her lover and threw his head at her. She was now under attack.

You're messing with the wrong woman...

The Shovel Bitch moved to the center of the room and swung her shovel into the corners, blindly attacking the intruder. No matter where she struck, her shovel blade never connected with a person.

Is somebody even there...

She attacked every inch of the shack, but there was no sign of anyone else in the room with her. She was beginning to wonder if there was no one there at all. She wondered if she accidentally decapitated Dog Boy herself, by being too rough with him during sex.

But then she heard it—a growling noise. The noise of some kind of animal or demon.

What is it... she said, backing away.

The growls became louder.

Then Shovel Bitch ran. She jumped out of the shack, running down the hill, calling for help.

Somebody... It's after me...

Animal claws slashed across her naked back and she fell to the ground. She turned and swung her shovel, but hit nothing.

Where the hell are you?

She swung the shovel again, swinging at the tiniest sounds, but nothing seemed to be there—just a deep growl that echoed from every direction at once.

What are you? A devil?

A current of air passed her face and then a claw cut open her neck. Shovel Bitch grabbed her throat. It was deep, deep enough to have killed her if she were mortal.

The Shovel Bitch swung her weapon one last time and then

her feet fell out from under her. A pickaxe broke both of her ankles and she crumpled to the ground.

Selena jumped on top of her chest, pinning her naked body to the ground. Then she pierced her claws into the bitch's clownish painted-on eyes and dug out her cold wet brains.

Dean carried Lance's skeletal body like a load of laundry without a laundry basket. Pieces of him kept falling off and getting left behind.

"Come on, bro," Dean said, moving as quietly as they could through the mutant town, trying not to attract attention. "Let's get out of here before Man-E-Faces gets back."

"Where are we going?" Lance said.

Dean turned one way, then the other. Lance's foot fell off.

"Let's go back the way we came, back to the campsite," Dean said.

"Good idea," Lance said. "They probably won't follow us that way."

"Yeah, and I left a bunch of beer back there," Dean said.

Lance's arm fell off.

"Bro, look out," Dean said, reaching down for the severed skeleton arm. "You keep losing shit."

"You're the one losing my shit. I can't move anything below my neck."

Dean stuffed the arm up into Lance's ribcage so it wouldn't fall off again. But just as he secured the arm, Lance's penis rolled onto the ground.

"Sorry, bro," Dean said. "I'm not picking *that* up."

He walked on.

"My dick? You're leaving my dick?"

"Sorry, dude, I'm not touching that thing," Dean said. "I'm not a homo."

Lance just rolled his eyes. He probably couldn't use it anymore anyway.

"What's that?" Dean asked.

He shined his light on something up the hill. In the distance, it looked like a person running around inside of the large houses up there. Not a mutant, it looked like one of their friends.

"Is that Selena?" Lance asked.

"It can't be," Dean said. "She died."

"Yeah, but so did we."

"*I'm* not dead. Maybe you're dead, but I've never been more alive in my life."

Lance looked at the giant hole in the back of Dean's head.

"Yeah, you're alive alright..." Lance said, as bits of brain dropped out of Dean's gaping wound.

"Should we check it out?" Dean asked.

"Yeah," Lance said. "If it's Selena we could use her help."

"Cool," Dean said. "Maybe she'll help us find the others, too."

Lance's other arm fell off.

"Oops, sorry, bro," Dean said. "I'll get that."

Dean couldn't reach down to pick up the arm without dropping more of Lance's parts, so he just kicked it every few feet as they walked up the hill.

"I need to rest a moment," Trent said.

He couldn't take the pain anymore. Walking on his mangled legs was excruciating. It felt like his flesh was being torn open with every step he took—though he knew it would've been a lot worse if he were still alive and his nerves were working at full capacity.

"Okay, take all the time you need," Lauren said, setting him down on a rock.

She put the shirt of glowing crystals in front of them, then sat next to Trent, squeezing as close to him as she could.

"Can you give me some room?" Trent said. She was nearly pushing him off the rock.

"Sure." She moved over for him, but only by an inch or two.

He stretched his legs until they were in the most relaxed, least agonizing position possible.

"I'm hungry," Trent said. "How the hell am I still hungry when I'm dead?"

"I might still have some of the delicious food I made," Lauren said excitedly.

"You have any cookies?" he asked. "I'm not eating one of those gross fucking meat pies."

Lauren put her backpack in her lap and opened it. The mutant's severed head wiggled and drooled inside. She looked at Trent to make sure he didn't see the head, then pushed it aside to get at the cookies underneath. She chose the special cookie at the bottom of her bag. She had been saving it for a special occasion such as this.

"I have one left," she said. "The best one."

He took the cookie and removed the plastic wrap.

"Thanks," he said in the least sincere way he could muster.

As he put the cookie in his mouth, Lauren's eyes widened, staring closely at his lips. He was starving, so he shoveled it in as fast as he could. She loved that he gobbled up her food, especially when some ingredients came from her body. It was as if Trent thought she was so delicious that he had to devour her in only a few gulps.

"Wait a minute…" Trent said, after he swallowed most of the cookie. "What is this?"

"What?" she asked, rubbing his shoulder.

"I taste something," he said. "What did you put inside of this?"

She wondered what he tasted. It could have been from the scabs or pubic hairs she put inside of it, but she hoped her ejaculate was the strongest flavor. When she made food for this trip, food that she knew Trent would be eating, she wanted something special for his dessert, something that she hoped would turn him on.

"Just chocolate chips," she said, her face turned red as if she were suddenly feeling bashful.

Female ejaculation was something she heard about, but wasn't something she'd ever been able to accomplish. The week before, she read an article online that all women are capable of doing it, if they knew how to stimulate the g-spot just right. She read that these fluids actually issued from the woman's prostate gland upon orgasm and that both men and women were capable of having prostate orgasms, though men had to stimulate the gland through their anus. The article even suggested milking your prostate on a regular basis for health purposes.

"Why, what's it taste like?" Lauren asked, on the edge of her seat with anticipation.

She spent a whole night squatting over a bowl, milking her prostate into the cookie dough. A lot more fluid came out than she was expecting. She didn't even need to add extra water to the mix. She was so proud of herself when she was finished. The aroma was almost floral, like the scent of sunflower petals after they wilt. She knew it would make a delicious batch of cookies and prayed that Trent would have been able to taste her ejaculate when he consumed them.

"It tastes like… medicine," Trent said.

Lauren frowned. It wasn't her ejaculate that he tasted. It was just the drugs.

"Did you put…" Trent smelled the cookie. "*Roofies* in this cookie?"

She broke eye contact with him.

"You did, didn't you?" he yelled.

He was getting dizzy.

"Well, you wouldn't put out," she said. "What do you expect me to do?"

Trent would have strangled the woman, but he could hardly think straight anymore.

"How could you do something so horrible?" he asked, his voice becoming faint.

He blacked out and fell over. When she saw him helpless on the ground, Lauren flashed a giddy smile.

"I do whatever it takes to get what I want," she said to him. "You should remember that."

She zipped up her backpack and got to her feet.

"Now you're all mine."

Then Lauren dragged her unconscious slam piece to a more secluded section of the cave.

Where is everybody…

The Elder couldn't find anyone. Axe Face and Sickle Arms never reported in after the hunt. The Hunchback and The Shovel Bitch were supposed to meet her in the mushroom garden for afternoon chores but they never showed up. She worried something horrible might have happened to them.

What is going on?

Something was wrong. The Elder always knew when something was wrong. She hiked up the hill toward the mansion. It was where most of the children usually played. She wanted to keep an eye on them, make sure they were safe.

Darlings…

As she arrived to the mansion, the front door was wide open. She couldn't hear any of the girls whispering or laughing as she usually would.

Are you alright?

When she stepped inside, her foot squished into a human liver and slid across black blood on the floor.

Hello?

She panicked. It was definitely meat she slipped on.

She knelt down and felt the carpeting. Human body parts were scattered everywhere. Her hand smacked into something round. She grabbed it, felt around the edges. The Elder dropped it once she realized what it was—a child's head. But the head was quiet and still, no longer alive. The brain had been torn out through the neck.

No.... no...

There wasn't just one. Many brainless skulls littered the room. There were claw marks across their faces. It was as if some kind of animal attacked them and ate their brains right out of their heads.

The Elder couldn't believe it. Her children were dead. *Really* dead. Every single one of them.

It can't be...

She got to her feet and backed out of the house, trying not to slip in all the blood.

They're dead... They're all dead...

As she walked backwards out of the house, in shock from finding all of her loved ones torn to shreds, she didn't hear the beast coming up from behind.

Selena dropped the pickaxe into the rotten woman's skull. She cracked open the bone casing and drank out the brains. The jaguar in her had a taste for the mutant brains. Although most of the meat on their bodies was tough and rubbery, like jerky, their brains were extra tender and robust. The soft meat was almost fishy-tasting, richly aged in their skulls like fine wine in the bottle.

When she finished her meal, Selena licked her paws with a wide sandpapery tongue. Then she disappeared into the darkness.

"Are you sure she came this way?" Lance asked.

"Positive, bro," Dean said.

They made it to the top of the hill, but they didn't see Selena anywhere. There was just a corpse of an old dead woman.

"What happened to her?" Lance asked.

Dean examined the body. The back of her skull was cracked open like an egg and her brain was missing.

"What do you think did that?"

"I don't know, bro," Dean said. "I think something else lives down in these caves besides mutants."

"Like what?"

"Some kind of brain-eating monster or something," Dean said. Then he shined his light through the doorway of the house. It was littered with the bodies of the mutant children. "It went on a rampage here."

"What about Selena?" Lance asked. "Did it get her, too?"

"I don't know, bro. Probably. We should get out of here before whatever did this comes back."

When Dean turned to go back the way they came, a massive figure stood behind him. A cleaver extended from The Butcher's arm, aiming at Dean's throat.

"Dude, it's him…" Dean backed up.

But the mutant didn't follow. Inside of The Butcher's chest cavity, the Patriarchal Head saw the dead woman on the ground. His eyes widened, black goo like tears leaked from them. He moaned out, shocked to see her in such a state. The Butcher kneeled to the ground so that the head in his body could kiss The Elder's cheek. They were once the mother and father of the Turtle family, the leaders of their people. He couldn't believe she was gone.

A look of anger grew on the Patriarchal Head. The Butcher faced Dean. He would have his revenge on whoever did this to The Elder.

Dean backed through the doorway, not looking where he was going. He slammed Lance into the edge of the door, breaking his body in half. Lance cried out as everything from the pelvis down splatted on the floor.

"Sorry, bro," Dean said.

Dean didn't see all the body parts behind him until he stepped into what felt like a bowl. He looked down. His boot was stuck inside of a mutant little girl's severed head.

"Oh. Shit." Dean saw all the pieces of children scattered around him, trying to keep his balance in the kid guts.

The Patriarchal Head glared at Dean from The Butcher's chest cavity. He was even more furious when he saw all of his dead children on the floor. Dean held out his arms and shook his head.

"It wasn't me, bro," Dean said. "I didn't kill them all. Honest."

Dean casually shook his leg, trying to shake off the girl's severed head that was stuck to the bottom of his foot. It wouldn't come loose.

"I'd never do something like this. Uh…" He paused when he remembered what he did to two of the little girls only minutes ago. "Killing kids goes against the bro code."

He continued backing away, walking on the girl's head like a shoe, shaking his leg every few feet.

The Butcher pulled out another blade. It was a blood-stained knife long enough to cut a subterranean pig in half with one strike. The Head screamed as The Butcher charged Dean. The massive knife came down at Dean's shoulder, but the frat boy lifted Lance's body up to block the attack.

Lance screamed as the knife chopped into his skinless ribcage.

"Dude, don't use me as a shield!" Lance cried.

"Sorry, bro. I wasn't thinking."

But when The Butcher attacked the second time, Dean used his friend's broken body as a shield again.

"What did I just tell you?" Lance cried. "Stop!"

"It was just an accident, bro. I won't do it again."

The Butcher used both his knife and cleaver, swinging them one at a time, chopping at Dean but always hitting Lance by mistake.

"You keep doing it!" Lance cried as pieces of his body flew across the room. "Why do you keep doing it?"

"I can't help it, bro," Dean said. "It's instinctual and shit."

"Just run, dumbass!"

Dean turned and ran up the spiral staircase, clomping on the skull-shoe every step of the way.

"Not upstairs," Lance said. "It's a dead end."

"Too late, bro."

The Butcher attacked Dean's feet through the banister, but only hit the corner of the skull-shoe. The girl's head broke off and rolled down the steps. Dean kept going, dribbling milk all the way up the staircase.

Trent awoke with pain ripping through his body. He tried to get up, but could only move his head.

"Hello?" Trent called out.

The orange lighting grew brighter as Lauren stepped toward him.

"I'm right here, baby," she said.

"What's going on?" he asked. "What happened?"

"We're in Heaven," she said. "Together."

"What about the way out?" Trent said. "You said you found a way out."

"Oh, sorry... I lied about that. It was too dangerous out there with all the mutants hunting us, so I hid us somewhere they'd never find us."

She placed orange crystals around the cave, brightening the area. A gurgling head lay on a shelf looking down at them.

"What the hell is that?" Trent asked.

"I call him Porco," she said, rubbing her fingers along the severed living head. "He's my new pet."

"No," Trent said, nodding toward a pile of arms and legs. "*That.*"

She picked up one of the arms.

"Oh, these were your limbs," she said, folding her fingers into his, then kissing the knuckles. "You won't be needing these anymore."

When Trent's eyes adjusted to the light, he examined his body more carefully. He was lying naked on a large rock slab like a bed. His arms and legs were missing, hacked off by the bloody machete lying next to him.

"What the hell!" he cried.

Lauren stepped closer. Her skin was sliding off. Strips of flesh hung from her arms and shoulders, peeling like wallpaper.

"I buried us alive in here," she said. "We can never get out. No one can ever get in."

Trent looked around the cave. It was the size of a small bedroom. There were no exits. The only way out was a small passage that had recently been caved in, blocked by ten tons of rock.

She kissed his neck, rubbing her blistered fingers against his bare chest.

"We can be together forever, just like we always wanted." Lauren lay on the rock next to him, cuddling her head into his neck. "We're immortal. We can never die. So from here until eternity, we can just be together, holding each other, making love, snuggling."

When she pulled away from him, a strip of skin from her cheek stuck to his neck.

"It's our love tomb." She smiled, revealing a toothless mouth.

"We need a weapon," Dean said, as they ran into the master bedroom. "Help me look for a weapon."

The light on his helmet flickered, then went off.

"Damn it!"

Dean hit the light. It flickered on and off.

"Hurry up!" Lance cried.

When it came back on, Dean closed the door and locked it. Then he put Lance down and pushed the bed in front of the door. The smell of dust and urine rose from the mattress.

"That's not going to hold," Lance said from the floor.

"I just need to buy some time."

Dean searched the room, looking for something he could use to defend himself with. Mounted on the walls were old rifles that probably hadn't been used in a hundred years.

"Do they work?" Lance asked.

When Dean picked a gun off the wall, it fell apart in his hands. The pieces tumbled to the floor.

"Nope," Dean said.

Dean searched through cabinets and chests, trying to find some kind of weapon. The Butcher was outside the door, turning the knob, trying to get it open.

"You're not going to find anything," Lance said. "Don't bother. Just climb out the window."

"Well, if I can't find a weapon I'll fucking *MAKE* myself a weapon," Dean said. "I've played Dead Rising 2 like *five times*, bro. I know how to make badass zombie-killing weapons using just a mop handle and a toy truck."

"Dude, you've got like two minutes before he gets in," Lance said. "You don't have time to make anything. Let's just go out the window."

"Window…" Dean said, nodding his head.

Dean went to the window and took down the curtain rod. Then he grabbed some twine from a trunk.

"This will be awesome," Dean said. "I'm like fucking MacGyver and shit."

Dean tied the twine to the end of the curtain rod. Then he excitedly twirled it around as if it were a whip. When he realized getting whipped with the twine would be about as deadly as throwing dental floss at someone, he frowned at his results. The twine was too weak. He needed something stronger.

The Butcher smashed a hole in the door, cracking open the wood. The doorknob broke off and rolled across the floor.

"Let's go," Lance cried. "Come on, before the rest of my intestines fall out."

When Dean looked at Lance he saw exactly what he needed.

"Dude, you're brilliant," Dean said.

Dean went to Lance and grabbed his intestines, pulling them out of his lower body cavity.

"What the fuck!" Lance cried.

There weren't a lot of his intestines left. Most of them fell out in the slaughterhouse or when his pelvis broke off, but there was enough to meet Dean's purposes.

"This is going to be kickass," Dean said.

Like a rope, he tied the intestine to the end of the curtain rod. Then he grabbed the doorknob and tied it to the other end. The twine was used for extra support. Then he picked up Lance and strapped him to his back, using the leftover intestine like a belt.

"What the fuck are you doing?"

"Relax, bro," Dean said, putting on his most intense, serious face. "I got this."

When The Butcher broke into the room, Dean held out his new weapon. It was like a fishing pole with a metal ball on the end of it.

Dean stared down The Butcher. "I think it's about time we played a little game of EXTREME FUCKING TETHERBALL!"

Dean swung the weapon in a circle, the doorknob spinning over his head like a tetherball.

"It's like normal tetherball, only played way more extreme and intense," Dean said, explaining the sport to the monster. He figured they didn't have extreme tetherball in the pioneer days. "And you use a human intestine instead of a rope."

"You fucking idiot..." Lance groaned behind him.

The Butcher pushed the bed out of the way.

"You're dealing with the extreme tetherball master, bitch," Dean said. "Get ready, because I'm serving first!"

Before Dean could actually do anything, the doorknob fell off the end of the rope. It flew across the room, into The Butcher's shoveled out face, and nailed him right in the unprotected lower half of his brain.

Dean couldn't believe his eyes when The Butcher was knocked unconscious. He fell backward onto the floor.

"Hell yeah, bitch!" Dean said, taking complete credit for

the accident. "What did I tell you? Extreme tetherball *master*."

"Let's go," Lance yelled.

Dean climbed over the bed and passed the mutant's body. The other living heads were still conscious inside the chest cavity, glaring up at him.

"Booya, bitches!" Dean said to the heads.

The Butcher grabbed Dean's leg.

"Fuck!" Dean kicked the hand off.

The Butcher stood back up and raised his cleaver. His head lay to one side, still unconscious.

"Shit," Dean said, backing away. "It's the other heads… The other heads can control the body!"

Dean turned to run and The Butcher slashed at him with the cleaver. It hit Lance in the face.

"Come on, bro," Dean yelled. "Let's get out of here."

He ran down the spiral staircase. Lance gurgled and coughed blood onto the back of Dean's legs.

"Bro?"

Dean looked over his shoulder to see that Lance's lower jaw had been torn off. His tongue dangled out of the hole.

"Dude!" Dean cried.

Blood shot out of Lance's throat when he tried to speak.

"Don't worry, bro. We're almost home free."

Dean ran through the front door of the old mansion and froze in his tracks. Some kind of creature was out there, stalking toward the doorway.

"Selena?" Dean asked.

It looked like her, but she was different. She was half-animal.

"What happened to you?"

She was on all fours, growling, baring blood-soaked fangs. Her eyes were like those of a cat, her fingers ended in razor-sharp claws, and cat ears poked out of her dark hair. A tail grew out of her shorts and whipped against the back of her legs. Her torn clothes revealed patches of fur beginning to grow from her hips and shoulders, patterned with jaguar spots.

"Are you okay?"

Her mind seemed completely gone, overtaken by her inner beast. Dean took one step forward and her growls increased. Then she charged.

"Fuck this shit!"

Dean ran back into the house and slammed the door. Selena crashed into the wood, trying to ram it down. He held his weight against it, squishing Lance's face against the wood.

"She's gone batshit, bro," Dean yelled. "She's like a werejaguar or something."

The Butcher walked down the spiral staircase. Blood dripped from his cleaver. His head flopped to the side.

"Crap," Dean said. "We're surrounded."

Lance gurgled behind him.

As Selena clawed on the door, Dean looked around. The only exit to the room was a door on the far side, across the ocean of body parts.

"Let's go!"

Dean leapt from the door and ran. Slipping through the blood as he crossed the room, he didn't turn back until he reached the door on the other side.

Splinters of wood exploded into the air as the door burst open. Selena growled and charged into the room, racing toward the final mutant.

When Dean saw her, he realized she wasn't after him. She was after the mutant. She was the creature who killed The Elder and all of the children.

"Sweet, bra!" Dean cried in excitement.

He pumped his fist as the jaguar woman leapt through the air, aiming for The Butcher's jugular.

"Wait..." Dean said. "Wrong head!"

Selena decapitated The Butcher's head with her claws. It fell to the ground. But the mutant did not go down. He punched Selena so hard she flew across the room and crashed into the wall.

"The other heads control the body, too!" Dean yelled.

Selena got to her feet and dodged as The Butcher's cleaver chopped into the wall next to her head. She circled him, moving stealthily. But unlike her other prey, the Patriarchal Head in the mutant's chest cavity was not blind. He could see her perfectly. Her silence could not hide her from The Butcher.

"You fucking psycho bitch!" Trent cried. "I'm going to kill you!"

Trent head-butted the air in Lauren's direction. He didn't know how he was going to do it, but he was going to bite her throat out eventually. Once she came close enough.

"I love you so much, baby," she said, rubbing Trent's cheek. He tried to bite at her hand. "Our immortality will be better than going to Heaven."

"Are you fucking kidding me? This is *Hell*. I fucking hate—"

Before he could say *you*, his words were cut short by a tube getting shoved into his mouth. It was a tube from his scuba gear, the one that was connected to his oxygen tank. Lauren pushed it down his throat halfway to his stomach.

"Sorry, I'm sure you must be hungry," she said. "It's long past feeding time."

He whined and whipped his head as he tried to spit out the tube, but it was too deep.

"I didn't cut your limbs off because I was afraid you'd run away," she said. "I *know* you wouldn't run away. But I wanted to take care of you. I wanted you to *need* me."

Trent choked and gagged on the tube.

"When mother birds take care of their young, they do everything for them. They even digest their food for them. I want us to be like that. I want to feed you like a baby bird."

Water fell from Trent's eyes as Lauren put a finger in her throat, tickling her gag reflex. She brought the other end of the tube to her mouth, then she emptied the contents of her stomach down Trent's throat.

When Dean opened the door to the next room, he couldn't believe what he saw. The room was some kind of storage area filled with items from the modern age. There were flashlights, climbing gear, backpacks, tents, camping gear, hiking boots.

"All this stuff..." Dean said, digging through it. "There's stuff from hunters, campers, hikers, cavers."

He stopped searching, pausing in thought.

"Dude, you know what this means?"

Lance gurgled in response.

"The mutants must have hunted and killed these people in the mountains," Dean said. "That means they had to have gotten out of the cave somehow. There *has* to be another way out of the cave system."

Dean found a box filled with flashlights. He turned one of them on. It was three times as bright as the light on his helmet.

"We're set bro," Dean said. "We can get out of here."

Then he saw the hunting rifle in the corner. Dean went to it. The thing was fully loaded, with extra ammo. He lifted it up to his shoulder, flipped off the safety and looked through the scope.

"Hells, yeah," Dean said, pumping his fist. "Hells fucking yeah."

He was going to kill the fuck out of that Butcher mutant. That is, if Selena didn't kill the fuck out of him first.

"Selena? What did you do?"

Steven Renwood was beginning to regret adopting the jaguar girl. His wife was already on her last thread of patience with the girl, and he wasn't sure how she'd react to the dead dog on the kitchen floor.

"How many times did I tell you, Pichanga's a family member not a chew toy."

He knelt to the ground over the body. Then he removed his glasses and rubbed the stress out of his temples.

"Christ..."

The terrier was ripped apart. Its guts sprayed across the linoleum floor. It was like a cat leaving a dead mouse on your doorstep as a present. He knew his daughter didn't do it on purpose. It was just in her nature.

"Selena, come here," he called.

He knew she was in the next room listening. He could hear her sharpening her claws against the side of the living room couch.

"Selena!"

She stopped scratching. Then she hopped across the living room floor and peeked her head through the doorway to the kitchen, her kitty eyes shining at him.

"What did you do?"

She ducked her head behind the wall. Then slowly peeked her head out again.

"Stop being cute," he said. "This is serious."

She crawled into the kitchen and licked her hands.

"Look what you did to Pichanga," he said. "Do you know how upset your mother will be when she sees this? This is the third pet this year."

Selena looked away.

"You can't go around mauling every animal you see," he said. "It's horrible. It makes people sad."

A moth fluttered near her head, stealing her attention away. She swatted at it with her paws.

Although Steven was able to help young Selena gain control of most of her body, she kept some of the jaguar spirit with her at all times. It was as if she'd been a cat for so long she didn't know how to live without it.

"I don't want you killing anything else," Steven said. "Your mother loved this dog. Do you understand me?"

Selena licked her lips. A moth wing fell from her chin.

"No more killing things."

Without warning, Selena pounced up from the ground into his arms, digging her claws into his shoulders to support herself as she snuggled against his chest, purring.

"Goddamnit…" he said, not able to stay mad at her no matter what horrible thing she'd done.

He knew she wouldn't stop killing things until he completely cured her of the jaguar possession. Cats kill things. It's what they do. They're playful, selfish, and deadly. And they love to toy with the things they kill.

Selena ran at The Butcher's legs and cut a gash in his knee. It knocked him off balance so he wasn't able to swing in time. She growled and jumped him from behind, clawing open his back. The Butcher turned and swung his knife, but she ducked and raced to the other side of the room.

Come here, kitty… said The Patriarchal Head in a hissing whispery voice.

The other heads in the chest cavity gurgled and spit.

Selena lowered her head, growling, her tail whipping behind her.

Let me cut out your eyes…

Selena charged. When The Butcher slashed at her, she reached into the chest cavity and ripped out one of the heads. All of the mouths in the chest cavity opened in a scream as their brother was torn away. She ran off with it before The Butcher could stop her.

You witch… Give him back…

The ancient severed head opened his mouth to cry as Selena tore into his skull and chewed on his brain.

I'm going to gut you, kitty…

The head dangled from Selena's mouth by a rope of brain. She tossed it aside and crept around The Butcher, circling him.

I spent so many years protecting my family from the outside world…

The Butcher held out his blade, waiting for her to strike.

And then you come here and kill them all… They were meant to live forever…

He aimed his blade at her and she stared it down, growling at the weapon.

I promised them they'd live forever…

The jaguar woman backed up, getting ready to lunge.

Now I can only promise them revenge…

Selena jumped at The Butcher, aiming directly for the Patriarchal Head. But he snatched her by the neck, then he plunged the blade deep in her chest.

Die, kitty…

She kicked off of him and rolled to the ground. As she tried to get up, he chopped her in the forehead. Her skin split open but no blood spilled from the wound. There wasn't any blood in her body.

Now I'll gut you…

As The Butcher raised his cleaver to chop off Selena's head, the sound of a gunshot echoed through the room. The bullet hit the mutant in the shoulder.

"Get away from her, bro," Dean said, stepping into the room.

He had the hunting rifle pointed at the freak.

You can die first…

The Butcher turned to Dean, holding his blade out to one side.

"Put the knife down," Dean said. "I've got the gun, bitch."

The Butcher didn't drop his knife. He continued moving forward, blocking any chance Dean would have to run.

"Have it your way, bro."

Dean fired the rifle. The bullet hit him in the chest, missing all of the heads.

"Fuck…"

He cocked the weapon, putting another bullet in the chamber, then fired again. The bullet hit one of the heads in the cheek. He cocked and fired again. This time he missed the mutant's body completely.

"Dude, I suck at this..." Dean said, cocking the rifle.

Dean walked right up to the mutant, aimed the rifle between the eyes of the Patriarchal Head at point blank range. Then he fired. The bullet pierced through the monster's forehead, blowing his brains out the back of his skull.

"Boom!" Dean cried, as brains splattered against his hands and rifle.

The other five heads inside the body cavity raged. They took control of the body and grabbed the barrel of Dean's rifle, pushing it away from them.

"Oh, fuck..." Dean forgot he had to kill all the heads before The Butcher would die.

The Butcher raised his cleaver, aiming at his throat as the five heads screamed. Then Selena attacked him from behind. She dug her claws into his back and ripped out his spine.

"Whoa!" Dean cried.

His mouth was wide open as the mutant crumpled to the floor. The five heads were still alive and wiggling in the body, but the body could no longer function with its spine ripped out.

"That was *extreme*," Dean said.

She just stood there. The spinal column wiggled like a snake in her hand.

Lauren crawled on top of Trent's body.

"Now that you're fed, I want you to feed me."

Lauren removed her clothes. As she rubbed her body against him, one of her nipples slipped off and stuck to his chest like a wet leaf. She put his penis in her mouth, but it was flaccid. She licked, trying to get him erect, but nothing happened.

"I want you to put a baby in me," she said, using his fetish to turn him on. "Come on. Get me pregnant. We can fill this whole cave with babies."

It wasn't working. Trent didn't even bother looking at her. His eyes were on the living severed head.

"Put your seed in my womb," Lauren said. "Come on. Get hard and do it."

The severed head was set too close to the orange crystals. The flesh melted from its face, revealing skull beneath the liquid skin.

"What's going on?" Lauren tugged on his penis, rubbed her body against him. "Why aren't you hard? I want you to get me pregnant. Don't you want me to be your baby-making machine?"

But no matter what she did, Trent would not be aroused. He knew she could never really become pregnant again. Her womb was dead. It had been impaled by the mutant's sickle blade. He had no interest mating with a female who could not produce offspring.

"What?" Lauren read his body language and realized why he wasn't interested in her. "No… It doesn't matter." She rubbed her wounded stomach. "Just pretend it's still alive."

Lauren cried out in frustration. They were trapped in that tomb forever, but they could not make love, they could not have the eternity of physical bliss that she so desperately desired. She struggled on in vain, trying to give him an erection as her flesh continued to melt from her body.

When Selena dropped the mutant's spine, her eyes locked on Dean. She growled at the sight of him.

"Whoa, bra," Dean said, pointing the rifle at her. "I'm on your side, remember?"

She slinked toward him, her claws extended.

"I'll shoot," Dean said.

Selena walked straight up to the gun, baring her fangs. Then her growling turned to purring. She closed her eyes, stuck out her tongue, and licked the pieces of brain off the barrel of the rifle.

Dean just stood there, watching her lick the shaft of his weapon, with his mouth wide open.

"Dude," Dean said to Lance. "I don't have a furry fetish or nothing, but this is kind of hot."

Lance gurgled in response.

When she was finished, Selena turned around, got down on all fours and then hopped out of the house. All Dean could see was jaguar fur rapidly growing across the rest of her body as she disappeared into the darkness.

"I guess she's not coming back, bro," Dean said. "We're on our own."

He turned toward the storeroom, stepping over the corpse filled with wiggling heads.

"Let's pack up as much shit as we can and get out of here."

Lance gurgled as Dean grabbed a backpack and filled it with flashlights, climbing gear, and bullets.

"Dude, you know what? Caving kinda sucks. We should've gone white water rafting instead." He sighed. "Or just stayed home and watched Spartacus on HBO. That show's awesome."

Then Dean flexed his muscles and posed like a gladiator, holding out the hunting rifle like a sword.

EPILOGUE
SERENE DEAN

THE BRO CODE #219
A Bro never kills a kid, unless he's
mistaken it for a bloodthirsty midget.

Dean cracked open a beer and took a drink. It was cold. The cave acted like a refrigerator and kept it chilled. He leaned back against the rock, relaxing at their original campsite.

"Want one?"

Dean offered a beer to Gravy sitting next to him. Gravy shook his head.

"Nah, bro," Gravy said. "I'm good."

With his only working mangled hand, Gravy hit his bowl and breathed the smoke deep.

"It took fucking forever to get you out of that hole, bro," Dean said. "I hope you appreciate it."

Gravy exhaled.

"It was weird, bro," Gravy said. "I didn't even know I was still alive down there. I thought I died and was in the afterlife."

"Dude, really?"

"It was like a sensory deprivation chamber," Gravy said. "I felt nothing, I saw nothing, I heard nothing. With water filling my lungs I wasn't even breathing. I had nowhere else to go but deep into my head. It was like I entered another world."

"Sweet, bro."

"Yeah, it was all a dream, I guess. But it was more real than any lucid dream I ever had. It was a trip. In fact, after I smoke this bowl I think I want you to put me back. I'd rather live in those dreams forever than have to deal with this mangled body."

"Maybe that's what those heads were doing," Dean said.

"What heads?"

"Those heads."

Dean pointed at the dozens of living human heads on the ground surrounding the campsite. The heads were like an audience, facing them.

"Oh yeah, those heads…" Gravy said. "Where'd you get them all?"

"They were on some shelves in an underground church. I wondered what the hell they were all doing up there. At first, I thought it would be better to burn them, put them out of their misery. Who wants to live forever as a severed head? But maybe it's like you said—maybe they were living inside their minds, in dream worlds."

"Probably, bro," Gravy said, hitting his bowl again.

"Most of the town was just heads. There were some non-heads, too. But they must have been mobile so they could protect the heads from people who would fuck with them. I don't know. I don't think I'd want to be just a head."

"So where are the others?"

"I'm not sure," Dean said. "I looked everywhere for Trent and Lauren. They're nowhere to be found. I found Marta's remains. She didn't make it."

"Poor Giant Gonzales… What about her hot sister?"

Dean looked at the shining eyes of a jaguar woman staring at them across the chasm. She tossed them the corpse of a subterranean pig she killed, perhaps as a thank you gift for saving her from The Butcher back there.

"Selena's still alive," Dean said, watching Selena as she crawled back into the cave. "She's kind of gone feral, though."

Then Dean turned to Lance sitting on his other side. "And Lance is right here, of course."

Lance's meatless torso lay propped up against the rock, gurgling at them. His one remaining eye rolled in its socket.

"Want a beer, bro?" Dean asked Lance, holding out a Natty Ice.

Lance shook his head.

"Come on, bro, I'll help you with it."

Dean poured the beer down the jawless hole, over his dangling tongue.

"CHUG! CHUG! CHUG! CHUG!" Dean chanted, as he dumped the beer down Lance's throat, though most of it emptied through the cracks in his ribcage.

"So you really want me to toss you back in that hole before I go?" Dean asked.

"Yeah, fuck it," Gravy said. "I was riding a dragon with some big-breasted chick wearing a chainmail bikini. I really want to get back to that."

"Dude, that sounds awesome."

"It was. I got laid like twenty times."

"Sweet. I'll throw these other heads in the hole with you. That way they can stay in their dream worlds and don't need anyone protecting them."

He turned to Lance. "How about you, bro? You want to ride dragons with chainmail bikini chicks? I mean, you're never going to get laid looking like that anyway. You might as well get buried in a hole…"

Lance shook his head furiously. No way did he want to get buried in a hole like that. It was his absolute worst nightmare.

"Cool, you can keep Gravy company down there," Dean said.

Lance kept shaking his head, but Dean wasn't paying attention.

"How about you?" Gravy asked. "What are you going to do with your immortality? Just hang out in a cave by yourself?"

Dean took a swig of his beer.

"I thought about sticking around, bro," Dean said. "That jaguar chick could probably use a hot stud like me to keep her warm at nights. But, nah… I'm going to take off. Go back home."

"How are you going to leave?" Gravy asked. "I thought the immortality only worked in these mountains. Won't you die if you leave?"

"There's supposed to be a mineral down here somewhere that's responsible for the immortality. My plan is to find that and make a necklace out of it or something. If I make it portable

I can go wherever I want and still live forever. I don't have to be stuck here."

"Huh…" Gravy said. "So you'll become the immortal Extreme Dean, the dude who gets to live forever."

"Totally, bro. And it couldn't have happened to a more awesome guy, you know? Usually in movies it's always the extreme douchebags that get immortality, like Tom Cruise or Christopher Lambert. But this time it's me—the coolest bro in the world. I'm the complete *opposite* of a douchebag."

"I guess so…" Gravy wasn't really paying attention to him anymore.

"Generations of bros will get the opportunity to hang out with Extreme Dean. Since I'll never grow old, I'll just stay a bro forever. I'll change identities and join different Sig Alp chapters at different colleges around the country. After four years of awesome partying, I'll just start over somewhere else. I'll be a legend. I'll be the eternal bro. All the chicks will think I'm like a god and will totally want to sleep with me."

"Totally." Gravy gave him a high-five with his mangled hand.

"Or maybe I'll even do something important with my life. You know, something meaningful. What's the point of immortality if I don't do something awesome with it?"

"Don't know, bro."

"I've got hundreds of years," Dean said. "I can learn everything there is to know about science and physics. Eventually, I'll be all super smart and can invent something that will benefit the whole world. You know, like a cure for cancer or a space ship that can go warp speed."

"Or you can just stay home and get fucked up all the time."

"Yeah…" Dean nodded. "Or I can just stay home and get fucked up all the time…"

Dean chugged the last of his beer and crushed the can against his head.

"That would be *extreme*…"

BONUS SECTION

This is the part of the book where we would have published an afterword by the author but he insisted on drawing a comic strip instead for reasons we don't quite understand.

I hope you liked my new book *Clusterfuck*. Wasn't it just splendid?

It's me CM3!

My favorite part was where the main character turned out to be a robot crab viking in disguise.

A what?

just finished reading it

Then he jumped over that tanknado on his lazer bike.

Umm...

FACT: A tanknado is a tornado but it's full of tanks

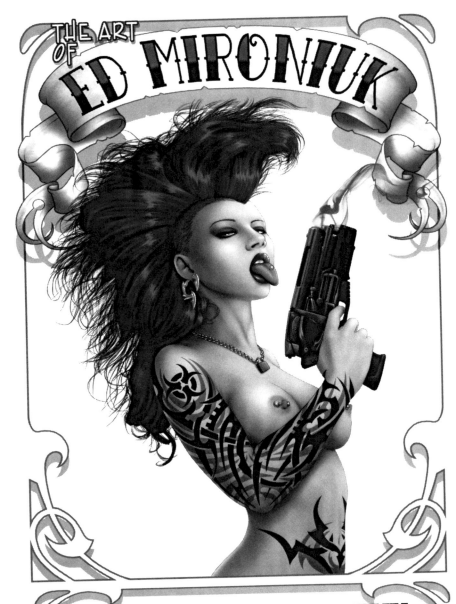

ABOUT THE AUTHOR

Carlton Mellick III is one of the leading authors of the bizarro fiction subgenre. Since 2001, his books have drawn an international cult following, despite the fact that they have been shunned by most libraries and chain bookstores.

He won the Wonderland Book Award for his novel, *Warrior Wolf Women of the Wasteland*, in 2009. His short fiction has appeared in *Vice Magazine, The Year's Best Fantasy and Horror #16, The Magazine of Bizarro Fiction,* and *Zombies: Encounters with the Hungry Dead,* among others. He is also a graduate of Clarion West, where he studied under the likes of Chuck Palahniuk, Connie Willis, and Cory Doctorow.

He lives in Portland, OR, the bizarro fiction mecca.

Visit him online at **www.carltonmellick.com**

BIZARRO BOOKS

CATALOG   SPRING 2013

ERASERHEAD PRESS

Your major resource for the bizarro fiction genre:

WWW.BIZARROCENTRAL.COM

Introduce yourselves to the bizarro fiction genre and all of its authors with the Bizarro Starter Kit series. Each volume features short novels and short stories by ten of the leading bizarro authors, designed to give you a perfect sampling of the genre for only $10.

BB-0X1
"The Bizarro Starter Kit" (Orange)
Featuring D. Harlan Wilson, Carlton Mellick III, Jeremy Robert Johnson, Kevin L Donihe, Gina Ranalli, Andre Duza, Vincent W. Sakowski, Steve Beard, John Edward Lawson, and Bruce Taylor. **236 pages $10**

BB-0X2
"The Bizarro Starter Kit" (Blue)
Featuring Ray Fracalossy, Jeremy C. Shipp, Jordan Krall, Mykle Hansen, Andersen Prunty, Eckhard Gerdes, Bradley Sands, Steve Aylett, Christian TeBordo, and Tony Rauch. **244 pages $10**

BB-0X2
"The Bizarro Starter Kit" (Purple)
Featuring Russell Edson, Athena Villaverde, David Agranoff, Matthew Revert, Andrew Goldfarb, Jeff Burk, Garrett Cook, Kris Saknussemm, Cody Goodfellow, and Cameron Pierce **264 pages $10**

BB-001 "The Kafka Effekt" D. Harlan Wilson — A collection of forty-four irreal short stories loosely written in the vein of Franz Kafka, with more than a pinch of William S. Burroughs sprinkled on top. **211 pages $14**

BB-002 "Satan Burger" Carlton Mellick III — The cult novel that put Carlton Mellick III on the map ... Six punks get jobs at a fast food restaurant owned by the devil in a city violently overpopulated by surreal alien cultures. **236 pages $14**

BB-003 "Some Things Are Better Left Unplugged" Vincent Sakwoski — Join The Man and his Nemesis, the obese tabby, for a nightmare roller coaster ride into this postmodern fantasy. **152 pages $10**

BB-005 "Razor Wire Pubic Hair" Carlton Mellick III — A genderless humandildo is purchased by a razor dominatrix and brought into her nightmarish world of bizarre sex and mutilation. **176 pages $11**

BB-007 "The Baby Jesus Butt Plug" Carlton Mellick III — Using clones of the Baby Jesus for anal sex will be the hip sex fetish of the future. **92 pages $10**

BB-010 "The Menstruating Mall" Carlton Mellick III — "The Breakfast Club meets Chopping Mall as directed by David Lynch." - Brian Keene **212 pages $12**

BB-011 "Angel Dust Apocalypse" Jeremy Robert Johnson — Meth-heads, man-made monsters, and murderous Neo-Nazis. "Seriously amazing short stories..." - Chuck Palahniuk, author of Fight Club **184 pages $11**

BB-015 "Foop!" Chris Genoa — Strange happenings are going on at Dactyl, Inc, the world's first and only time travel tourism company.
"A surreal pie in the face!" - Christopher Moore **300 pages $14**

BB-032 **"Extinction Journals" Jeremy Robert Johnson** — An uncanny voyage across a newly nuclear America where one man must confront the problems associated with loneliness, insane dieties, radiation, love, and an ever-evolving cockroach suit with a mind of its own. **104 pages $10**

BB-037 **"The Haunted Vagina" Carlton Mellick III** — It's difficult to love a woman whose vagina is a gateway to the world of the dead. **132 pages $10**

BB-043 **"War Slut" Carlton Mellick III** — Part "1984," part "Waiting for Godot," and part action horror video game adaptation of John Carpenter's "The Thing." **116 pages $10**

BB-047 **"Sausagey Santa" Carlton Mellick III** — A bizarro Christmas tale featuring Santa as a piratey mutant with a body made of sausages. 124 pages $10

BB-048 **"Misadventures in a Thumbnail Universe" Vincent Sakowski** — Dive deep into the surreal and satirical realms of neo-classical Blender Fiction, filled with television shoes and flesh-filled skies. **120 pages $10**

BB-053 **"Ballad of a Slow Poisoner" Andrew Goldfarb** — Millford Mutterwurst sat down on a Tuesday to take his afternoon tea, and made the unpleasant discovery that his elbows were becoming flatter. **128 pages $10**

BB-055 **"Help! A Bear is Eating Me" Mykle Hansen** — The bizarro, heartwarming, magical tale of poor planning, hubris and severe blood loss... **150 pages $11**

BB-056 **"Piecemeal June" Jordan Krall** — A man falls in love with a living sex doll, but with love comes danger when her creator comes after her with crab-squid assassins. **90 pages $9**

BB-058 **"The Overwhelming Urge" Andersen Prunty** — A collection of bizarro tales by Andersen Prunty. **150 pages $11**

BB-059 **"Adolf in Wonderland" Carlton Mellick III** — A dreamlike adventure that takes a young descendant of Adolf Hitler's design and sends him down the rabbit hole into a world of imperfection and disorder. **180 pages $11**

BB-061 **"Ultra Fuckers" Carlton Mellick III** — Absurdist suburban horror about a couple who enter an upper middle class gated community but can't find their way out. **108 pages $9**

BB-062 **"House of Houses" Kevin L. Donihe** — An odd man wants to marry his house. Unfortunately, all of the houses in the world collapse at the same time in the Great House Holocaust. Now he must travel to House Heaven to find his departed fiancee. **172 pages $11**

BB-064 **"Squid Pulp Blues" Jordan Krall** — In these three bizarro-noir novellas, the reader is thrown into a world of murderers, drugs made from squid parts, deformed gun-toting veterans, and a mischievous apocalyptic donkey. **204 pages $12**

BB-065 **"Jack and Mr. Grin" Andersen Prunty** — "When Mr. Grin calls you can hear a smile in his voice. Not a warm and friendly smile, but the kind that seizes your spine in fear. You don't need to pay your phone bill to hear it. That smile is in every line of Prunty's prose." - Tom Bradley. **208 pages $12**

BB-066 **"Cybernetrix" Carlton Mellick III** — What would you do if your normal everyday world was slowly mutating into the video game world from Tron? **212 pages $12**

BB-072 **"Zerostrata" Andersen Prunty** — Hansel Nothing lives in a tree house, suffers from memory loss, has a very eccentric family, and falls in love with a woman who runs naked through the woods every night. **144 pages $11**

BB-073 "The Egg Man" Carlton Mellick III — It is a world where humans reproduce like insects. Children are the property of corporations, and having an enormous ten-foot brain implanted into your skull is a grotesque sexual fetish. Mellick's industrial urban dystopia is one of his darkest and grittiest to date. **184 pages $11**

BB-074 "Shark Hunting in Paradise Garden" Cameron Pierce — A group of strange humanoid religious fanatics travel back in time to the Garden of Eden to discover it is invested with hundreds of giant flying maneating sharks. **150 pages $10**

BB-075 "Apeshit" Carlton Mellick III - Friday the 13th meets Visitor Q. Six hipster teens go to a cabin in the woods inhabited by a deformed killer. An incredibly fucked-up parody of B-horror movies with a bizarro slant. **192 pages $12**

BB-076 "Fuckers of Everything on the Crazy Shitting Planet of the Vomit At smosphere" Mykle Hansen - Three bizarro satires. Monster Cocks, Journey to the Center of Agnes Cuddlebottom, and Crazy Shitting Planet. **228 pages $12**

BB-077 "The Kissing Bug" Daniel Scott Buck — In the tradition of Roald Dahl, Tim Burton, and Edward Gorey, comes this bizarro anti-war children's story about a bohemian conenose kissing bug who falls in love with a human woman. **116 pages $10**

BB-078 "MachoPoni" Lotus Rose — It's My Little Pony... *Bizarro* style! A long time ago Poniworld was split in two. On one side of the Jagged Line is the Pastel Kingdom, a magical land of music, parties, and positivity. On the other side of the Jagged Line is Dark Kingdom inhabited by an army of undead ponies. **148 pages $11**

BB-079 "The Faggiest Vampire" Carlton Mellick III — A Roald Dahl-esque children's story about two faggy vampires who partake in a mustache competition to find out which one is truly the faggiest. **104 pages $10**

BB-080 "Sky Tongues" Gina Ranalli — The autobiography of Sky Tongues, the biracial hermaphrodite actress with tongues for fingers. Follow her strange life story as she rises from freak to fame. **204 pages $12**

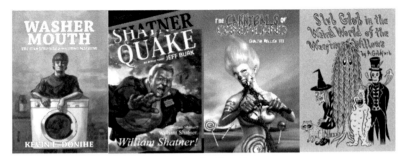

BB-081 **"Washer Mouth" Kevin L. Donihe** - A washing machine becomes human and pursues his dream of meeting his favorite soap opera star. **244 pages $11**

BB-082 **"Shatnerquake" Jeff Burk** - All of the characters ever played by William Shatner are suddenly sucked into our world. Their mission: hunt down and destroy the real William Shatner. **100 pages $10**

BB-083 **"The Cannibals of Candyland" Carlton Mellick III** - There exists a race of cannibals that are made of candy. They live in an underground world made out of candy. One man has dedicated his life to killing them all. **170 pages $11**

BB-084 **"Slub Glub in the Weird World of the Weeping Willows"** **Andrew Goldfarb** - The charming tale of a blue glob named Slub Glub who helps the weeping willows whose tears are flooding the earth. There are also hyenas, ghosts, and a voodoo priest **100 pages $10**

BB-085 **"Super Fetus" Adam Pepper** - Try to abort this fetus and he'll kick your ass! **104 pages $10**

BB-086 **"Fistful of Feet" Jordan Krall** - A bizarro tribute to spaghetti westerns, featuring Cthulhu-worshipping Indians, a woman with four feet, a crazed gunman who is obsessed with sucking on candy, Syphilis-ridden mutants, sexually transmitted tattoos, and a house devoted to the freakiest fetishes. **228 pages $12**

BB-087 **"Ass Goblins of Auschwitz" Cameron Pierce** - It's Monty Python meets Nazi exploitation in a surreal nightmare as can only be imagined by Bizarro author Cameron Pierce. **104 pages $10**

BB-088 **"Silent Weapons for Quiet Wars" Cody Goodfellow** - "This is high-end psychological surrealist horror meets bottom-feeding low-life crime in a techno-thrilling science fiction world full of Lovecraft and magic..." -John Skipp **212 pages $12**

BB-089 "Warrior Wolf Women of the Wasteland" Carlton Mellick III — Road Warrior Werewolves versus McDonaldland Mutants...post-apocalyptic fiction has never been quite like this. **316 pages $13**

BB-091 "Super Giant Monster Time" Jeff Burk — A tribute to choose your own adventures and Godzilla movies. Will you escape the giant monsters that are rampaging the fuck out of your city and shit? Or will you join the mob of alien-controlled punk rockers causing chaos in the streets? What happens next depends on you. **188 pages $12**

BB-092 "Perfect Union" Cody Goodfellow — "Cronenberg's THE FLY on a grand scale: human/insect gene-spliced body horror, where the human hive politics are as shocking as the gore." -John Skipp. **272 pages $13**

BB-093 "Sunset with a Beard" Carlton Mellick III — 14 stories of surreal science fiction. **200 pages $12**

BB-094 "My Fake War" Andersen Prunty — The absurd tale of an unlikely soldier forced to fight a war that, quite possibly, does not exist. It's Rambo meets Waiting for Godot in this subversive satire of American values and the scope of the human imagination. **128 pages $11**

BB-095 "Lost in Cat Brain Land" Cameron Pierce — Sad stories from a surreal world. A fascist mustache, the ghost of Franz Kafka, a desert inside a dead cat. Primordial entities mourn the death of their child. The desperate serve tea to mysterious creatures. A hopeless romantic falls in love with a pterodactyl. And much more. **152 pages $11**

BB-096 "The Kobold Wizard's Dildo of Enlightenment +2" Carlton Mellick III — A Dungeons and Dragons parody about a group of people who learn they are only made up characters in an AD&D campaign and must find a way to resist their nerdy teenaged players and retarded dungeon master in order to survive. 232 **pages $12**

BB-098 "A Hundred Horrible Sorrows of Ogner Stump" Andrew Goldfarb — Goldfarb's acclaimed comic series. A magical and weird journey into the horrors of everyday life. **164 pages $11**

BB-099 **"Pickled Apocalypse of Pancake Island" Cameron Pierce**—A demented fairy tale about a pickle, a pancake, and the apocalypse. **102 pages $8**

BB-100 **"Slag Attack" Andersen Prunty**— Slag Attack features four visceral, noir stories about the living, crawling apocalypse. A slag is what survivors are calling the slug-like maggots raining from the sky, burrowing inside people, and hollowing out their flesh and their sanity. **148 pages $11**

BB-101 **"Slaughterhouse High" Robert Devereaux**—A place where schools are built with secret passageways, rebellious teens get zippers installed in their mouths and genitals, and once a year, on that special night, one couple is slaughtered and the bits of their bodies are kept as souvenirs. **304 pages $13**

BB-102 **"The Emerald Burrito of Oz" John Skipp & Marc Levinthal** —OZ IS REAL! Magic is real! The gate is really in Kansas! And America is finally allowing Earth tourists to visit this weird-ass, mysterious land. But when Gene of Los Angeles heads off for summer vacation in the Emerald City, little does he know that a war is brewing...a war that could destroy both worlds. **280 pages $13**

BB-103 **"The Vegan Revolution... with Zombies" David Agranoff** — When there's no more meat in hell, the vegans will walk the earth. **160 pages $11**

BB-104 **"The Flappy Parts" Kevin L Donihe**—Poems about bunnies, LSD, and police abuse. You know, things that matter. 132 **pages $11**

BB-105 **"Sorry I Ruined Your Orgy" Bradley Sands**—Bizarro humorist Bradley Sands returns with one of the strangest, most hilarious collections of the year. **130 pages $11**

BB-106 **"Mr. Magic Realism" Bruce Taylor**—Like Golden Age science fiction comics written by Freud, *Mr. Magic Realism* is a strange, insightful adventure that spans the furthest reaches of the galaxy, exploring the hidden caverns in the hearts and minds of men, women, aliens, and biomechanical cats. **152 pages $11**

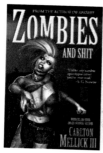   

BB-107 "Zombies and Shit" Carlton Mellick III—"Battle Royale" meets "Return of the Living Dead." Mellick's bizarro tribute to the zombie genre. **308 pages $13**

BB-108 "The Cannibal's Guide to Ethical Living" Mykle Hansen— Over a five star French meal of fine wine, organic vegetables and human flesh, a lunatic delivers a witty, chilling, disturbingly sane argument in favor of eating the rich.. **184 pages $11**

BB-109 "Starfish Girl" Athena Villaverde—In a post-apocalyptic underwater dome society, a girl with a starfish growing from her head and an assassin with sea anenome hair are on the run from a gang of mutant fish men. **160 pages $11**

BB-110 "Lick Your Neighbor" Chris Genoa—Mutant ninjas, a talking whale, kung fu masters, maniacal pilgrims, and an alcoholic clown populate Chris Genoa's surreal, darkly comical and unnerving reimagining of the first Thanksgiving. **303 pages $13**

BB-111 "Night of the Assholes" Kevin L. Donihe—A plague of assholes is infecting the countryside. Normal everyday people are transforming into jerks, snobs, dicks, and douchebags. And they all have only one purpose: to make your life a living hell.. **192 pages $11**

BB-112 "Jimmy Plush, Teddy Bear Detective" Garrett Cook—Hard- boiled cases of a private detective trapped within a teddy bear body. **180 pages $11**

BB-113 "The Deadheart Shelters" Forrest Armstrong—The hip hop lovechild of William Burroughs and Dali... **144 pages $11**

BB-114 "Eyeballs Growing All Over Me... Again" Tony Raugh— Absurd, surreal, playful, dream-like, whimsical, and a lot of fun to read. **144 pages $11**

BB-115 "Whargoul" Dave Brockie — From the killing grounds of Stalingrad to the death camps of the holocaust. From torture chambers in Iraq to race riots in the United States, the Whargoul was there, killing and raping. **244 pages $12**

BB-116 "By the Time We Leave Here, We'll Be Friends" J. David Osborne — A David Lynchian nightmare set in a Russian gulag, where its prisoners, guards, traitors, soldiers, lovers, and demons fight for survival and their own rapidly deteriorating humanity. **168 pages $11**

BB-117 "Christmas on Crack" edited by Carlton Mellick III — Perverted Christmas Tales for the whole family! . . . as long as every member of your family is over the age of 18. **168 pages $11**

BB-118 "Crab Town" Carlton Mellick III — Radiation fetishists, balloon people, mutant crabs, sail-bike road warriors, and a love affair between a woman and an H-Bomb. This is one mean asshole of a city. Welcome to Crab Town. **100 pages $8**

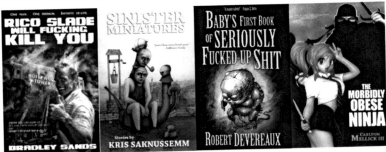

BB-119 "Rico Slade Will Fucking Kill You" Bradley Sands — Rico Slade is an action hero. Rico Slade can rip out a throat with his bare hands. Rico Slade's favorite food is the honey-roasted peanut. Rico Slade will fucking kill everyone. A novel. **122 pages $8**

BB-120 "Sinister Miniatures" Kris Saknussemm — The definitive collection of short fiction by Kris Saknussemm, confirming that he is one of the best, most daring writers of the weird to emerge in the twenty-first century. **180 pages $11**

BB-121 "Baby's First Book of Seriously Fucked up Shit" Robert Devereaux — Ten stories of the strange, the gross, and the just plain fucked up from one of the most original voices in horror. **176 pages $11**

BB-122 "The Morbidly Obese Ninja" Carlton Mellick III — These days, if you want to run a successful company . . . you're going to need a lot of ninjas. **92 pages $8**

BB-123 **"Abortion Arcade" Cameron Pierce** — An intoxicating blend of body horror and midnight movie madness, reminiscent of early David Lynch and the splatterpunks at their most sublime. **172 pages $11**

BB-124 **"Black Hole Blues" Patrick Wensink** — A hilarious double helix of country music and physics. **196 pages $11**

BB-125 **"Barbarian Beast Bitches of the Badlands" Carlton Mellick III** — Three prequels and sequels to *Warrior Wolf Women of the Wasteland.* **284 pages $13**

BB-126 **"The Traveling Dildo Salesman" Kevin L. Donihe** — A nightmare comedy about destiny, faith, and sex toys. Also featuring Donihe's most lurid and infamous short stories: *Milky Agitation, Two-Way Santa, The Helen Mower, Living Room Zombies,* and *Revenge of the Living Masturbation Rag.* **108 pages $8**

BB-127 **"Metamorphosis Blues" Bruce Taylor** — Enter a land of love beasts, intergalactic cowboys, and rock 'n roll. A land where Sears Catalogs are doorways to insanity and men keep mysterious black boxes. Welcome to the monstrous mind of Mr. Magic Realism. **136 pages $11**

BB-128 **"The Driver's Guide to Hitting Pedestrians" Andersen Prunty** — A pocket guide to the twenty-three most painful things in life, written by the most well-adjusted man in the universe. **108 pages $8**

BB-129 **"Island of the Super People" Kevin Shamel** — Four students and their anthropology professor journey to a remote island to study its indigenous population. But this is no ordinary native culture. They're super heroes and villains with flesh costumes and out-landish abilities like self-detonation, musical eyelashes, and microwave hands. **194 pages $11**

BB-130 **"Fantastic Orgy" Carlton Mellick III** — Shark Sex, mutant cats, and strange sexually transmitted diseases. Featuring the stories: *Candy-coated, Ear Cat, Fantastic Orgy, City Hobgoblins,* and *Porno in August.* **136 pages $9**

BB-131 "Cripple Wolf" Jeff Burk — Part man. Part wolf. 100% crippled. Also including *Punk Rock Nursing Home, Adrift with Space Badgers, Cook for Your Life, Just Another Day in the Park, Frosty and the Full Monty*, and *House of Cats*. **152 pages $10**

BB-132 "I Knocked Up Satan's Daughter" Carlton Mellick III — An adorable, violent, fantastical love story. A romantic comedy for the bizarro fiction reader. **152 pages $10**

BB-133 "A Town Called Suckhole" David W. Barbee — Far into the future, in the nuclear bowels of post-apocalyptic Dixie, there is a town. A town of derelict mobile homes, ancient junk, and mutant wildlife. A town of slack jawed rednecks who bask in the splendors of moonshine and mud boggin'. A town dedicated to the bloody and demented legacy of the Old South. A town called Suckhole. **144 pages $10**

BB-134 "Cthulhu Comes to the Vampire Kingdom" Cameron Pierce — What you'd get if H. P. Lovecraft wrote a Tim Burton animated film. **148 pages $11**

BB-135 "I am Genghis Cum" Violet LeVoit — From the savage Arctic tundra to post-partum mutations to your missing daughter's unmarked grave, join visionary madwoman Violet LeVoit in this non-stop eight-story onslaught of full-tilt Bizarro punk lit thrills. **124 pages $9**

BB-136 "Haunt" Laura Lee Bahr — A tripping-balls Los Angeles noir, where a mysterious dame drags you through a time-warping Bizarro hall of mirrors. **316 pages $13**

BB-137 "Amazing Stories of the Flying Spaghetti Monster" edited by Cameron Pierce — Like an all-spaghetti evening of Adult Swim, the Flying Spaghetti Monster will show you the many realms of His Noodly Appendage. Learn of those who worship him and the lives he touches in distant, mysterious ways. **228 pages $12**

BB-138 "Wave of Mutilation" Douglas Lain — A dream-pop exploration of modern architecture and the American identity, *Wave of Mutilation* is a Zen finger trap for the 21st century. **100 pages $8**

BB-139 "Hooray for Death!" Mykle Hansen — Famous Author Mykle Hansen draws unconventional humor from deaths tiny and large, and invites you to laugh while you can. **128 pages $10**

BB-140 "Hypno-hog's Moonshine Monster Jamboree" Andrew Goldfarb — Hicks, Hogs, Horror! Goldfarb is back with another strange illustrated tale of backwoods weirdness. **120 pages $9**

BB-141 "Broken Piano For President" Patrick Wensink — A comic masterpiece about the fast food industry, booze, and the necessity to choose happiness over work and security. **372 pages $15**

BB-142 "Please Do Not Shoot Me in the Face" Bradley Sands — A novel in three parts, *Please Do Not Shoot Me in the Face: A Novel*, is the story of one boy detective, the worst ninja in the world, and the great American fast food wars. It is a novel of loss, destruction, and--incredibly--genuine hope. **224 pages $12**

BB-143 "Santa Steps Out" Robert Devereaux — Sex, Death, and Santa Claus ... The ultimate erotic Christmas story is back. **294 pages $13**

BB-144 "Santa Conquers the Homophobes" Robert Devereaux — "I wish I could hope to ever attain one-thousandth the perversity of Robert Devereaux's toenail clippings." - Poppy Z. Brite **316 pages $13**

BB-145 "We Live Inside You" Jeremy Robert Johnson — "Jeremy Robert Johnson is dancing to a way different drummer. He loves language, he loves the edge, and he loves us people. These stories have range and style and wit. This is entertainment... and literature."- Jack Ketchum **188 pages $11**

BB-146 "Clockwork Girl" Athena Villaverde — Urban fairy tales for the weird girl in all of us. Like a combination of Francesca Lia Block, Charles de Lint, Kathe Koja, Tim Burton, and Hayao Miyazaki, her stories are cute, kinky, edgy, magical, provocative, and strange, full of poetic imagery and vicious sexuality. **160 pages $10**

BB-147 "Armadillo Fists" Carlton Mellick III — A weird-as-hell gangster story set in a world where people drive giant mechanical dinosaurs instead of cars. **168 pages $11**

BB-148 "Gargoyle Girls of Spider Island" Cameron Pierce — Four college seniors venture out into open waters for the tropical party weekend of a lifetime. Instead of a teenage sex fantasy, they find themselves in a nightmare of pirates, sharks, and sex-crazed monsters. **100 pages $8**

BB-149 "The Handsome Squirm" by Carlton Mellick III — Like Franz Kafka's *The Trial* meets an erotic body horror version of *The Blob*. **158 pages $11**

BB-150 "Tentacle Death Trip" Jordan Krall — It's *Death Race 2000* meets H. P. Lovecraft in bizarro author Jordan Krall's best and most suspenseful work to date. **224 pages $12**

BB-151 "The Obese" Nick Antosca — Like Alfred Hitchcock's *The Birds*... but with obese people. **108 pages $10**

BB-152 "All-Monster Action!" Cody Goodfellow — The world gave him a blank check and a demand: Create giant monsters to fight our wars. But Dr. Otaku was not satisfied with mere chaos and mass destruction.... **216 pages $12**

BB-153 "Ugly Heaven" Carlton Mellick III — Heaven is no longer a paradise. It was once a blissful utopia full of wonders far beyond human comprehension. But the afterlife is now in ruins. It has become an ugly, lonely wasteland populated by strange monstrous beasts, masturbating angels, and sad man-like beings wallowing in the remains of the once-great Kingdom of God. **106 pages $8**

BB-154 "Space Walrus" Kevin L. Donihe — Walter is supposed to go where no walrus has ever gone before, but all this astronaut walrus really wants is to take it easy on the intense training, escape the chimpanzee bullies, and win the love of his human trainer Dr. Stephanie. **160 pages $11**

BB-155 **"Unicorn Battle Squad" Kirsten Alene** — Mutant unicorns. A palace with a thousand human legs. The most powerful army on the planet. **192 pages $11**

BB-156 **"Kill Ball" Carlton Mellick III** — In a city where all humans live inside of plastic bubbles, exotic dancers are being murdered in the rubbery streets by a mysterious stalker known only as Kill Ball. **134 pages $10**

BB-157 **"Die You Doughnut Bastards" Cameron Pierce** — The bacon storm is rolling in. We hear the grease and sugar beat against the roof and windows. The doughnut people are attacking. We press close together, forgetting for a moment that we hate each other. **196 pages $11**

BB-158 **"Tumor Fruit" Carlton Mellick III** — Eight desperate castaways find themselves stranded on a mysterious deserted island. They are surrounded by poisonous blue plants and an ocean made of acid. Ravenous creatures lurk in the toxic jungle. The ghostly sound of crying babies can be heard on the wind. **310 pages $13**

BB-159 **"Thunderpussy" David W. Barbee** — When it comes to high-tech global espionage, only one man has the balls to save humanity from the world's most powerful bastards. He's Declan Magpie Bruce, Agent 00X. **136 pages $11**

BB-160 **"Papier Mâché Jesus" Kevin L. Donihe** — Donihe's surreal wit and beautiful mind-bending imagination is on full display with stories such as All Children Go to Hell, Happiness is a Warm Gun, and Swimming in Endless Night. **154 pages $11**

BB-161 **"Cuddly Holocaust" Carlton Mellick III** — The war between humans and toys has come to an end. The toys won. **172 pages $11**

BB-162 **"Hammer Wives" Carlton Mellick III** — Fish-eyed mutants, oceans of insects, and flesh-eating women with hammers for heads. Hammer Wives collects six of his most popular novelettes and short stories. **152 pages $10**

Lightning Source UK Ltd.
Milton Keynes UK
UKOW05f1117021213

222215UK00001B/178/P